HAUNTING
TALES

HAUNTING TALES

edited by
Barbara Ireson

illustrated by Freda Woolf

E. P. Dutton & Co., Inc.   New York

First published in the U.S.A. 1974 by E. P. Dutton & Co., Inc.
Collection copyright © 1973 by Faber and Faber Limited
Illustrations copyright © 1973 by Faber and Faber Limited

Library of Congress Cataloging in Publication Data

Ireson, Barbara, comp.   Haunting tales

CONTENTS: Palmer, G., and Lloyd, N. Huw.—Leodhas, S. N.
The man who didn't believe in ghosts. —Manning-Sanders, R.
Hans and his master. —Arthur, R. The haunted trailer. [etc.]

1. Ghost stories. [1. Ghost stories]
I. Woolf, Freda, illus.   II. Title.
PZ5.I6Hau3   823'.01   [Fic]   74-7222   ISBN 0-525-31533-0

Printed in the U.S.A.   First Edition
10 9 8 7 6 5 4 3 2 1

Acknowledgments

Thanks are due to the following authors, publishers, and others for permission to include the stories named:

"A Long Day Without Water" by Joan Aiken. Reprinted by permission of A. M. Heath & Company Ltd. and Brandt & Brandt.

"The Haunted Trailer" by Robert Arthur from *Alfred Hitchcock's Ghostly Gallery* by permission of Random House, Inc.

"Uncle Einar" by Ray Bradbury. Copyright 1955 by Ray Bradbury. Reprinted by permission of A. D. Peters and Company and Harold Matson Co., Inc.

"The Twilight Road" by H. F. Brinsmead from *Miscellany Four* edited by Edward Blishen, published by Oxford University Press; first American publication by Franklin Watts, Inc., 1968.

"Jimmy Takes Vanishing Lessons" by Walter R. Brooks from *Jimmy Takes Vanishing Lessons*. Copyright 1950 by Walter R. Brooks. Reprinted by permission of Alfred A. Knopf, Inc.

"The Ghostly Earl" by R. Chetwynd-Hayes. Printed by permission of the author.

"Through the Veil" by Sir Arthur Conan Doyle. Reprinted by permission of John Murray and Jonathan Clowes Ltd.

Acknowledgments

"Faithful Jenny Dove" by Eleanor Farjeon, copyright Collins, 1925. Reprinted by permission of David Higham Associates Ltd.

"The Crossways" from *The Collected Short Stories of L. P. Hartley*. Copyright © 1968 by L. P. Hartley, Hamish Hamilton Ltd.

"The Man Who Didn't Believe in Ghosts" from *Ghosts Go Haunting* by Sorche Nic Leodhas. Copyright © 1965 by Leclaire G. Alger. Reprinted by permission of Holt, Rinehart and Winston, Inc.

"Hans and His Master" from *The Book of Ghosts and Goblins* by Ruth Manning-Sanders, published by Methuen and Co. Ltd. Reprinted by permission of Ruth Manning-Sanders and David Higham Associates Ltd.

"Huw" from *The Obstinate Ghost* by Geoffrey Palmer and Noel Lloyd. Reprinted by permission of the authors and the Hamlyn Publishing Group Ltd.

"The Demon King" by J. B. Priestley. Reprinted by permission of the author.

"Fiddler, Play Fast, Play Faster" from *The Long Christmas* by Ruth Sawyer. Copyright 1941, © 1969 by Ruth Sawyer. Reprinted by permission of The Viking Press, Inc.

"Master Ghost and I" by Barbara Softly. Reprinted by permission of the author.

"The Magic Shop" from *The Complete Short Stories of H. G. Wells*. Reprinted by permission of the Trustees of the Estate of H. G. Wells.

Contents

Contents

HAUNTING
TALES

Huw

Geoffrey Palmer and Noel Lloyd

If you had asked me a couple of months ago whether or not I believed in ghosts I could not have given you a straight answer. I would probably have said, "Well, yes and no . . ." and gone on to explain that I could not answer one way or another because I had never actually seen such a thing, and though lots of odd things undoubtedly happen from time to time most of them surely have a rational explanation.

But that would have been a couple of months ago. Ask me the same question today and I would not hesitate to answer, "Yes, I *do* believe in ghosts, and what's more, I'm not a bit frightened of them." If you are wondering what happened to make me so definite I'd like to tell you all about it. I still find the whole thing very hard to accept, but I must accept it because it was real—it did happen.

It all began when my young brother Bryn invited me to spend a few days with him at Aberystwyth in Wales, where he was studying at the University. As I was between jobs my time was my own; and as a Welshman compelled to live in London the chance of spending some time in my home country was too good to miss. I accepted my brother's offer and decided to drive leisurely up through Shropshire and enter Wales by Snowdonia National Park instead of taking the quickest route.

The weather was good and I enjoyed the journey to the north-west. The Shropshire hills and valleys brought me into touch with that special, unassuming loveliness that is one of the charming features of the English countryside. I even went out of my way to visit Clunton, Clunbury, Clungunford and Clun, just to discover whether they are, as Housman claims, "the quietest places under the sun". They were pretty quiet.

At last I headed west into Wales, keeping well away from the major roads, choosing instead any road that looked barely wide enough to take a car, hoping to reach Dolgellau, the friendly little town in a valley that is protected by Cader Idris. The trouble with driving aimlessly, enjoying the scenery and refusing to hurry, is that it is very easy to lose track of time—which is what happened to me. Daylight began to fade and the sky filled up with smoky clouds. There was a spatter of rain on the windscreen. The road was little more than a cart track and the country was very hilly. I thought I had better get on to a decent road as quickly as possible and head for Bala, leaving Dolgellau until the next day. At that point I realized I was running out of petrol.

It was quite dark by the time I had reached the main road and the petrol situation was serious. My map did not show any villages for several miles and I thought it quite likely that I would have to spend the night huddled up in the car in the middle of the Welsh mountains. Fortunately, this unpleasant vision faded when my lights picked out a solitary petrol pump by the side of a grey stone cottage. Of course, this little wayside petrol station was closed, but I was able to drag the owner away from his television set and persuade him to fill my tank.

I had only travelled a couple of miles farther when I saw

the boy. By now the rain was very heavy and visibility was poor, but I saw him perfectly clearly as he stood by the side of the road, hands in pockets, looking towards the car. I pulled up and opened the on-side door.

"Missed your bus?" I called, taking it for granted that buses did run along this road. He didn't answer, but with a slight movement shook his head. He looked to be about thirteen or fourteen years old; he was tall and dressed in jeans and a black jacket buttoned up to his neck. His face was startling in its pallor.

"Do you want a lift?" I went on. "If so, jump in." This was no time to indulge in aimless conversation and the boy's lack of interest rather irritated me. I pushed the door open a little more, wondering whether he was going to accept my offer, but he slid into the passenger seat without hesitation. I reached across him, closed the door and snapped the safety lock.

"What a night!" I said. "Have you missed your bus?" I asked him again—I could think of no other reason why a lad of his age should be standing in such a lonely spot on such a night.

He said nothing and I had to bite my lips to prevent myself making a sarcastic remark about the cat having bitten his tongue. I'll try once more, I thought. "Where are you going? Where can I drop you?"

This time he did answer me—in Welsh, and I mentally apologized to him for misunderstanding his silence. Perhaps he did not speak English very well, although clearly he understood it. "I'm afraid I know only a few words of Welsh," I said, "though I recognized the word 'trees'— something trees—can you translate?"

"Stricken," he answered in a husky adolescent's voice.

"Stricken Trees—that's an odd name. I can't remember

anything like that on the map, either in English or Welsh. Is it a local name?"

"Yes," he said.

"And is it far?"

"No."

What marvellous dialogue, I thought, hoping that Stricken Trees was *very* near. I couldn't stand much more yes-ing and no-ing. Still, he was company of a sort, and talking to someone made a change from listening to the tyres swishing over the wet road.

"Well, you'd better tell me when we get there," I said, "otherwise you'll find yourself in Bala." At that he twisted a little in his seat and turned to look at me. Ah, the first sign of life, I thought. Perhaps he's got a girl-friend in Bala and wouldn't mind being taken on there.

But the boy was showing agitation, not pleasure.

"What's the matter?" I asked.

"Don't go to Bala, mister," he said, with a sort of quivering urgency in his tone. "Not tonight. . . ."

I could not help laughing at the intensity of his entreaty and my laugh was accompanied by a long roll of thunder. "Why not? There's nowhere to stay before Bala, and I am so tired and my joints ache with the damp that I don't feel like driving the extra twenty miles or so to Dolgellau."

"Don't go to Bala, mister," he repeated.

"It's not as bad as that," I said jokingly. "Haven't you ever been there?"

"Not the last time," he said. "I never got there, you see."

I didn't see, but I let the subject drop. Frankly, I was beginning to feel a bit uneasy. I wondered if the boy was perhaps a bit simple—he was very unlike any fourteen-year-old I had ever met. "What's your name?" I asked, mainly for something to say.

"Huw," he replied. As he made no further contribution to the conversation I gave up and drove on in silence.

About ten minutes later, during which time I had, as I thought, been concentrating on the road, I remembered my passenger. "Huw, this place—Stricken Trees—are we anywhere near it?" My eyes were glued to the winding road and I could not tell whether he had heard me. "Huw!" I said, raising my voice. "Are you asleep? Are we anywhere near Stricken Trees?" Then the back of my neck tightened as though suddenly gripped in a vice, and without turning my head I knew. . . . I pulled the car into the side of the road to make absolutely sure. Huw was no longer sitting by my side.

I remember my feelings as if it had all taken place an hour ago. First, a quick stab of fear, then puzzlement as I tried the door and found it still locked, then an amused relief when I decided what had happened. Obviously Huw had told me where to stop, had got out and left me to continue alone. I had been guilty of falling asleep at the wheel—a constant fear of those who drive long distances alone. I had been driving by instinct . . . and could thank my guardian angel that the absence of any other vehicle had prevented an accident. "Let this be a lesson to you," I told myself. "You'd better stop at the next village for a rest and a snack." I let in the clutch and drove on, and within five minutes had reached a tiny village.

There was an inn among the dozen or so houses, and I parked the car and went in. An elderly lady sat behind the high counter, knitting. The small bar, hot and smoke-filled, was crowded with men puffing at pipes and talking in Welsh. But the landlady spoke to me in English with a musical lilt that seemed to embrace the whole scale. "Good evening, sir, *terrible* weather, and what can I get you?" She slid off her stool and put down the knitting.

"A pint of bitter, please," I said. "And could you possibly make me a sandwich? I haven't eaten for hours."

The landlady disappeared into the back room and soon returned with the thickest, juiciest roast-beef sandwich I have ever eaten. It was a most welcome sight and I tucked into it eagerly. The other customers took little notice of me after their first casual glances, but Mrs. Cadwallader as the landlady was called, and I got on famously. As it turned out I bought my milk from her brother's dairy at the corner of my road in London, and she had heard about my aged Auntie Blodwen who lived at the top of a hill in Flintshire and made lace that was known throughout North Wales. When I told her that I intended to spend the night in Bala she was delighted. "Beautiful town," she said, "and if you want a *lovely* place to stay, Morgan Llyfnant Arms is my brother-in-law. The rooms overlook some fine gardens and on fine days you can see the lake and the linen is as crisp and clean as Snowdon's white cap!"

"The Llyfnant Arms it shall be," I promised. Talk of Bala had brought back vividly to my mind my strange passenger from Stricken Trees. Mrs. Cadwallader had turned to do something at the back of the bar and I raised my voice slightly. "By the way," I asked, "do you know a young lad from these parts named Huw?"

Every sound in the room suddenly faded. Mrs. Cadwallader, her back still turned to me, seemed to freeze. I could feel every eye swivel round and fix on the back of my head. I felt as though I had committed a crime—though what it was I had no idea. I blundered on. "And where is the place called Stricken Trees?"

When Mrs. Cadwallader turned round her eyes were full of sympathy, though not for me, as I soon realized, for she was looking past me into the room. "It's all right now, Mr. Griffiths," she said softly. "Don't you worry."

I shifted my position to see who Mr. Griffiths was and to guess why he shouldn't worry. From a solid group at the back there came forward a tiny wizened man with a skull-like face. Dark mournful eyes were the only living feature in it. When he spoke his voice was rich and deep, like an orator's. It was odd hearing it emerge from his spare frame.

"You have seen Huw tonight."

I didn't know whether he had made a statement or asked a question, but I felt like a schoolboy before a stern headmaster. "Yes, I gave him a lift about twelve miles back, to a place called Stricken Trees. To be honest, I don't remember dropping him."

"No, you wouldn't," Mr. Griffiths said, smiling grimly.

"I think I was overtired and dropped off to sleep for a few seconds."

"What did he say?"

"Not a lot," I replied. "He was a silent lad—at the awkward age, I suppose. Oh, he did tell me not to go to Bala tonight." I expected smiles when I said that, but the only smile in the room was my own. There was another silent spell before Mr. Griffiths spoke again. "Then don't go to Bala tonight. . . ." He gave a curious sound like a strangled sob and with shoulders bowed he moved slowly across the room and went out into the night.

One man from the group got up as if to follow him, but another clutched his sleeve. "No, Dai, let him be. Nobody can help."

The others muttered agreement, so Dai sat down again. From that moment the atmosphere changed. No longer distant and clannish, the men crowded round me, asked me my name, where I came from, my profession, my taste in music and books, as if they were all trainee television interviewers, but never a word did they utter about Huw or Stricken Trees. I soon understood that they were de-

liberately avoiding those two topics, so I tried to probe the mystery. But every question was met by a chorus of false laughs.

"Huw? Only Ted Griffiths's boy."

"Worries about him, see?"

"Very close, that family."

"Have another drink?"

"No, thank you," I said. "Only one pint when I'm driving. But what have the Griffiths family got against Bala? I'm looking forward to seeing Morgan Llyfnant Arms."

More false laughter—even from Mrs. Cadwallader too. "Have another beer," was all I could get out of them. I had to get away. There was a mystery, but obviously I wasn't going to be let into the secret. I thanked the landlady, said good night to the men and promised I'd call again when I was in that part of the country. I was relieved to get back to my car, even though the rain was still tumbling down and the dark clouds were scurrying across the sky like crowds going to a football match.

Away from the village lights it was pitch-dark again. I tried to quell my uneasiness by humming *Men of Harlech*, but before I had got to the end there was an ominous splutter from the engine. Please don't break down, I willed—not here; but the car stopped decisively, with a final spiteful chuckle. I was just about to get out and peer beneath the bonnet when the truth dawned on me. I was quite out of petrol! The needle registered an empty tank. It was impossible, but a fact.

Bristling with anger I went to the back of the car. The cap of the petrol tank was missing. Somebody had siphoned out all the six gallons I had bought at the wayside pump. I wished that I was not too old to burst into tears. As it was I had to clench my fists to contain my feelings.

Then I caught a glimpse of someone standing by a wooden pole at the side of the road. It was Huw, peering at me, his white face caught in the headlights.

I dashed towards him. "Huw!" I cried. "What's going on? Who stole my petrol? Was it you or that strange father of yours? Huw—where are you? Don't play tricks on me, for heaven's sake!"

But it was useless to keep on. He had disappeared. All that remained of Huw was a voice whispering in my ear, "Don't go to Bala tonight, mister. . . ."

I'm not going anywhere tonight, I thought despairingly, except to a makeshift bed in the back of the car. Idly I looked at the spot where Huw had been standing and noticed a painted board at the top of the wooden pole. Out of curiosity I got a torch from the car and shone it on to the board. I gave a gasp when the words on it were visible.

DAFYDD FARM 100 YARDS
BED & BREAKFAST
DAIRY PRODUCE

Well, if not a silver lining, this was at least a slightly less leaden one. I grabbed my case from the back seat, locked the car and trudged the hundred yards to Dafydd Farm, heedless of the rain and the ankle-deep mud.

Mrs. Jenkinson did not seem at all surprised to receive a visitor at such a late hour and welcomed me warmly. The farmhouse kitchen was scrubbed and spotless, and soon I was sitting down to a meal of ham and eggs that tasted better than anything the best four-star hotel could provide.

Mrs. Jenkinson hovered around me as I ate, making sure that I had everything I needed, and I found myself telling her the story of Huw, his father, my empty petrol tank and the strange behaviour of the men in the inn. She nodded knowingly several times, and when she had put a huge dish of apple tart and clotted cream in front of me she sat down at the opposite side of the table.

"I dare say it all seems very mysterious to you, sir," she began, "but I think I can make things a bit clearer. Huw is a ghost. . . ." She uttered the words in a matter-of-fact way as though she might have been saying, "Huw is a boy. . . ." She smiled at my start of surprise and went on, "The people in the village delude themselves that he only exists in the mind of his father, but he's a real ghost. I've seen him myself, and spoken to him, and I'm not one to imagine things, I can tell you."

"I'm sure you're not," I said. "Where does Stricken Trees come into the story?"

"That is where the Griffiths family lives. Years ago the trees outside their cottage were struck by lightning. Not a leaf has grown on them since, but the skeletons still stand there, bent and withered like rheumaticky old men. As for Huw—three years ago it happened—when the boy was thirteen. Ted Griffiths always maintained that he was delicate and wouldn't allow him to play out with the other boys, though when Huw got the chance to climb trees and kick a football it was clear that he was as strong as the rest of them. One day the travelling circus came to Bala. Huw wanted to go with his pals, but his father wouldn't hear of it. Said the night air might affect his chest and a lot of foolish things like that. I remember seeing the party set off in Wyn Evans's old bus, excited as only children can be at the thought of seeing clowns and tight-rope walkers, lions and elephants. Huw waved them off and went back sadly to Stricken Trees. But he never arrived home because little Billy Price Top-shop had left his new bicycle leaning against his front wall, and as Huw passed by, looking both ways—it suddenly seemed as though the temptation was too much for him. He took the bike and rode off after the bus like the wind.

"If he had stopped to think he would have realized that there was no chance of getting to Bala in time for the circus as it's near enough twenty miles away and up and down hill all the way. But Huw *didn't* think. He just went on pedalling for all he was worth. He was about half-way to Bala when the tragedy happened—a chance in a thousand, it was. A huge boulder rolled down from the hill and knocked him off the bike into the path of a car coming towards him.

"He was hurt very badly. The people in the car were frantic with worry. They wrapped him up in a blanket, put him in the car and drove him to Stricken Trees as fast as they could—Huw was conscious at first and able to tell them where he lived. But by the time they had got there he was dead.

"His father nearly went out of his mind with grief and since then has shrunk away almost to nothing. Huw was the apple of his eye and he had little else to live for. Nowadays the only sign of life he shows is when he thinks Huw's ghost is about. Then he walks the roads seeking the boy, calling his name and asking forgiveness for not letting him go in the bus."

"Does Huw always warn people away from Bala, as he did me?" I asked.

"Now there's funny," said Mrs. Jenkinson. "I haven't heard of him doing that before. I wonder why he didn't want you to go there. . . ."

Even with so much to think about I slept well that night between sheets as Snowdon-white as those at Morgan Llyfnant Arms. Before I finally sank into sleep I wished I could give Huw a lift again. I would have been more understanding.

The next morning, after a wonderful breakfast, I set off early. Mr. Jenkinson, fortunately, was able to replace the missing petrol. The aimless wanderings of the mountain sheep kept my mind on the serious business of driving, though I was able to marvel at the beauty of the towering mountains on one side of the road and the deep rich valleys on the other. When I saw the policeman ahead of me he seemed strangely out of place—directing traffic in that lonely spot surely wasn't necessary, I thought. He waved me to a halt and it was almost like being back in London.

"Sorry, sir," he said, when I poked my head out of the window. "I'm afraid you can't go any farther. Road to Bala's closed."

"But I must get there," I protested. "When will it be open again?"

"Couldn't say exactly, sir, but it'll be some time, I reckon."

"Has there been an accident?" For some reason my thoughts flew to Huw sprawled on the road with a car coming towards him.

"More an act of God, I'd say, sir."

"What *has* happened then?"

The policeman jerked a thumb behind him to the corner I had been approaching. "Landslide last night in all that rain. Near on half a mountain came down on the road and slid over into the valley. Thank your lucky stars you didn't start out any earlier yesterday and weren't anywhere near here last night, sir, or you'd never have got to Bala—*never*."

Huw, I thought, you can siphon the petrol out of my tank any time you like if your motive is always as good as it was last night. I reversed the car and drove back to find Stricken Trees. When Mr. Griffiths knew that Huw's ghost had saved my life his pride in his son would surely lighten his grief and give him the courage to face his loss.

So you see, that is why I believe in ghosts and why, if they are at all like Huw, there's no need to be afraid of them.

The Man Who Didn't Believe in Ghosts

Sorche Nic Leodhas

In a town not far from Edinburgh there was a house that was said to be haunted. It wasn't the sort of house you'd think would attract a ghost at all. It was only a two-storey cottage with a garret, and it was far too neat and pretty for ghosts to care much about. The outside walls of it were painted white and its casement windows had diamond-shaped panes to them. There was a climbing rose trained over the front door, and there was a flower garden before the house and a kitchen garden behind it, with a pear tree and an apple tree and a small green lawn. Who'd ever think that a ghost would choose to bide in a place like that? But folks did say it was haunted, all the same.

The house had belonged to an old lawyer with only one child, a daughter. Folk old enough to remember her still say that there never was another lass as bonny as her in the town. The old man loved her dearly but she died early. There was an old sad story told about her being in love with the son of an old laird who did not favour the match. The poor lad died of a fever while they were still courting, and not long after she died too—folk said of a broken heart.

After that the old man lived alone in the house, with a woman coming in each day to take care of it. There wasn't a word said about ghosts in the old man's time. He'd not have put up with it for a minute.

When the old lawyer died, there was nobody left that was kin to him but a second cousin several times removed. So to keep the property in the family, the old man left all he had to the cousin, including the house, of course.

The young man was grateful, but as he was not married, he had little use for a house. The lodgings he was living in suited him fine. So he put the renting of the house into an agent's hands. The rent money would make a nice little nest egg against the time when he decided he would like to get married. When that time came he'd want the house for himself.

It was the folks the agent found to live in the house that started all the talk about ghosts. At first they were very well pleased with the house, but as time passed they began to notice queer things were happening in it. Doors would open and close again, with nobody at all near them. When the young wife was dusting the spare bedroom, she heard drawers being pulled open and shut again behind her, but when she turned about to look, no one at all was there.

Things were lifted and put down again before the tenants' very eyes, but they couldn't see who was lifting them or putting them down. They came to have the feeling there was somebody always in the house with them. Of course, they tried to be sensible about it, but it gave them a terribly eerie feeling. As for getting a maid to stay, it couldn't be done! The maids all said that they felt that someone was always looking over their shoulders while they worked, and every time they set something down, it got itself moved to another place. They wouldn't take it upon themselves to say why, but they'd take whatever pay was coming to them, and go. And they did.

The end of the tenants' stay in the house came upon the day when the young wife came into the sitting-room to find her wee lad rolling his ball across the floor. Every time the ball reached the middle of the room it seemed to turn and roll itself back to him, as if someone who couldn't be seen were playing with him. But when he looked up at his mother and laughed and said "Bonny lady!" 'twas more than she could bear. She caught him up in her arms and ran out of the door to one of the neighbours, and no one could persuade her to set foot in the house again. So her husband went to the agent and told him they were sorry, but the way things were, they'd have to give up the house.

The young man to whom the house had been left was a very matter-of-fact young fellow. He didn't believe in ghosts. He was quite put out because the story had got round that there were ghosts in the house. Of course, the young couple who had lived there couldn't be depended on not to talk about what had happened. It wouldn't have been according to human nature for them to keep quiet about it. What made it awkward was that by this time the young man had found a lass he wanted to marry, but unfortunately she had heard the story. And she did believe in ghosts.

She said that she loved him dearly and would like very much to marry him. But she told him flatly that she could never, *never* bring herself to live in a haunted house.

Then the young man told her that he would go and live in the house himself, just to prove that there were no ghosts in it. Anyway, he didn't believe in ghosts. So he left his lodgings and moved in and got himself settled comfortably in his house.

Well, the doors did open and close of themselves, but that didn't daunt him. He just took them off their hinges and rehung them. They went on opening and closing just the same, but he said that was only because of a flaw in the walls.

He had to admit to himself that he heard drawers opening and closing, and latches of cupboards clicking shut. There was a tinkling in the china closet, too, as if someone were moving the cups and plates about. And once or twice he thought he heard water running in the scullery. But when he looked, every tap was shut off tight. Besides, he knew there was no one but himself in the house. So he said that old houses were always full of queer noises because of the foundations settling, and paid them no more heed.

Even when a book he had just closed and laid on the table opened itself again, and leaves turned over slowly as if someone were looking at them, he told himself that it was just a puff of wind from the window did it, although afterwards he remembered that the windows were closed at the time.

But still he didn't believe in ghosts.

So he went on living in the house and trying to persuade his sweetheart to marry him and come and live there with him. And, of course, to convince her that the house wasn't haunted at all. But he had no luck, for she wouldn't be persuaded.

Well, things went on in this unsatisfactory way until his summer holidays came round. He decided, now that he had the time for it, to do something he'd been meaning to do and never got round to. There were a lot of clothes in the attic that had belonged to the old lawyer and his daughter. It seemed sinful to leave them there to moulder away when some poor body'd be glad to have them. So what he was going to do was to pack them all up and send them to the Missionary Society where a good use would be found for them.

He went up to the garret and found some empty boxes, and began to pack the clothes. They were all hanging in tall presses, ranged around the room. He packed the old lawyer's clothes first. There were a good many of them, suits and coats and boots and shoes, all of the best quality, to say nothing of a quantity of warm underclothing in boxes neatly stacked on the floors of the presses. When he had taken everything out and folded it neatly, he packed the boxes and set them out of his way, and turned to the press that held the dead lass's clothes. When he opened the first press there was a sound uncommonly like a sigh. It gave him a start for a moment, but then he laughed and told himself that it was only the silk of garments brushing against each other in the breeze made by the opening door. He began to take them out, one by one, and to fold them and gently lay them in the box he'd set ready for them. It made him feel a little bit sad and sentimental to be handling the dresses that had been worn by the pretty young thing who had died so young and so long ago.

He'd laid away five or six of them when he came to one frock that seemed strangely heavy for the material of which it was made. It was a light, crisp cotton sprigged with flowers still bright in spite of the years it had hung in the press. He thought that a dress like that should have had almost no weight at all, so he looked it over curiously. Perhaps a brooch or a buckle was the answer? Then he found a pocket set in the seam of the skirt, and in the pocket a small red book and a letter. It was a letter of the old style, with no envelope, and the dead girl's name and address on the outer folded sheet. He laid the dress aside and, taking his find to the low-set window, he sat down on the floor to read what he had found. He was not a man to read other people's letters and secrets, but something made him feel that it was right to do so now.

He read the letter first. It said:

My dear love:

Although they have not told me I know that I am very ill. It may be that we shall not meet again in this world. If I should die I beg of you to make them promise that when you, too, are dead we shall lie together side by side.

Your true love

The young man sat for a while, thinking of the letter, wondering how it had come to the lass, remembering that he had heard that the old laird was hard set against the match. Then he took up the little red book and opened it. The little book was a sort of day-by-day diary with the date printed at the top of each page. It had begun as a sort of housekeeping journal. There was a lot in it about household affairs. There were records of sewing done, of jars of pickles and jams laid by, and about the house being turned out and cleaned from end to end, and such things. But through it all was the story of a young girl's heart. She told about meeting the laird's son, where they first met and when he first spoke to her of love and what they said and how they planned to marry as soon as the old laird could be persuaded to give his consent to the match. Although he was against it, they thought he might be brought over in time.

But they had no time, poor young things! Soon after, the diary told of the letter that John the Carrier had brought her, that had frightened her terribly. And the next page said only, "My love is dead." Page after page was empty after that. Then towards the end of the little book she had written: "I know that I am going to die. I asked my father today to promise to beg the laird to let me lie beside my love when I am dead, but he only turned away and would not answer. I am afraid his pride will not let him ask a favour of one who would not accept me into his family. But, oh my love, if he does not, I'll find a way to bring things right. I'll never rest until I do."

And that was all.

The young man raised his eyes from the page and repeated thoughtfully, "I'll never rest until I do."

It was then and there that he began to believe in ghosts!

He put the diary and the letter into his pocket, and leaving everything just as it was in the garret, he went downstairs. The packing could wait for another day. He had something better to do. As he went he thought of the old lawyer living there day after day with the ghost of his dead daughter mutely beseeching him to do what his pride would never let him do.

"Well, I have no pride at all," the young man said.

He packed a bag and put on his hat and coat, and started for the station. But as he went out of the door, he turned and put his head back in and called, "Do not fret yourself any longer, lass! You can rest now. I'll find the way to bring things right."

At the station he was fortunate enough to find a train that would take him where he wanted to go. When he got off the train he asked about the village for news of the laird. Och, the old laird was long dead, folk told him, and a rare old amadan that one was, though they shouldn't be saying it of the dead. But the new laird, him that was the old laird's nephew, had the estate now, and a finer man you'd not be finding should you search for a year and a day.

So up to the castle the young man went. When he got there he found the new laird as reasonable a man as he could hope to find. So he gave him the letter and the diary and let him read the story for himself. Then he told him about his house and the ghost in it that would not rest until she had her way.

The old laird's nephew listened gravely, and at the end

of the young man's story he sighed and said, "Fifty years! Fifty long years! What a weary time to wait. Poor lass."

The old laird's nephew believed in ghosts himself.

He called his solicitors at once and got them to work. They were so quick about it that by the time the young man got back home after paying a visit to the old laird's nephew who asked him to stay till all was settled, the two lovers were reunited at last and lay together side by side in the old laird's family tomb.

When he got home he could tell the minute he stepped through the door that there was no one there but himself. There was no more trouble with the doors, and the only sounds were the ordinary sounds that he made himself.

He finally persuaded the lass he wanted to marry to come for supper one night and bring along the old aunt she lived with. The aunt prided herself on having such a keen scent for ghosts that she could actually smell one if it was in a house. So they came, and as soon as they were all settled at the supper table the aunt looked all around the room and sniffed two or three times.

"Ghosts! Nonsense, my dear!" she said to the young man's lass firmly. "There isn't a single ghost in this house. You may be sure I'd know at once, if there were!"

That satisfied the young lady. So, soon she and the young man were married. They lived together so happily in the house that folks completely forgot that it had ever been said that it was haunted. It didn't look at all like the kind of house that would ever have a ghost. Only the young man remembered.

He really did believe in ghosts, after all.

Hans and His Master

Ruth Manning-Sanders

There was once a rich old gentleman who was no better than he should be, and he died and was buried in the family vault. But that wasn't the end of him. Every night his ghost came up into the house and made such an uproar that no one could sleep: he stamped here, he clattered there; he rattled and banged and flung things about, till all the household were nigh crazy with terror.

The gracious lady, his widow, was grieved at heart. And one day when she had gone down into the kitchen, she said, "Ah, why cannot my late husband find rest, so that you and I, my poor servants, might have at least a little peace?"

Well now, sitting in the kitchen, drinking his soup, was old Hans, the coachman. And he spoke up and said, "If the gracious lady will leave the matter to me, I think I know of a remedy. But for a couple of days I must have a hundred gold pieces, and also a coffin. I will lay me down in the coffin; and if the gracious lady will have me carried into the vault, coffin and all, and set alongside of my master I will soon find out why my poor master can't rest in his grave."

Now Hans was the oldest servant of the house, and his lady liked and trusted him. So she gave him the hundred gold pieces, and ordered a coffin to be made for him. And whilst the coffin was in the making, Hans took the gold pieces and buried them in the stable. Then, when the coffin was ready, Hans got into it, stretched himself out, and bade them put on the lid. And that they did, and carried the coffin down to the vault, and laid it beside the coffin of the master.

And Hans lay quiet in his coffin through the day and through the evening, until the great clock in the stable yard struck midnight.

And as the last stroke of the clock died away, Hans heard the lid of his master's coffin burst open; so he immediately banged up the lid of his own coffin likewise. Then the master sat up in his coffin, and Hans sat up in *his* coffin. Then the master climbed out of his coffin, and so did Hans.

There they stood, master and man, looking at one another.

"Hans, Hans," said the master, "how came you here?"

"Exactly as you did, gracious master," said Hans. "I am dead and buried, and waiting humbly to serve you as I did in life."

"And where are you going now, Hans?"

"Exactly where you are going, gracious master, humbly to serve you."

"But I am going up to the house, Hans, for I have still something to see to."

"That I have also, gracious master, and just for that reason I can find no rest in my coffin."

"But what in the world can you have to see about, Hans?"

"It's this way, gracious master (humbly to serve you); I had a little sum of money put by and I buried it in the stable. Now I must just go and have a look, for I fear that thieves may have taken it."

"I too have a fear on my mind, Hans. So come, we will go together."

So the master led the way to the door of the vault, and Hans followed. And when they reached that door, the master slipped through the keyhole.

"Come along, Hans," said he.

"Ah, good master—humbly to serve you—I can't come, the keyhole is too narrow."

Then the master put his hand on the lock of the door; the door sprang open, and Hans stepped through. But the master shook his head and said, "Hans, Hans, what is this? I fear you are not dead!"

"Not dead, gracious master? Most certainly I am dead! But the manner of the flesh still clings about me, and I have yet to learn the way of ghosts."

"That may be, Hans—but it is strange."

"Don't shake your gracious head, master; I shall soon learn."

"That may be, Hans," said the master again. And they crossed the courtyard together. And when they came to the door of the house, the master chuckled and said, "First let us go through the rooms and frighten the women."

And he led the way to the kitchen.

And there again he slipped through the keyhole. But again he had to open the door before Hans could follow him.

"Oh Hans, Hans," said he, "this is very strange! I fear you are not dead after all!"

"Not dead, master—humbly to serve you! Didn't you see me get out of my coffin? A coffin is made for the dead, not for the living. But the hours of my death are short, and the hours of my life long, and the ways of the living are not cast aside in a moment."

"Well, now to work," said the master. And he went

to the dresser, snatched down one thing after the other, and flung everything on the floor. And what he saw his master doing, Hans did likewise: pots, dishes, plates, cups and saucers, knives and forks went flying; chairs and tables were overturned. The racket they made woke the whole household; the master chuckled and chuckled; Hans roared with laughter. But the strange thing was that whatever the master overturned put itself right again, and the things he threw from the dresser bounced up and set themselves in their proper place, sound and whole; whereas what Hans threw down was smashed into a thousand pieces, and the pieces remained strewed about the floor.

Then the master shook his head once more, and said, "Hans, Hans, my mind misgives me. I fear you are not dead!"

"Not dead, gracious master, not dead, how can that be, and me laid in my coffin? It is only that my life is not yet far distant, and so my hand is still heavy. I was never quick like you to learn new ways. Give me but a little time, and my hand will be as light as yours."

"Maybe, maybe," said the master. "But come, the night passes. Let us get on with the game."

And he led Hans from room to room, snatched the pictures from the walls, overturned the furniture, and threw everything pell-mell, making such an uproar that the people in the house put their fingers in their ears, drew the bedclothes over their heads, and lay quaking in sheer terror.

"Now," said the master at last, "I think they are scared enough, so we will go down to the cellar."

And down to the cellar he went, and Hans followed.

The master wasn't chuckling any more, he was sighing and groaning. "Hans," said he, "I will show you my trouble."

He laid his hand on a huge cask, and the cask moved from its place as lightly as a bubble; and there, underneath it, a hole opened in the cellar floor, and from the hole rose up a huge cauldron full of gold.

"Hans, Hans," groaned the master, "this gold is the cause of my trouble, and because of it my soul can find no rest. It was entrusted to me to bestow upon an orphanage, but I kept it for myself and hid it here. Ah, Hans, Hans, if the orphans could but get this gold, then I might have peace. But all in vain I groan and sigh: the orphans can never get it, for no living man knows that it is here. So here it must remain to all eternity; and to all eternity must I sigh and groan, and play the fool—if, by so doing, I may forget my sorrows for a few brief moments."

Then the master waved his hand over the cauldron. It sank once more, and the ground covered it. He touched the cask with his finger, and the cask moved back into its place as lightly as a bubble.

"Now, Hans," sighed the master, "we will see to your affair."

So they went to the stable, and there Hans took a spade and began to dig in the corner where he had buried his hundred gold pieces.

"Hans," said the master, "why do you dig?"

"To find the gold that I buried, master."

"Oh Hans, Hans, I fear you are not dead! The dead has only to wave a hand and the money will come out by itself."

"Not dead, gracious master—humbly to serve you! Not dead! Most surely I am dead! Did you not see me in my coffin? But I have not yet fully learned how I must go on, and so I dig as I did in life."

Then Hans dug up all his gold, and counted it coin by coin.

"Yes," said he, "it is all here. And now I must bury it again."

And he began shovelling back the earth over the gold, slowly and carefully, taking his time.

"Work quicker, work quicker!" cried the master. "For soon the cocks will crow, and then we must lie down in our coffins."

But Hans was not to be hurried, however much his master fretted and fumed. However, at last he filled in the earth over his gold, and patted the earth smooth, and laid down his spade.

Cock-a-doodle-do! Faint, hoarse and sleepy, a cock crowed from the poultry yard.

"Hans, Hans, did you hear that? The grey cock has crowed! We must hasten to our coffins!"

"I will come, gracious master—humbly to serve you. I will come very soon. But first I am going back up into the house to frighten the people just a little bit more. For that is great fun, gracious master, and to remember it will make me laugh when I have to lie down in my coffin."

And Hans ran up into the house and began to throw things about, making all the noise he could. But the master stood at the house door, wringing his hands.

Cock-a-doodle-doo-oo! Out in the poultry house there came a glimmer of dawn light. A cock stirred on his perch, and crowed between sleep and waking.

"Hans, Hans, did you hear that? The red cock has crowed! If you don't come at once I shall leave you and go alone, for it is time we were back in our coffins!"

Now Hans wished for nothing better than that his master should go and leave him, so he flung a few dishes from the dresser and shouted, "I come directly, gracious master, I come directly! But first a little more fun!"

Cock-a-doodle-doo! Cock-a-doodle-doo! Cock-a-doodle-

doo! The rising sun darted a ray of light up from behind the courtyard wall; the ray flashed through the window of the poultry house, and three cocks crowed clear and loud.

"Hans, Hans, the grey cock has crowed, the red cock has crowed, the white cock has crowed, and the dawn has come!" The wailing voice of the master grew fainter and fainter, and was silent. He had gone back to his coffin in the vault.

Now the house was very quiet. Hans tiptoed up to his mistress's door and called, "Mistress, gracious mistress, wake up!"

"It is easy to wake, Hans, when one has not slept," answered the gracious widowed lady. And she opened her door and came out.

Then Hans told her all that had happened. And she called her servants, and everyone went down to the cellar. There, after much heaving and straining, they managed to move the great cask from its place. And then they took spades and pickaxes and dug and dug, and at last unearthed the cauldron full of gold. They packed the gold into sacks; and even before the mistress sat down to breakfast, she had the sacks of gold carried to the orphanage.

After that the house was put in order. And on the following night, and on every night thereafter, the gracious widowed lady and her servants were able to sleep peacefully in their beds. Never again did the master come to make the night hideous with his uproar. Only, on the first night, Hans waked from his sleep to find the master standing by his bed.

"Hans, Hans," said the master, "I fear you have sadly deceived me! And yet I am grateful to you, my valiant servant, because what you have done was to my greatest good. By your means the wrong has been righted; and now I can go to my rest."

The Haunted Trailer

Robert Arthur

It was inevitable, of course. Bound to happen some day. But why did it have to happen to me? What did *I* do to deserve the grief? And I was going to be married, too. I sank my last thousand dollars into that trailer, almost. In it Monica and I were going on a honeymoon tour of the United States. We were going to see the country. I was going to write, and we were going to be happy as two turtle-doves.

Ha!

Ha ha!

If you detect bitterness in that laughter, I'll tell you why I'm bitter.

Because it had to be me, Mel—for Melvin—Mason who became the first person in the world to own a haunted trailer!

Now, a haunted castle is one thing. Even an ordinary haunted house can be livable in. In a castle, or a house, if there's a ghost around, you can lock yourself in the bedroom and get a little sleep. A nuisance, yes. But nothing a man couldn't put up with.

In a trailer, though! What are you going to do when you're sharing a trailer, even a super-de-luxe model with four built-in bunks, a breakfast nook, a complete bathroom, a radio, electric range, and easy chair, with a ghost? Where can you go to get away from it?

Ha!

Ha ha!

I've heard so much ghostly laughter the last week that I'm laughing myself that way now.

There I was. I had the trailer. I had the car to pull it, naturally. I was on my way to meet Monica in Hollywood, where she was living with an aunt from Iowa. And twelve miles west of Albany, the first night out, my brand-new, spic-and-span trailer picks up a hitch-hiking haunt!

But maybe I'd better start at the beginning. It happened this way. I bought the trailer in New England—a Custom Clipper, with chrome and tan outside trim, for $2,998. I hitched it on behind my car and headed westwards, happier than a lark when the dew's on the thorn. I'd been saving up for this day for two years, and I felt wonderful.

I took it easy, getting the feel of the trailer, and so I didn't make very good time. I crossed the Hudson river just after dark, trundled through Albany in a rainstorm, and half an hour later pulled off the road into an old path between two big rocks to spend the night.

The thunder was rolling back and forth overhead, and the lightning was having target practice with the trees. But I'd picked out a nice secluded spot and I made myself comfortable. I cooked up a tasty plate of beans, some coffee, and fried potatoes. When I had eaten I took off my shoes, slumped down in the easy chair, lit a cigarette, and leaned back.

"Ah!" I said aloud. "Solid comfort. If only Monica were here, how happy we would be."

But she wasn't, so I picked up a book.

It wasn't a very good book. I must have dozed off. Maybe I slept for a couple of hours. Maybe three. Anyway, I woke with a start, the echo of a buster of a thunderbolt still rattling the willow pattern tea-set in the china cupboard. My hair was standing on end from the electricity in the air.

Then the door banged open, a swirl of rain swept in, and the wind—anyway, I thought it was the wind—slammed the door to. I heard a sound like a ghost—there's no other way to describe it—of a sigh.

"Now this," said the voice, "is something like!"

I had jumped up to shut the door, and I stood there with my unread book in my hand, gaping. The wind had blown a wisp of mist into my trailer and the mist, instead of evaporating, remained there, seeming to turn slowly and to settle into shape. It got more and more solid until . . .

Well, you know. It was a spectre. A haunt. A homeless ghost.

The creature remained there, regarding me in a decidedly cool manner.

"Sit down, chum," it said, "and don't look so pop-eyed. You make me nervous. This is my first night indoors in fifteen years, and I wanta enjoy it."

"Who—" I stammered—"who——"

"I'm not," the spectre retorted, "a brother owl, so don't who-who at me. What do I look like?"

"You look like a ghost," I told him.

"Now you're getting smart, chum. I *am* a ghost. What *kind* of a ghost do I look like?"

I inspected it more closely. Now that the air inside my trailer had stopped eddying, it was reasonably firm of outline. It was a squat, heavy-set ghost, attired in ghostly garments that certainly never had come to it new. He wore the battered ghost of a felt hat, and a stubble of ghostly beard showed on his jowls.

"You look like a tramp ghost," I answered with distaste, and my uninvited visitor nodded.

"Just what I am, chum," he told me. "Call me Spike Higgins. Spike for short. That was my name before it happened."

"Before what happened?" I demanded. The ghost wafted across the trailer to settle down on a bunk, where he lay down and crossed his legs, hoisting one foot encased in a battered ghost of a shoe into the air.

"Before I was amachoor enough to fall asleep riding on top of a truck, and fall off right here fifteen years ago," he told me. "Ever since I been forced to haunt this place. I wasn't no Boy Scout, so I got punished by bein' made to stay here in one spot. Me, who never stayed in one spot two nights running before!

"I been gettin' kind of tired of it the last couple of years. They wouldn't even lemme haunt a house. No, I hadda do all my haunting out in th' open, where th' wind an' rain could get at me, and every dog that went by could bark at me. Chum, you don't know what it means to me that you've picked this place to stop."

"Listen," I said firmly, "you've got to get out of here!"

The apparition yawned.

"Chum," he said, "you're the one that's trespassin', not me. This is my happy hunting ground. Did I ask you to stop here?"

"You mean," I asked between clenched teeth, "that you won't go? You're going to stay here all night?"

"Right, chum," the ghost grunted. "Gimme a call for 6 a.m." He closed his eyes, and began snoring in an artificial and highly insulting manner.

Then I got sore. I threw the book at him, and it bounced off the bunk without bothering him in the least. Spike Higgins opened an eye and leered at me.

"Went right through me," he chortled. "Instead of me goin' through it. Ha ha! Ha ha ha! Joke."

43

"You—" I yelled, in a rage. "You—stuff!"

And I slammed him with the chair cushion, which likewise went through him without doing any damage. Spike Higgins opened both eyes and stuck out his tongue at me.

Obviously I couldn't hurt him, so I got control of myself.

"Listen," I said craftily. "You say you are doomed to haunt this spot for ever? You can't leave?"

"Forbidden to leave," Spike answered. "Why?"

"Never mind," I gritted. "You'll find out."

I snatched up my raincoat and hat and scrambled out into the storm. If that ghost was doomed to remain in that spot for ever, I wasn't. I got into the car, got the motor going, and backed out of there. It took a lot of manœuvring in the rain, with mud underwheel, but I made it. I got straightened out on the concrete and headed westwards.

I didn't stop until I'd covered twenty miles. Then, beginning to grin as I thought of the shock the ghost of Spike Higgins must have felt when I yanked the trailer from underneath him, I parked on a stretch of old, unused road and then crawled back into the trailer again.

Inside, I slammed the door and . . .

Ha!

Ha ha!

Ha ha ha!

Yes, more bitter laughter. Spike Higgins was still there, sound asleep and snoring.

I muttered something under my breath. Spike Higgins opened his eyes sleepily.

"Hello," he yawned. "Been having fun?"

"Listen," I finally got it out. "I—thought—you—were—doomed—to—stay—back—there—where—I—found—you—for ever!"

The apparition yawned again.

"Your mistake, chum. I didn't say I was doomed to stay. I said I was forbidden to leave. I didn't leave. You hauled me away. It's all your responsibility and I'm a free agent now."

"You're a what?"

"I'm a free agent. I can ramble as far as I please. I can take up hoboing again. You've freed me. Thanks, chum. I won't forget."

"Then—then——" I sputtered. Spike Higgins nodded.

"That's right. I've adopted you. I'm going to stick with you. We'll travel together."

"But you can't!" I cried out, aghast. "Ghosts don't travel around! They haunt houses—or cemeteries—or maybe woods. But——"

"What do you know about ghosts?" Spike Higgins's voice held sarcasm. "There's all kinds of ghosts, chum. Includin' hobo ghosts, tramp ghosts with itchin' feet who can't stay put in one spot. Let me tell you, chum, a 'bo ghost like me ain't never had no easy time of it.

"Suppose they do give him a house to haunt? All right, he's got a roof over his head, but there he is, stuck. Houses don't move around. They don't go places. They stay in one spot till they rot.

"But things are different now. You've helped bring in a new age for the brotherhood of spooks. Now a fellow can haunt a house and be on the move at the same time. He can work at his job and still see the country. These trailers are the answer to a problem that's been bafflin' the best minds in the spirit world for thousands of years. It's the newest thing, the latest and best. Haunted trailers. I tell you, we'll probably erect a monument to you at our next meeting. The ghost of a monument, anyway."

Spike Higgins had raised up on an elbow to make his speech. Now, grimacing, he lay back.

"That's enough, chum," he muttered. "Talking uses up my essence. I'm going to merge for a while. See you in the morning."

"Merge with what?" I asked. Spike Higgins was already so dim I could hardly see him.

"Merge with the otherwhere," a faint, distant voice told me, and Spike Higgins was gone.

I waited a minute to make sure. Then I breathed a big sigh of relief. I looked at my raincoat, at my wet feet, at the book on the floor, and knew it had all been a dream. I'd been walking in my sleep. Driving in it too. Having a nightmare.

I hung up the raincoat, slid out of my clothes, and got into a bunk.

I woke up late, and for a moment felt panic. Then I breathed easily again. The other bunk was untenanted. Whistling, I jumped up, showered, dressed, ate, and got under way.

It was a lovely day. Blue sky, wind, sunshine, birds singing. Thinking of Monica, I almost sang with them as I rolled down the road. In a week I'd be pulling up in front of Monica's aunt's place in Hollywood and tooting the horn . . .

That was the moment when a cold draught of air sighed along the back of my neck, and the short hairs rose.

I turned, almost driving into a hay wagon. Beside me was a misty figure.

"I got tired of riding back there alone," Spike Higgins told me. "I'm gonna ride up front a while an' look at th' scenery."

"You—you——" I shook with rage so that we nearly ran off the road. Spike Higgins reached out, grabbed the wheel in tenuous fingers, and jerked us back on to our course again.

"Take it easy, chum," he said. "There's enough competition in this world I'm in, without you hornin' into th' racket."

I didn't say anything, but my thoughts must have been written on my face. I'd thought he was just a nightmare. But he was real. A ghost had moved in with me, and I hadn't the faintest idea how to move him out.

Spike Higgins grinned with a trace of malice.

"Sure, chum," he said. "It's perfectly logical. There's haunted castles, haunted palaces, and haunted houses. Why not a haunted trailer?"

"Why not haunted ferry-boats?" I demanded with bitterness. "Why not haunted Pullmans? Why not haunted trucks?"

"You think there ain't?" Spike Higgins's misty countenance registered surprise at my ignorance. "Could I tell you tales! There's a haunted ferry-boat makes the crossing at Poughkeepsie every stormy night at midnight. There's a haunted private train on the Atchison, Sante Fé. Pal of mine haunts it. He always jumped trains, but he was a square dealer, and they gave him the private train for a reward.

"Then there's a truck on the New York Central that never gets where it's going. Never has yet. No matter where it starts out for, it winds up some place else. Bunch of my buddies haunt it. And another truck on the Southern Pacific that never has a train to pull it. Runs by itself. It's driven I dunno how many signalmen crazy, when they saw it go past right ahead of a whole train. I could tell you——"

"Don't!" I ordered. "I forbid you to. I don't want to hear."

"Why, sure, chum," Spike Higgins agreed. "But you'll get used to it. You'll be seein' a lot of me. Because where thou ghost, I ghost. Pun." He gave a ghostly chuckle and relapsed into silence. I drove along, my mind churning. I had to get rid of him. *Had* to. Before we reached California, at the very latest. But I didn't have the faintest idea in the world how I was going to.

Then, abruptly, Spike Higgins's ghost sat up straight. "Stop!" he ordered. "Stop, I say!"

We were on a lonely stretch of road, bordered by old cypresses, with weed-grown marshland beyond. I didn't see any reason for stopping. But Spike Higgins reached out and switched off the ignition. Then he slammed on the emergency brake. We came squealing to a stop, and just missed going into a ditch.

"What did you do that for?" I yelled. "You almost ditched us! Confound you, you ectoplasmic, hitch-hiking nuisance! If I ever find a way to lay hands on you——"

"Quiet, chum!" the apparition told me rudely. "I just seen an old pal of mine. Slippery Samuels. I ain't seen him since he dropped a bottle of nitro just as he was gonna break into a bank in Mobile sixteen years ago. We're gonna give him a ride."

"We certainly are not!" I cried. "This is my car, and I'm not picking up any more——"

"It may be your car," Spike Higgins sneered, "but I'm the resident haunt, and I got full powers to extend hospitality to any buddy ghosts I want, see? Rule 11, subdivision c. Look it up. Hey, Slippery, climb in!"

A finger of fog pushed through the partly open window of the car at his hail, enlarged, and there was a second apparition on the front seat with me.

The newcomer was long and lean, just as shabbily dressed as Spike Higgins, with a ghostly countenance as mournful as a Sunday School picnic on a rainy day.

"Spike, you old son of a gun," the second spook murmured, in hollow tones that would have brought goose-flesh to a statue. "How've you been? What're you doing here? Who's he?"—nodding at me.

"Never mind him," Spike said disdainfully. "I'm haunting his trailer. Listen, whatever became of the old gang?"

"Still hoboing it," the long, lean apparition sighed. "Nitro Nelson is somewhere around. Pacific Pete and Buffalo Benny are lying over in a haunted jungle somewhere near Toledo. I had a date to join 'em, but a storm blew me back to Wheeling a couple of days ago."

"Mmm," Spike Higgins's ghost muttered. "Maybe we'll run into 'em. Let's go back in my trailer and do a little chinning. As for you, chum, make camp any time you want. Ta ta."

The two apparitions oozed through the back of the car and were gone. I was boiling inside, but there was nothing I could do.

I drove on for another hour, went through Toledo, then stopped at a wayside camp. I paid my dollar, picked out a spot, and parked.

But when I entered the trailer, the ghosts of Spike Higgins and Slippery Samuels, the bank robber, weren't there. Nor had they shown up by the time I finished dinner. In fact I ate, washed, and got into bed with no sign of them.

Breathing a prayer that maybe Higgins had abandoned me to go back to 'boing it in the spirit world, I fell asleep. And began to dream. About Monica ...

When I woke, there was a sickly smell in the air, and the heavy staleness of old tobacco smoke.

I opened my eyes. Luckily, I opened them prepared for the worst. Even so, I wasn't prepared well enough.

Spike Higgins was back. Ha ! Ha ha ! Ha ha ha ! I'll say he

49

was back. He lay on the opposite bunk, his eyes shut, his mouth open, snoring. Just the ghost of a snore, but quite loud enough. On the bunk above him lay his bank-robber companion. In the easy chair was slumped a third apparition, short and stout, with a round, whiskered face. A tramp spirit, too.

So was the ghost stretched out on the floor, gaunt and cadaverous. So was the small, mournful spook in the bunk above me, his ectoplasmic hand swinging over the side, almost in my face. Tramps, all of them. Hobo spooks. Five hobo phantoms asleep in my trailer!

And there were cigarette butts in all the ash trays, and burns on my built-in writing desk. The cigarettes apparently had just been lit and let burn. The air was choking with stale smoke, and I had a headache I could have sold for a fire alarm, it was ringing so loudly in my skull.

I knew what had happened. During the night Spike Higgins and his pal had rounded up some more of their ex-hobo companions. Brought them back. To *my* trailer. Now—I was so angry I saw all five of them through a red haze that gave their ectoplasm a ruby tinge. Then I got hold of myself. I couldn't throw them out. I couldn't harm them. I couldn't touch them.

No, there was only one thing I could do. Admit I was beaten. Take my loss and quit while I could. It was a bitter pill to swallow. But if I wanted to reach Monica, if I wanted to enjoy the honeymoon we'd planned, I'd have to give up the fight.

I got into my clothes. Quietly I sneaked out, locking the trailer behind me. Then I hunted for the owner of the trailer camp, a lanky man, hard-eyed, but well dressed. I guessed he must have money.

"Had sort of a party last night, hey?" he asked me, with a leering wink. "I seen lights, an' heard singing, long after midnight. Not loud, though, so I didn't bother you. But it looked like somebody was havin' a high old time."

I gritted my teeth.

"That was me," I said, "I couldn't sleep. I got up and turned on the radio. Truth is, I haven't slept a single night in that trailer. I guess I wasn't built for trailer life. That job cost me $2,998 new, just three days ago. I've got the bill-of-sale. How'd you like to buy it for fifteen hundred, and make two hundred easy profit on it?"

He gnawed his lip, but knew the trailer was a bargain. We settled for thirteen-fifty. I gave him the bill-of-sale, took the money, uncoupled, got into the car, and left there.

As I turned the bend in the road, heading westwards, there was no sign that Spike Higgins's ghost was aware of what had happened.

I even managed to grin as I thought of his rage when he woke up to find I had abandoned him. It was almost worth the money I'd lost to think of it.

Beginning to feel better, I stepped on the accelerator, piling up miles between me and that trailer. At least I was rid of Spike Higgins and his friends.

Ha!

Ha ha!

Ha ha ha!

That's what I thought.

About the middle of the afternoon I was well into Illinois. It was open country, and monotonous, so I turned on my radio. And the first thing I got was a police broadcast.

"All police, Indiana and Illinois! Be on the watch for a tan-and-chrome trailer, stolen about noon from a camp near Toledo. The thieves are believed heading west in it. That is all."

I gulped. It couldn't be! But—it sounded like my trailer, all right. I looked in my rear-vision mirror, apprehensively. The road behind was empty. I breathed a small sigh of relief. I breathed it too soon. For at that moment, round a curve half a mile behind me, something swung into sight and came racing down the road after me.

The trailer.

Ha!

Ha ha!

There it came, a tan streak that zipped round the curve and came streaking after me, zigzagging wildly from side to side of the road, doing at least sixty—without a car pulling it.

My flesh crawled, and my hair stood on end. I stepped on the accelerator. Hard. And I picked up speed in a hurry. In half a minute I was doing seventy, and the trailer was still gaining. Then I hit eighty—and passed a motor-cycle cop parked beside the road.

I had just a glimpse of his pop-eyed astonishment as I whizzed past, with the trailer chasing me fifty yards behind. Then, kicking on his starter, he slammed after us.

Meanwhile, in spite of everything the car would do, the trailer pulled up behind me and I heard the coupling clank as it was hitched on. At once my speed dropped. The trailer was swerving dangerously, and I had to slow. Behind me the cop was coming, siren open wide, but I didn't worry about him because Spike Higgins was materializing beside me.

"Whew!" he said, grinning at me. "My essence feels all used up. Thought you could give Spike Higgins and his pals the slip, huh? You'll learn, chum, you'll learn. That trooper looks like a tough baby. You'll have fun trying to talk yourself out of this."

"Yes, but see what it'll get *you*, you ectoplasmic excrescence!" I raged at him. "The trailer will be stored away in some county garage for months as evidence while I'm being held for trial on the charge of stealing it. And how'll you like haunting a garage?"

Higgins's face changed.

"Say, that's right," he muttered. "My first trip for fifteen years, too."

He put his fingers to his lips, and blew the shrill ghost of a whistle. In a moment the car was filled with cold, clammy draughts as Slippery Samuels and the other three apparitions appeared in the seat beside Higgins.

Twisting and turning and seeming to intermingle a lot, they peered out at the cop, who was beside the car now, one hand on his gun butt, trying to crowd me over to the shoulder.

"All right, boys!" Higgins finished explaining. "You know what we gotta do. Me an' Slippery'll take the car. You guys take the trailer!"

They slipped through the open windows like smoke. Then I saw Slippery Samuels holding on to the left front bumper, and Spike Higgins holding on to the right, their ectoplasm streaming out horizontal to the road, stretched and thinned by the air rush. And an instant later we began to move with a speed I had never dreamed of reaching.

We zipped ahead of the astonished cop, and the speedometer needle began to climb again. It took the trooper an instant to believe his eyes. Then with a yell he yanked out his gun and fired. A bullet bumbled past; then he was too busy trying to overtake us again to shoot.

The speedometer said ninety now, and was still climbing. It touched a hundred and stuck there. I was trying to pray when down the road a mile away I saw a sharp curve, a bridge, and a deep river. I froze. I couldn't even yell.

We came up to the curve so fast that I was still trying to move my lips when we hit it. I didn't make any effort to take it. Instead I slammed on the brakes and prepared to plough straight ahead into a fence, a stand of young poplars, and the river.

But just as I braked, I heard Spike Higgins's ghostly scream, "Allay-OOP!"

And before we reached the ditch, car and trailer swooped up in the air. An instant later at a height of a hundred and fifty feet, we hurtled straight westwards over the river and the town beyond.

I'd like to have seen the expression on the face of the motor-cycle cop then. As far as that goes, I'd like to have seen my own.

Then the river was behind us, and the town, and we were swooping down towards a dank, gloomy-looking patch of woods through which ran an abandoned railway line. A moment later we struck earth with a jouncing shock and came to rest.

Spike Higgins and Slippery Samuels let go of the bumpers and straightened themselves up. Spike Higgins dusted ghostly dust off his palms and leered at me.

"How was that, chum?" he asked. "Neat, hey?"

"How——" I stuttered—"how——"

"Simple," Spike Higgins answered. "Anybody that can tip tables can do it. Just levitation, 'at's all. Hey, meet the boys. You ain't been introduced yet. This is Buffalo Benny, this one is Toledo Ike, this one Pacific Pete."

The fat spook, the cadaverous one, and the melancholy little one appeared from behind the car, and smirked as Higgins introduced them. Then Higgins waved a hand impatiently.

"C'm on, chum," he said. "There's a road there that takes us out of these woods. Let's get going. It's almost dark, and we don't wanna spend the night here. This used to be in Dan Bracer's territory."

"Who's Dan Bracer?" I demanded, getting the motor going, because I was as anxious to get away from there as Spike Higgins's spook seemed to be.

"Just a railway dick," Spike Higgins said, with a distinctly uneasy grin. "Toughest bull that ever kicked a poor 'bo off a freight."

"So mean he always drank black coffee," Slippery Samuels put in, in a mournful voice. "Cream turned sour when he picked up the jug."

"Not that we was afraid of him——" Buffalo Benny, the fat apparition, squeaked. "But——"

"We just never liked him," Toledo Ike croaked, a sickly look on his ghostly features. "O' course, he ain't active now. He was retired a couple of years back, an' jes' lately I got a rumour he was sick."

"Dyin'," Pacific Pete murmured hollowly.

"Dyin'." They all sighed the word, looking apprehensive. Then Spike Higgins's ghost scowled truculently at me.

"Never mind about Dan Bracer," he snapped. "Let's just get goin' out of here. And don't give that cop no more thought. You think a cop is gonna turn in a report that a car and trailer he was chasin' suddenly sailed up in the air an' flew away like an aeroplane? Not on your sweet life. He isn't gonna say nothing to nobody about it."

Apparently he was right, because after I had driven out of the woods, with some difficulty, and on to a secondary highway, there was no further sign of pursuit. I headed westwards again, and Spike Higgins and his pals moved back to the trailer, where they lolled about, letting my cigarettes burn and threatening to call the attention of the police to me when I complained.

I grew steadily more morose and desperate as the Pacific Coast, and Monica, came nearer. I was behind schedule, due to Spike Higgins's insistence on my taking a round-about route so they could see the Grand Canyon, and no way to rid myself of the obnoxious haunts appeared. I couldn't even abandon the trailer. Spike Higgins had been definite on that point. It was better to haul a haunted trailer around than to have one chasing you, he pointed out, and shuddering at the thought of being pursued by a trailer full of ghosts wherever I went, I agreed.

But if I couldn't get rid of them, it meant no Monica, no marriage, no honeymoon. And I was determined that nothing as insubstantial as a spirit was going to interfere with my life's happiness.

Just the same, by the time I had driven over the mountains and into California, I was almost on the point of doing something desperate. Apparently sensing this, Spike Higgins and the others had been on their good behaviour. But I could still see no way to get rid of them.

It was early afternoon when I finally rolled into Hollywood, haggard and unshaven, and found a trailer camp, where I parked. Heavy-hearted, I bathed and shaved and put on clean clothes. I didn't know what I was going to say to Monica, but I was already several days behind schedule, and I couldn't put off ringing her.

There was a telephone in the camp office. I looked up Ida Bracer—her aunt's name—in the book, then put through the call.

Monica herself answered. Her voice sounded distraught.

"Oh, Mel," she exclaimed, as soon as I announced myself, "where have you been? I've been expecting you for days."

"I was delayed," I told her, bitterly. "Spirits. I'll explain later."

"Spirits?" Her tone seemed cold. "Well, anyway, now that you're here at last, I must see you at once. Mel, Uncle Dan is dying."

"Uncle Dan?" I echoed.

"Yes, Aunt Ida's brother. He used to live in Iowa, but a few months ago he was taken ill, and he came out to be with Aunt and me. Now he's dying. The doctor says it's only a matter of hours."

"Dying?" I repeated again. "Your Uncle Dan, from Iowa, dying?"

Then it came to me. I began to laugh. Exultantly.

"I'll be right over!" I said, and hung up.

Still chuckling, I hurried out and unhitched my car. Spike Higgins stared at me suspiciously.

"Just got an errand to do," I said airily. "Be back soon."

"You better be," Spike Higgins's ghost said. "We wanta drive around and see those movie stars' houses later on."

Ten minutes later Monica herself, trim and lovely, was opening the door for me. In high spirits, I grabbed her round the waist, and kissed her. She turned her cheek to me, then, releasing herself, looked at me strangely.

"Mel," she frowned, "what in the world is wrong with you?"

"Nothing," I carolled. "Monica darling, I've got to talk to your uncle."

"But he's too sick to see anyone. He's sinking fast, the doctor says."

"All the more reason why I must see him," I told her, and pushed into the house. "Where is he, upstairs?"

I hurried up, and into the sickroom. Monica's uncle, a big man with a rugged face and a chin like the prow of a battleship, was in bed, breathing stertorously.

"Mr. Bracer!" I said, breathless, and his eyes opened slowly.

"Who're you?" a voice as raspy as a shovel scraping a concrete floor growled.

"I'm going to marry Monica," I told him. "Mr. Bracer, have you ever heard of Spike Higgins? Or Slippery Samuels? Or Buffalo Benny, Pacific Pete, Toledo Ike?"

"Heard of 'em?" A bright glow came into the sick man's eyes. "Ha! I'll say I have. And laid hands on 'em, too, more'n once. But they're dead now."

"I know they are," I told him. "But they're still around. Mr. Bracer, how'd you like to meet up with them again?"

"Would I!" Dan Bracer murmured, and his hands clenched in unconscious anticipation. "Ha!"

"Then," I said, "if you'll wait for me in the cemetery the first night after—after—well, anyway, wait for me, and I'll put you in touch with them."

The ex-railway detective nodded. He grinned broadly, like a tiger viewing its prey and eager to be after it. Then he lay back, his eyes closed, and Monica, running in, gave a little gasp.

"He's gone!" she said.

"Ha ha!" I chuckled. "Ha ha ha! What a surprise this is going to be to certain parties."

The funeral was held in the afternoon, two days later. I didn't see Monica much in the interim. In the first place, though she hadn't known her uncle well, and wasn't particularly grieved, there were a lot of details to be attended to. In the second place, Spike Higgins and his pals kept me on the jump. I had to drive around Hollywood, to all the stars' houses, to Malibou Beach, Santa Monica, Laurel Canyon, and the various studios, so they could sightsee.

Then, too, Monica rather seemed to be avoiding me, when I did have time free. But I was too inwardly gleeful at the prospect of getting rid of the ghosts of Higgins and his pals to notice.

I managed to slip away from Higgins to attend the funeral of Dan Bracer, but could not help grinning broadly, and even at times chuckling, as I thought of his happy anticipation of meeting Spike Higgins and the others again. Monica eyed me oddly, but I could explain later. It wasn't quite the right moment to go into details.

After the funeral, Monica said she had a headache, so I promised to come round later in the evening. I returned to the trailer to find Spike Higgins and the others sprawled out, smoking my cigarettes again. Higgins looked at me with dark suspicion.

"Chum," he said, "we wanta be hitting the road again. We leave tomorrow, get me?"

"Tonight, Spike," I said cheerfully. "Why wait? Right after sunset you'll be on your way. To distant parts. Tra la, tra le, tum tum te tum."

He scowled, but could think of no objection. I waited impatiently for sunset. As soon as it was thoroughly dark, I hitched up and drove out of the trailer camp, heading for the cemetery where Dan Bracer had been buried that afternoon.

Spike Higgins was still surly, but unsuspicious until I drew up and parked by the low stone wall at the nearest point to Monica's uncle's grave. Then, gazing out at the darkness-shadowed cemetery, he looked uneasy.

"Say," he snarled, "whatcha stoppin' here for? Come on, let's be movin'."

"In a minute, Spike," I said. "I have some business here." I slid out and hopped over the low wall.

"Mr. Bracer!" I called. "Mr. Bracer!"

I listened, but a long freight rumbling by half a block distant, where the Union Pacific lines entered the city, drowned out any sound. For a moment I could see nothing. Then a misty figure came into view among the headstones.

"Mr. Bracer!" I called as it approached. "This way!"

The figure headed towards me. Behind me Spike Higgins, Slippery Samuels and the rest of the ghostly crew were pressed against the wall, staring apprehensively into the darkness. And they were able to recognize the dim figure approaching before I could be sure of it.

"Dan Bracer!" Spike Higgins choked, in a high, ghostly squeal.

"It's him!" Slippery Samuels groaned.

"In the spirit!" Pacific Pete wailed. "Oh oh oh oh OH!"

They tumbled backwards, with shrill squeaks of dismay. Dan Bracer's spirit came forward faster. Paying no attention to me, he took off after the retreating five.

Higgins turned and fled, wildly, with the others at his heels. They were heading towards the railway line, over which the freight was still rumbling, and Dan Bracer was now at their heels. Crowding each other, Higgins and Slippery Samuels and Buffalo Benny swung on to a passing truck, with Pacific Pete and Toledo Ike catching wildly at the rungs of the next.

They drew themselves up to the top of the trucks, and stared back. Dan Bracer's ghost seemed, for an instant, about to be left behind. But one long ectoplasmic arm shot out. A ghostly hand caught the rail of the guard's van, and Dan Bracer swung aboard. A moment later, he was running forward along the tops of the trucks, and up ahead of him, Spike Higgins and his pals were racing towards the engine.

That was the last I saw of them—five phantom figures fleeing, the sixth pursuing in happy anticipation. Then they were gone out of my life, heading east.

Still laughing to myself at the manner in which I had rid myself of Spike Higgins's ghost, and so made it possible for Monica and me to be married and enjoy our honeymoon trailer trip after all, I drove to Monica's aunt's house.

"Melvin!" Monica said sharply, as she answered my ring. "What are you laughing about now?"

"Your uncle," I chuckled. "He——"

"My uncle!" Monica gasped. "You—you fiend! You laughed when he died! You laughed all during his funeral! Now you're laughing because he's dead!"

"No, Monica!" I said. "Let me explain. About the spirits, and how I——"

Her voice broke.

"Forcing your way into the house—laughing at my poor Uncle Dan—laughing at his funeral——"

"But, Monica!" I cried. "It isn't that way at all. I've just been to the cemetery, and——"

"And you came back laughing," Monica retorted. "I never want to see you again. Our engagement is broken. And worst of all is the *way* you laugh. It's so—so ghostly! So spooky. Blood-chilling. Even if you hadn't done the other things, I could never marry a man who laughs like that. So here's your ring. And good-bye."

Leaving me staring at the ring in my hand, she slammed the door. And that was that. Monica is very strong-minded, and what she says, she means. I couldn't even try to explain. About Spike Higgins. And how I'd unconsciously come to laugh that way through associating with five phantoms. After all, I'd just rid myself of them for good. And the only way Monica would ever have believed my story would have been from my showing her Spike Higgins's ghost himself.

Ha!

Ha ha!

Ha ha ha ha!

If you know anyone who wants to buy a practically unused trailer, cheap, let them get in touch with me.

The Magic Shop

H. G. Wells

I had seen the Magic Shop from afar several times; I had passed it once or twice, a shop window of alluring little objects, magic balls, magic hens, wonderful cones, ventriloquist dolls, the material of the basket trick, packs of cards that *looked* all right, and all that sort of thing, but never had I thought of going in until one day, almost without warning, Gip hauled me by my finger right up to the window, and so conducted himself that there was nothing for it but to take him in. I had not thought the place was there, to tell the truth—a modest-sized frontage in Regent Street, between the picture shop and the place where the chicks run about just out of patent incubators—but there it was sure enough. I had fancied it was down nearer the Circus, or round the corner in Oxford Street or even in Holborn; always over the way and a little inaccessible it had been, with something of the mirage in its position; but here it was now quite indisputably, and the fat end of Gip's pointing finger made a noise upon the glass.

"If I was rich," said Gip, dabbing a finger at the Disappearing Egg, "I'd buy myself that. And that"—which was The Crying Baby, Very Human—"and that," which was a mystery, and called, so a neat card asserted, "Buy One and Astonish Your Friends."

"Anything," said Gip, "will disappear under one of those cones. I have read about it in a book.

"And there, Dadda, is the Vanishing Halfpenny—only they've set it this way up so's we can't see how it's done."

Gip, dear boy, inherits his mother's breeding, and he did not propose to enter the shop or worry in any way; only, you know, quite unconsciously he lugged my finger doorward, and he made his interest clear.

"That," he said, and pointed to the Magic Bottle.

"If you had that?" I said; at which promising inquiry he looked up with a sudden radiance.

"I could show it to Jessie," he said, thoughtful as ever of others.

"It's less than a hundred days to your birthday, Gibbles," I said, and laid my hand on the door-handle.

Gip made no answer, but his grip tightened on my finger, and so we came into the shop.

It was no common shop this; it was a magic shop, and all the prancing precedence Gip would have taken in the matter of mere toys was wanting. He left the burthen of the conversation to me.

It was a little, narrow shop, not very well lit, and the door-bell pinged again with a plaintive note as we closed it behind us. For a moment or so we were alone and could glance about us. There was a tiger in papier mâché on the glass case that covered the low counter—a grave, kind-eyed tiger that waggled his head in a methodical manner; there were several crystal spheres, a china hand holding magic cards, a stock of magic fish-bowls in various sizes, and an immodest magic hat that shamelessly displayed its springs. On the door were magic mirrors; one to draw you out long and thin, one to swell your head and vanish your legs, and one to make you short and fat like a draught; and while we were laughing at these the shopman, as I suppose, came in.

At any rate, there he was behind the counter—a curious,

sallow, dark man, with one ear larger than the other and a chin like the toecap of a boot.

"What can we have the pleasure?" he said, spreading his long, magic fingers on the glass case; and so with a start we were aware of him.

"I want," I said, "to buy my little boy a few simple tricks."

"Legerdemain?" he asked. "Mechanical? Domestic?"

"Anything amusing?" said I.

"Um!" said the shopman, and scratched his head for a moment as if thinking. Then, quite distinctly, he drew from his head a glass ball. "Something in this way?" he said, and held it out.

The action was unexpected. I had seen the trick done at entertainments endless times before—it's part of the common stock of conjurers—but I had not expected it here. "That's good," I said, with a laugh.

"Isn't it?" said the shopman.

Gip stretched out his disengaged hand to take this object and found merely a blank palm.

"It's in your pocket," said the shopman, and there it was!

"How much will that be?" I asked.

"We make no charge for glass balls," said the shopman, politely. "We get them"—he picked one out of his elbow as he spoke—"free." He produced another from the back of his neck, and laid it beside its predecessor on the counter. Gip regarded his glass ball sagely, then directed a look of inquiry at the two on the counter, and finally brought his round-eyed scrutiny to the shopman, who smiled. "You may have those too," said the shopman, "and, if you *don't* mind, one from my mouth. *So!*"

Gip counselled me mutely for a moment, and then in a profound silence put away the four balls, resumed my reassuring finger, and nerved himself for the next event.

"We get all our smaller tricks in that way," the shopman remarked.

I laughed in the manner of one who subscribes to a jest. "Instead of going to the wholesale shop," I said. "Of course, it's cheaper."

"In a way," the shopman said. "Though we pay in the end. But not so heavily—as people suppose.... Our larger tricks, and our daily provisions and all the other things we want, we get out of that hat.... And you know, sir, if you'll excuse my saying it, there *isn't* a wholesale shop, not for Genuine Magic goods, sir. I don't know if you noticed our inscription—The Genuine Magic Shop." He drew a business card from his cheek and handed it to me. "Genuine," he said, with his finger on the word, and added, "There is absolutely no deception, sir."

He seemed to be carrying out the joke pretty thoroughly, I thought.

He turned to Gip with a smile of remarkable affability. "You, you know, are the Right Sort of Boy."

I was surprised at his knowing that, because, in the interests of discipline, we keep it rather a secret even at home; but Gip received it in unflinching silence, keeping a steadfast eye on him.

"It's only the Right Sort of Boy gets through that doorway."

And, as if by way of illustration, there came a rattling at the door, and a squeaking little voice could be faintly heard. "Nyar! I warn 'a go in there, Dadda, I WARN 'a go in there. Ny-a-a-ah!" and then the accents of a downtrodden parent, urging consolations and propitiations. "It's locked, Edward," he said.

"But it isn't," said I.

"It is, sir," said the shopman, "always—for that sort of

child," and as he spoke we had a glimpse of the other youngster, a little, white face, pallid from sweet-eating and over-sapid food, and distorted by evil passions, a ruthless little egotist, pawing at the enchanted pane. "It's no good, sir," said the shopman, as I moved, with my natural helpfulness, doorward, and presently the spoilt child was carried off howling.

"How do you manage that?" I said, breathing a little more freely.

"Magic!" said the shopman, with a careless wave of the hand, and behold! sparks of coloured fire flew out of his fingers and vanished into the shadows of the shop.

"You were saying," he said, addressing himself to Gip, "before you came in, that you would like one of our 'Buy One and Astonish your Friends' boxes?"

Gip, after a gallant effort, said "Yes".

"It's in your pocket."

And leaning over the counter—he really had an extraordinarily long body—this amazing person produced the article in the customary conjurer's manner. "Paper," he said, and took a sheet out of the empty hat with the springs; "string," and behold his mouth was a string-box, from which he drew an unending thread, which when he had tied his parcel he bit off—and, it seemed to me, swallowed the ball of string. And then he lit a candle at the nose of one of the ventriloquist's dummies, stuck one of his fingers (which had become sealing-wax red) into the flame, and so sealed the parcel. Then there was the Disappearing Egg, he remarked, and produced one from within my coat-breast and packed it, and also The Crying Baby, Very Human. I handed each parcel to Gip as it was ready, and he clasped them to his chest.

He said very little, but his eyes were eloquent; the clutch of his arms was eloquent. He was the playground of unspeakable emotions. These, you know, were *real* Magics.

Then, with a start, I discovered something moving about in my hat—something soft and jumpy. I whipped it off, and a ruffled pigeon—no doubt a confederate—dropped out and ran on the counter, and went, I fancy, into a cardboard box behind the papier mâché tiger.

"Tut, tut!" said the shopman, dexterously relieving me of my head-dress; "careless bird, and—as I live—nesting!"

He shook my hat, and shook out into his extended hand two or three eggs, a large marble, a watch, about half a dozen of the inevitable glass balls, and then crumpled, crinkled paper, more and more and more, talking all the time of the way in which people neglect to brush their hats *inside* as well as out, politely, of course, but with a certain personal application. "All sorts of things accumulate, sir. . . . Not *you*, of course, in particular. . . . Nearly every customer. . . . Astonishing what they carry about with them. . . ." The crumpled paper rose and billowed on the counter more and more and more, until he was nearly hidden from us, until he was altogether hidden, and still his voice went on and on. "We none of us know what the fair semblance of a human being may conceal, sir. Are we all then no better than brushed exteriors, white sepulchres——"

His voice stopped—exactly like when you hit a neighbour's gramophone with a well-aimed brick, the same instant silence, and the rustle of the paper stopped, and everything was still. . . .

"Have you done with my hat?" I said, after an interval.

There was no answer.

I stared at Gip, and Gip stared at me, and there were our distortions in the magic mirrors, looking very rum, and grave, and quiet. . . .

"I think we'll go now," I said. "Will you tell me how much all this comes to? . . .

"I say," I said, on a rather louder note, "I want the bill; and my hat, please."

It might have been a sniff from behind the paper pile. . . .

"Let's look behind the counter, Gip," I said. "He's making fun of us."

I led Gip round the head-wagging tiger, and what do you think there was behind the counter? No one at all! Only my hat on the floor, and a common conjurer's lop-eared white rabbit lost in meditation, and looking as stupid and crumpled as only a conjurer's rabbit can do. I resumed my hat, and the rabbit lolloped a lollop or so out of my way.

"Dadda!" said Gip, in a guilty whisper.

"What is it, Gip?" said I.

"I *do* like this shop, Dadda."

"So should I," I said to myself, "if the counter wouldn't suddenly extend itself to shut one off from the door." But I didn't call Gip's attention to that. "Pussy!" he said, with a hand out to the rabbit as it came lolloping past us; "Pussy, do Gip a magic!" and his eyes followed it as it squeezed through a door I had certainly not remarked a moment before. Then this door opened wider, and the man with one ear larger than the other appeared again. He was smiling still, but his eye met mine with something between amusement and defiance. "You'd like to see our showroom, sir," he said, with an innocent suavity. Gip tugged my finger forward. I glanced at the counter and met the shopman's eye again. I was beginning to think the magic just a little too genuine. "We haven't *very* much time," I said. But somehow we were inside the showroom before I could finish that.

"All goods of the same quality," said the shopman, rubbing his flexible hands together, "and that is the Best. Nothing in the place that isn't genuine Magic, and warranted thoroughly rum. Excuse me, sir!"

I felt him pull at something that clung to my coat sleeve, and then I saw he held a little, wriggling red demon by the tail—the little creature bit and fought and tried to get at his hand—and in a moment he tossed it carelessly behind a counter. No doubt the thing was only an image of twisted india-rubber, but for the moment . . . ! And his gesture was exactly that of a man who handles some petty biting bit of vermin. I glanced at Gip, but Gip was looking at a magic rocking-horse. I was glad he hadn't seen the thing. "I say," I said, in an undertone, and indicating Gip, and the red demon with my eyes, "you haven't many things like *that* about, have you?"

"None of ours! Probably brought it with you," said the shopman—also in an undertone, and with a more dazzling smile than ever. "Astonishing what people *will* carry about with them unawares!" And then to Gip, "Do you see anything you fancy here?"

There were many things that Gip fancied there.

He turned to this astonishing tradesman with mingled confidence and respect. "Is that a Magic Sword?" he said.

"A Magic Toy Sword. It neither bends, breaks, nor cuts the fingers. It renders the bearer invincible in battle against anyone under eighteen. Half a crown to seven and sixpence, according to size. These panoplies on cards are for juvenile knights-errant and very useful—shield of safety, sandals of swiftness, helmet of invisibility."

"Oh, Daddy!" gasped Gip.

I tried to find out what they cost, but the shopman did not heed me. He had got Gip now; he had got him away from my finger; he had embarked upon the exposition of all his confounded stock, and nothing was going to stop him. Presently I saw with a qualm of distrust and something like jealousy that Gip had hold of this person's finger as usually he has hold of mine. No doubt the fellow was interesting, I thought, and had an interestingly faked lot of stuff, really *good* faked stuff, still . . .

I wandered after them, saying very little, but keeping an eye on this prestidigital fellow. After all, Gip was enjoying it. And no doubt when the time came to go we should be able to go quite easily.

It was a long, rambling place, that showroom, a gallery broken up by stands and stalls and pillars, with archways leading off to other departments, in which the queerest-looking assistants loafed and stared at one, and with perplexing mirrors and curtains. So perplexing, indeed, were these that I was presently unable to make out the door by which we had come.

The shopman showed Gip magic trains that ran without steam or clockwork, just as you set the signals, and then some very, very valuable boxes of soldiers that all came alive directly you took off the lid and said . . . I myself haven't a very quick ear and it was a tongue-twisting sound, but Gip—he has his mother's ear—got it in no time. "Bravo!" said the shopman, putting the men back into the box unceremoniously and handing it to Gip. "Now," said the shopman, and in a moment Gip had made them all alive again.

"You'll take that box?" asked the shopman.

"We'll take that box," said I, "unless you charge its full value. In which case it would need a Trust Magnate——"

"Dear heart! *No!*" and the shopman swept the little men back again, shut the lid, waved the box in the air, and there it was, in brown paper, tied up and—*with Gip's full name and address on the paper!*

The shopman laughed at my amazement.

"This is the genuine magic," he said. "The real thing."

"It's a little too genuine for my taste," I said again.

After that he fell to showing Gip tricks, odd tricks, and still odder the way they were done. He explained them, he turned them inside out, and there was the dear little chap nodding his busy bit of a head in the sagest manner.

I did not attend as well as I might. "Hey, presto!" said the Magic Shopman, and then would come the clear small "Hey, presto!" of the boy. But I was distracted by other things. It was being borne in upon me just how tremendously rum this place was; it was, so to speak, inundated by a sense of rumness. There was something a little rum about the fixtures even, about the ceiling, about the floor, about the casually distributed chairs. I had a queer feeling that whenever I wasn't looking at them straight they went askew, and moved about, and played a noiseless puss-in-the-corner behind my back. And the cornice had a serpentine design with masks—masks altogether too expressive for proper plaster.

Then abruptly my attention was caught by one of the odd-looking assistants. He was some way off and evidently unaware of my presence—I saw a sort of three-quarter length of him over a pile of toys and through an arch—and, you know, he was leaning against a pillar in an idle sort of way doing the most horrid things with his features! The particular horrid thing he did was with his nose. He did it just as though he was idle and wanted to amuse himself. First of all it was a short, blobby nose, and then suddenly he shot it out like a telescope, and then out it flew and became thinner and thinner until it was like a long, red, flexible whip. Like a thing in a nightmare it was! He flourished it about and flung it forth as a fly-fisher flings his line.

My instant thought was that Gip mustn't see him. I turned about, and there was Gip quite preoccupied with the shopman, and thinking no evil. They were whispering together and looking at me. Gip was standing on a little stool, and the shopman was holding a sort of big drum in his hand.

"Hide and seek, Dadda!" cried Gip. "You're He!"

And before I could do anything to prevent it, the shopman had clapped the big drum over him.

I saw what was up directly. "Take that off," I cried, "this instant! You'll frighten the boy. Take it off!"

The shopman with the unequal ears did so without a word, and held the big cylinder towards me to show its emptiness. And the little stool was vacant! In that instant my boy had utterly disappeared! . . .

You know, perhaps, that sinister something that comes like a hand out of the unseen and grips your heart about. You know it takes your common self away and leaves you tense and deliberate, neither slow nor hasty, neither angry nor afraid. So it was with me.

I came up to this grinning shopman and kicked his stool aside.

"Stop this folly!" I said. "Where is my boy?"

"You see," he said, still displaying the drum's interior, "there is no deception——"

I put out my hand to grip him, and he eluded me by a dexterous movement. I snatched again, and he turned from me and pushed open a door to escape. "Stop!" I said, and he laughed, receding. I leapt after him—into utter darkness.

Thud!

"Lor' bless my 'eart! I didn't see you coming, sir!"

I was in Regent Street, and I had collided with a decent-looking working man; and a yard away, perhaps, and looking a little perplexed with himself, was Gip. There was some sort of apology, and then Gip had turned and come to me with a bright little smile, as though for a moment he had missed me.

And he was carrying four parcels in his arm!

He secured immediate possession of my finger.

For the second I was rather at a loss. I stared round to see the door of the magic shop, and, behold, it was not there! There was no door, no shop, nothing, only the common pilaster between the shop where they sell pictures and the window with the chicks! . . .

I did the only thing possible in that mental tumult; I walked straight to the kerbstone and held up my umbrella for a cab.

" 'Ansoms," said Gip, in a note of culminating exultation.

I helped him in, recalled my address with an effort, and got in also. Something unusual proclaimed itself in my tail-coat pocket, and I felt and discovered a glass ball. With a petulant expression I flung it into the street.

Gip said nothing.

For a space neither of us spoke.

"Dadda!" said Gip, at last, "that *was* a proper shop!"

I came round with that to the problem of just how the whole thing had seemed to him. He looked completely undamaged—so far, good; he was neither scared nor unhinged, he was simply tremendously satisfied with the afternoon's entertainment, and there in his arms were the four parcels.

Confound it! what could be in them?

"Um!" I said. "Little boys can't go to shops like that every day."

He received this with his usual stoicism, and for a moment I was sorry I was his father and not his mother, and so couldn't suddenly there, *coram publico*, in our hansom, kiss him. After all, I thought the thing wasn't so very bad.

But it was only when we opened the parcels that I really began to be reassured. Three of them contained boxes of soldiers, quite ordinary lead soldiers, but of so good a quality as to make Gip altogether forget that originally these parcels had been Magic Tricks of the only genuine sort, and the fourth contained a kitten, a little living white kitten, in excellent health and appetite and temper.

I saw this unpacking with a sort of provisional relief. I hung about in the nursery for quite an unconscionable time . . .

That happened six months ago. And now I am beginning to believe it is all right. The kitten had only the magic natural to all kittens, and the soldiers seem as steady a company as any colonel could desire. And Gip——?

The intelligent parent will understand that I have to go cautiously with Gip.

But I went so far as this one day. I said, "How would you like your soldiers to come alive, Gip, and march about by themselves?"

"Mine do," said Gip. "I just have to say a word I know before I open the lid."

"Then they march about alone?"

"Oh, *quite*, Dadda. I shouldn't like them if they didn't do that."

I displayed no unbecoming surprise, and since then I have taken occasion to drop in upon him once or twice, unannounced, when the soldiers were about, but so far I have never discovered them performing in anything like a magical manner. . . .

It is so difficult to tell.

There's also a question of finance. I have an incurable

habit of paying bills. I have been up and down Regent Street several times, looking for that shop. I am inclined to think, indeed, that in that matter honour is satisfied, and that, since Gip's name and address are known to them, I may very well leave it to these people, whoever they may be, to send in their bill in their own time.

John Charrington's Wedding

E. Nesbit

No one ever thought that May Forster would marry John Charrington; but he thought differently, and things which John Charrington intended had a queer way of coming to pass. He asked her to marry him before he went up to Oxford. She laughed and refused him. He asked her again next time he came home. Again she laughed, tossed her dainty blonde head, and again refused. A third time he asked her; she said it was becoming a confirmed bad habit, and laughed at him more than ever.

John was not the only man who wanted to marry her: she was the belle of our village coterie, and we were all in love with her more or less; it was a sort of fashion, like heliotrope ties or Inverness capes. Therefore we were as much annoyed as surprised when John Charrington walked into our little local Club—we held it in a loft over the saddler's, I remember—and invited us all to his wedding.

"Your wedding?"

"You don't mean it?"

"Who's the happy pair? When's it to be?"

John Charrington filled his pipe and lighted it before he replied. Then he said:

"I'm sorry to deprive you fellows of your only joke—but Miss Forster and I are to be married in September."

"You don't mean it?"

"He's got the mitten again, and it's turned his head."

"No," I said, rising, "I see it's true. Lend me a pistol someone—or a first-class fare to the other end of Nowhere. Charrington has bewitched the only pretty girl in our twenty-mile radius. Was it mesmerism, or a love-potion, Jack?"

"Neither, sir, but a gift you'll never have—perseverance—and the best luck a man ever had in this world."

There was something in his voice that silenced me, and all chaff of the other fellows failed to draw him further.

The queer thing about it was that when we congratulated Miss Forster, she blushed and smiled and dimpled, for all the world as though she were in love with him, and had been in love with him all the time. Upon my word, I think she had. Women are strange creatures.

We were all asked to the wedding. In Brixham everyone who was anybody knew everybody else who was anyone. My sisters were, I truly believe, more interested in the *trousseau* than the bride herself, and I was to be best man. The coming marriage was much canvassed at afternoon tea-tables, and at our little Club over the saddler's, and the question was always asked. "Does she care for him?"

I used to ask that question myself in the early days of their engagement, but after a certain evening in August I never asked it again. I was coming home from the Club through the churchyard. Our church is on a thyme-grown hill, and the turf about it is so thick and soft that one's footsteps are noiseless.

I made no sound as I vaulted the low lichened wall, and threaded my way between the tombstones. It was at the same instant that I heard John Charrington's voice, and saw Her. May was sitting on a low flat gravestone, her face turned towards the full splendour of the western sun. Its expression ended, at once and for ever, any question of love for him; it was transfigured to a beauty I should not have believed possible, even to that beautiful little face.

John lay at her feet, and it was his voice that broke the stillness of the golden August evening.

"My dear, my dear, I believe I should come back from the dead if you wanted me!"

I coughed at once to indicate my presence, and passed on into the shadow fully enlightened.

The wedding was to be early in September. Two days before I had to run up to town on business. The train was late, of course, for we are on the South-Eastern, and as I stood grumbling with my watch in my hand, whom should I see but John Charrington and May Forster. They were walking up and down the unfrequented end of the platform, arm in arm, looking into each other's eyes, careless of the sympathetic interest of the porters.

Of course I knew better than to hesitate a moment before burying myself in the booking-office, and it was not till the train drew up at the platform, that I obtrusively passed the pair with my Gladstone, and took the corner in a first-class smoking-carriage. I did this with as good an air of not seeing them as I could assume. I pride myself on my discretion, but if John were travelling alone I wanted his company. I had it.

"Hullo, old man," came his cheery voice as he swung his bag into my carriage; "here's luck; I was expecting a dull journey!"

"Where are you off to?" I asked, discretion still bidding me turn my eyes away, though I saw, without looking, that hers were red-rimmed.

"To old Branbridge's," he answered, shutting the door and leaning out for a last word with his sweetheart.

"Oh, I wish you wouldn't go, John," she was saying in a low, earnest voice. "I feel certain something will happen."

"Do you think I should let anything happen to keep me, and the day after tomorrow our wedding-day?"

"Don't go," she answered, with a pleading intensity which would have sent my Gladstone on to the platform and me after it. But she wasn't speaking to me. John Charrington was made differently; he rarely changed his opinions, never his resolutions.

He only stroked the little ungloved hands that lay on the carriage door.

"I must, May. The old boy's been awfully good to me, and now he's dying I must go and see him, but I shall come home in time for——" the rest of the parting was lost in a whisper and in the rattling lurch of the starting train.

"You're sure to come?" she spoke as the train moved.

"Nothing shall keep me," he answered; and we steamed out. After he had seen the last of the little figure on the platform he leaned back in his corner and kept silence for a minute.

When he spoke it was to explain to me that his god-father, whose heir he was, lay dying at Peasmarsh Place, some fifty miles away, and had sent for John, and John had felt bound to go.

"I shall be surely back tomorrow," he said, "or, if not, the day after, in heaps of time. Thank Heaven, one hasn't to get up in the middle of the night to get married nowa-days!"

"And suppose Mr. Branbridge dies?"

"Alive or dead I mean to be married on Thursday!" John answered, lighting a cigar and unfolding The Times.

At Peasmarsh station we said "good-bye", and he got out, and I saw him ride off; I went on to London, where I stayed the night.

When I got home the next afternoon, a very wet one, by the way, my sister greeted me with:

"Where's Mr. Charrington?"

"Goodness knows," I answered testily. Every man, since Cain, has resented that kind of question.

"I thought you might have heard from him," she went on, "as you're to give him away tomorrow."

"Isn't he back?" I asked, for I had confidently expected to find him at home.

"No, Geoffrey,"—my sister Fanny always had a way of jumping to conclusions, especially such conclusions as were least favourable to her fellow-creatures—"he has not returned, and, what is more, you may depend upon it he won't. You mark my words, there'll be no wedding tomorrow."

My sister Fanny has a power of annoying me which no other human being possesses.

"You mark my words," I retorted with asperity, "you had better give up making such a thundering idiot of yourself. There'll be more wedding tomorrow than ever you'll take the first part in." A prophecy which, by the way, came true.

But though I could snarl confidently to my sister, I did not feel so comfortable when late that night, I, standing on the doorstep of John's house, heard that he had not returned. I went home gloomily through the rain. Next morning brought a brilliant blue sky, gold sun, and all such softness of air and beauty of cloud as go to make up a perfect day. I woke with a vague feeling of having gone to bed anxious, and of being rather averse to facing that anxiety in the light of full wakefulness.

But with my shaving-water came a note from John which relieved my mind and sent me up to the Forsters with a light heart.

May was in the garden. I saw her blue gown through the hollyhocks as the lodge gates swung to behind me. So I did not go up to the house, but turned aside down the turfed path.

"He's written to you too," she said, without preliminary greeting, when I reached her side.

"Yes, I'm to meet him at the station at three, and come straight on to the church."

Her face looked pale, but there was a brightness in her eyes, and a tender quiver about the mouth that spoke of renewed happiness.

"Mr. Branbridge begged him so to stay another night that he had not the heart to refuse," she went on. "He is so kind, but I wish he hadn't stayed."

I was at the station at half-past two. I felt rather annoyed with John. It seemed a sort of slight to the beautiful girl who loved him, that he should come as it were out of breath, and with the dust of travel upon him, to take her hand, which some of us would have given the best years of our lives to take.

But when the three o'clock train glided in, and glided out again having brought no passengers to our little station, I was more than annoyed. There was no other train for thirty-five minutes; I calculated that, with much hurry, we might just get to the church in time for the ceremony; but, oh, what a fool to miss that first train! What other man could have done it?

That thirty-five minutes seemed a year, as I wandered round the station reading the advertisements and the time-tables, and the company's bye-laws, and getting more and more angry with John Charrington. This confidence in his own power of getting everything he wanted the minute he wanted it was leading him too far. I hate waiting. Everyone does, but I believe I hate it more than anyone else. The three-thirty-five was late, of course.

I ground my pipe between my teeth and stamped with

impatience as I watched the signals. Click. The signal went down. Five minutes later I flung myself into the carriage that I had brought for John.

"Drive to the church!" I said, as someone shut the door. "Mr. Charrington hasn't come by this train."

Anxiety now replaced anger. What had become of the man? Could he have been taken suddenly ill? I had never known him have a day's illness in his life. And even so he might have telegraphed. Some awful accident must have happened to him. The thought that he had played her false never—no, not for a moment—entered my head. Yes, something terrible had happened to him, and on me lay the task of telling his bride. I almost wished the carriage would upset and break my head so that someone else might tell her, not I, who—but that's nothing to do with this story.

It was five minutes to four as we drew up at the church-yard gate. A double row of eager onlookers lined the path from lychgate to porch. I sprang from the carriage and passed up between them. Our gardener had a good front place near the door. I stopped.

"Are they waiting still, Byles?" I asked, simply to gain time, for of course I knew they were by the waiting crowd's attentive attitude.

"Waiting, sir? No, no, sir; why, it must be over by now."

"Over! Then Mr. Charrington's come?"

"To the minute, sir; must have missed you somehow, and I say, sir," lowering his voice, "I never see Mr. John the least bit so afore, but my opinion is he's been drinking pretty free. His clothes was all dusty and his face like a sheet. I tell you I didn't like the looks of him at all, and the folks inside are saying all sorts of things. You'll see, some-thing's gone very wrong with Mr. John, and he's tried liquor. He looked like a ghost, and in he went with his eyes straight before him, with never a look or a word for none of us: him that was always such a gentleman!"

I had never heard Byles make so long a speech. The crowd in the churchyard were talking in whispers and getting ready rice and slippers to throw at the bride and bridegroom. The ringers were ready with their hands on the ropes to ring out the merry peal as the bride and bridegroom should come out.

A murmur from the church announced them; out they came. Byles was right. John Charrington did not look himself. There was dust on his coat, his hair was disarranged. He seemed to have been in some row, for there was a black mark above his eyebrow. He was deathly pale. But his pallor was not greater than that of the bride, who might have been carved in ivory—dress, veil, orange blossoms, face and all.

As they passed out the ringers stooped—there were six of them—and then, on the ears expecting the gay wedding peal, came the slow tolling of the passing bell.

A thrill of horror at so foolish a jest from the ringers passed through us all. But the ringers themselves dropped the ropes and fled like rabbits out into the sunlight. The bride shuddered, and grey shadows came about her mouth, but the bridegroom led her on down the path where the people stood with the handfuls of rice; but the handfuls were never thrown, and the wedding-bells never rang. In vain the ringers were urged to remedy their mistake: they protested with many whispered expletives that they would see themselves further first.

In a hush like the hush in the chamber of death the bridal pair passed into their carriage and its door slammed behind them.

Then the tongues were loosed. A babel of anger, wonder, conjecture from the guests and the spectators.

"If I'd seen his condition, sir," said old Forster to me as we drove off, "I would have stretched him on the floor of the church, sir, by Heaven I would, before I'd have let him marry my daughter!"

Then he put his head out of the window.

"Drive like hell," he cried to the coachman; "don't spare the horses."

He was obeyed. We passed the bride's carriage. I forbore to look at it, and old Forster turned his head away and swore. We reached home before it.

We stood in the hall doorway, in the blazing afternoon sun, and in about half a minute we heard wheels crunching the gravel. When the carriage stopped in front of the steps old Forster and I ran down.

"Great Heaven, the carriage is empty! And yet——"

I had the door open in a minute, and this is what I saw . . .

No sign of John Charrington; and of May, his wife, only a huddled heap of white satin lying half on the floor of the carriage and half on the seat.

"I drove straight here, sir," said the coachman, as the bride's father lifted her out; "and I'll swear no one got out of the carriage."

We carried her into the house in her bridal dress and drew back her veil. I saw her face. Shall I ever forget it? White, white and drawn with agony and horror, bearing such a look of terror as I have never seen since except in dreams. And her hair, her radiant blonde hair, I tell you it was white like snow.

As we stood, her father and I, half mad with the horror and mystery of it, a boy came up the avenue—a telegraph boy. They brought the orange envelope to me. I tore it open.

Mr. Charrington *was thrown from the dogcart on his way to the station at half-past one. Killed on the spot!*

And he was married to May Forster in our parish church at *half-past three*, in presence of half the parish.

"*I shall be married, dead or alive!*"

What had passed in that carriage on the homeward drive? No one knows—no one will ever know. Oh, May! oh, my dear!

Before a week was over they laid her beside her husband in our little churchyard on the thyme-covered hill—the churchyard where they had kept their love-trysts.

Thus was accomplished John Charrington's wedding.

The Ghostly Earl

R. Chetwynd-Hayes

My name is Charles Henry Fitzroy Carruthers, eighth Earl of Rillington, and I died some two hundred and forty years ago. That's right, I am a ghost. I wander the halls of Rillington Castle and when I meet people not accustomed to ghostly apparitions, they usually either scream to high heavens or take to their heels and run as though the hounds of hell were after them. Silly really, because I wouldn't harm a fly and, dash it all, a fellow has every right to wander his own castle without a stupid maid-servant screaming her head off. So I was pleasantly surprised when I met a little girl who treated me, if not with respect, at least as a respectable disembodied being.

Her name was Clare and she was the daughter of the present owner, that is to say, she was my great-great-great-great-great-great-great-grand-daughter.

"Don't start screaming," I said.

"I've no intention of screaming and I know who you are," she told me.

"Do you?" I said.

"Yes." She walked calmly up to me and began to examine my attire, which, if you are interested, is quite something: blue brocade coat with full skirt, white cravat, lace frills at the wrists, crimson waistcoat with silk knee-breeches to match, scarlet high-heeled shoes and, to top it all, a powdered wig. Altogether, I would say,

88

without undue conceit, I am a pretty handsome ghost. But the little wretch giggled.

"You do look funny," she announced.

"Indeed," I said coldly, rising to my full height, five feet six inches in my high heels. "I am glad you are amused."

"You are the famous ghost of Rillington Castle," she stated. "I've heard all about you."

I felt much better then and treated her to one of my rare smiles.

"Yes, I am the *famous* ghost."

"Daddy has only just inherited the castle," she went on, "so this is my first day here. Grandad and he weren't on talking terms, that's why we have never met before. My name is Clare."

My heart warmed to her father whom I seemed to remember as an untidy little boy. The old Earl and I had never got on. He refused to believe I existed, even after I spent all one night standing at the foot of his bed making faces at him. He had the audacity to say I was the result of too much port wine.

"You were a very wicked man when you were alive," Clare went on, "and spent all your time in drinking and gambling until a brave man called Sir Hulbert Makepiece killed you in a duel."

"That's a lie," I protested, "a deliberate lie made up by those Makepieces to further their own ends. I wasn't wicked. Oh, I'll grant you I drank a bottle or two and I might have played the occasional game of cards, but no more than was expected of a man in my position. And as for the duel! It was murder."

"Murder!" Clare gasped. "You mean Sir Hulbert . . .?"

"Waited for me one night in the long gallery and ran me through the heart with his rapier. He afterwards stabbed himself in the arm, then placed a sword in my dead hand and said he was only defending himself. That's why I haunt the castle. Can't rest, you see."

"Why?" she inquired.

"Why!" For a moment I was speechless. "You haven't been listening. I was foully murdered, my good name was besmirched, and you ask why I haunt the castle."

"Well, I think it's silly," she stated, "going round frightening people for something that happened two hundred and fifty years ago. You ought to be ashamed."

"You've been very badly brought up," I said, "and badly educated into the bargain. You must understand that there are certain formalities to be fulfilled before I can rest. You see, Sir Hulbert owed me a lot of money, that's why he killed me. He lost three thousand pounds playing cards in one night. He couldn't pay me."

"It sounds all very wicked to me," Clare remarked. "Mother says people shouldn't gamble."

"Not if they can't pay their debts," I retorted, "and three feet of cold steel is not my idea of legal currency."

"Well"—Clare sat down and swung her foot—"there isn't much you can do about it now. After all, Sir Hulbert has been dead for close on two hundred years."

"That's all you know about it, Miss Know-All. A debt of honour is inherited by the payee's heirs and successors. For two hundred and fifty years I have been looking for a Makepiece to settle the score."

Just then I heard footsteps and, knowing how most adults react to their first sight of me, I erred on the side of caution and vanished.

Clare seemed rather put out by my disappearance. She was looking round the room with a disappointed expression as the door opened and her mother entered. She was a pretty woman of about thirty-five, with fair hair and blue eyes, and she seemed a little cross.

"Clare, I've been looking for you everywhere. What are you doing up here?"

Clare said with a sly smile:

"You'll never believe me if I tell you."

"Well, try me," her mother answered.

"I've been talking to the ghost."

"The what?"

"The ghost. The wicked eighth earl, only he says he wasn't wicked. Sir Hulbert Makepiece murdered him in the long gallery."

"Oh, Clare!" Her mother sat down, momentarily helpless with laughter. "What am I going to do with you? That imagination of yours and those wild, impossible stories. Don't you realize there is no ghost and, as for that matter, the story of the wicked earl is probably only a myth. The earl was probably just another weak young man who gambled and drank too much, then got himself killed in a silly duel. One thing is certain—he's been dead and buried these past two hundred and fifty years and isn't likely to bother us now."

"Mummy"—Clare displayed admirable patience—"I saw him and spoke to him, and he said he was looking for a present-day Makepiece to pay a debt of honour."

"It sounds very romantic"—the countess rose—"and certainly very ghostlike, but I should have to see him for myself before I believe a word of it."

I was tempted. All I needed to do was to materialize and, stap-me-vitals, she would soon believe in ghosts. That was the trouble—her belief would take on vocal expression and I can't abide screaming women. So I overcame my natural impulse and remained invisible, much to the disgust of Clare, who looked reproachfully round the room.

In order not to try my forbearance further I passed through the nearest wall, then ascended to the battlements, my favourite haunt, for it is usually windy up there and living people are apt to give it a wide berth. I paced up and down the parapet, looked down upon the town which basked in the evening sunlight a few miles away, and remembered that in my day it had been but a small village, every cottage, every acre of ground for as far as the eye could see, my property. Yes, I had been a weakling, a fool. I should not have become involved with people like Sir Hulbert Makepiece. I should not have gambled. . . . The evening wind whistled round the battlements and suddenly I felt very lonely.

Later on I came down and made my way through empty rooms and along dark corridors until I reached the present earl's living quarters. He was seated on the left of a huge fireplace where logs were burning. His lady reclined opposite. The earl looked a little like me and I thought we might well get on together. On his lap he had a jumble of papers and he was frowning.

"There's no avoiding the issue," he said. "The old place must go."

"Can't we raise the money somehow?" Lady Rillington asked. "You know it will break all our hearts to lose the castle."

"My dear girl"—the earl shuffled his papers—"do you imagine I haven't tried everything? Death duties alone amount to twenty-five thousand pounds, and the old man had the place mortgaged for another ten thousand. Where can I raise thirty-five thousand? No, there's nothing else for it, I'll have to close with Wilkinson."

"You mean sell the castle to that dreadful creature?" Lady Rillington half rose from her chair. "Charles, he is so . . ."

Lord Rillington grimaced. " 'Fraid I've no option, my dear. Few people have that kind of money these days, or if they have, they aren't keen to buy a great old place like this."

"But"—Lady Rillington sank back again—"he's so objectionable, so overbearing. The thought of that man owning all this . . ."

I did not wait to hear any more, but drifted through the nearest wall, my very soul sick with apprehension. The Rillingtons had owned the castle since the foundations were laid eight hundred years ago, this was where generations had been born, had fought, sometimes killed, and often died. The prospect of a stranger, possibly some common fellow bloated with ill-gotten wealth, striding the battlements, gorging himself in the great dining hall, snoring in the red bedroom, made me tremble with rage and, involuntarily, I gave vent to a mighty roar that caused several doors to fly open and sent a highly-strung kitchen-maid into hysterics. I found Clare standing in the doorway of her bedroom and, knowing her to be a level-headed young person, I instantly materialized.

"Did you make that awful noise?" she asked.

"Yes," I said, "I did."

"That was very naughty of you," she said gravely. "You've frightened everyone out of their wits. All but me, of course. Why did you do it?"

"Your father is going to sell the castle," I growled, "to some base-born fellow called Wilkinson."

"How do you know?"

"I listened. Your father was telling your mother all about it."

She looked very shocked. "You mean, you eaves-dropped on a private conversation?"

"Of course I eavesdropped. What is the point of being invisible if you don't listen to what people are saying? Don't ask silly questions. Now, who is this fellow—Wilkinson?"

"I think you had better come into my room," said Clare, standing aside for me to enter, which was quite unnecessary for I could have walked right through her. "If someone comes along and sees you standing there, they'll probably faint or scream."

I walked into the room and seated myself on the bed. "Well," I asked, once Clare had closed the door, "who is he?"

"He's not very nice"—she shook her head sadly—"but very rich. He's big and fat, and breathes all over you."

"I know the type," I nodded. "There was a certain moneylender in my day. I remember I had occasion to

94

boot him down the main staircase, but that's by the way. Why should Wilkinson want to buy Rillington Castle?"

"He wants to transform it into a holiday hotel. Turn the supper room into a restaurant, the ballroom into a kind of popular dance hall, have jazz concerts on the lawn. . . . Why are you tearing your hair?"

"Turn the castle into a house of entertainment, an inn, a hostel?" If I had needed breath I most certainly would have been gasping for it. "If that fellow sets foot inside the front door I'll turn his hair white, I'll make myself appear as a grinning skeleton just as he's about to eat his dinner. I'll whisper in his ear when he goes to bed. I'll sit on his chest and wipe his forehead with a dead hand, I'll . . ."

"Stop," Clare stamped her foot. "You'll do nothing of the kind. I won't have you frightening people, not even an unpleasant man like Mr. Wilkinson. It would be like a strong man hitting a weak one and wouldn't do any good anyhow. So behave yourself and try to think of some practical way in which you can help Daddy raise the money."

"But he wants thirty-five thousand pounds," I objected. "I've no head for finance. A nobleman isn't supposed to concern himself with money."

"Daddy's a nobleman and he's got to, and he isn't half so clever as you are. Now you'd better disappear, I hear Mummy coming."

Mr Wilkinson arrived next day, having invited himself for the week-end, and never have I seen a man who so badly needed haunting. He was fat, red-faced, bald, and, whenever he came near someone smaller than himself, like a woman or a child, he leant over and breathed on them. He did it to Clare.

"And whom have we here?" He bent down until his repulsive face was but a few inches from hers. "It's the little lady herself, I do declare. And how are you, my dear, how are you?"

"Very well, sir," Clare replied with that remarkable self-control that I so much admired. "Thank you very much."

"And you, my dear?" This was to Lady Rillington and I saw her husband's lips tighten. "You look blooming. Blooming." And he leant over and breathed.

"I am quite well, thank you, Mr. Wilkinson," she said coolly.

"Harry to my friends," he boomed. "Don't stand on ceremony. After all, I'll own the old place soon and that sort of makes me one of the family."

"I think," said Lord Rillington, "it would be better all round if we kept our relationship on a business footing, Mr. Wilkinson. No sentiment in business, I believe you once said."

This barb penetrated even Wilkinson's thick skin and he frowned.

"As you please, Rillington. As you please." He looked round the great hall, eyed the grand staircase that Elizabeth I had once climbed, then said: "I think I'll pull out all that oak panelling, makes the place too dark. Paint the walls a nice bright pink, get a jukebox in, have a soft-drinks bar along that wall. Attract the youngsters."

"Oh, you can't," Lady Rillington breathed.

"But I can. I will." He turned slowly and he was not smiling any more; his little eyes were like blue ice. "Of course, you can always sell to someone else, if you can find another buyer. Or maybe . . ." He smiled now, a nasty, insinuating smirk. "Or maybe you have managed to raise fifty thousand pounds, my price, remember?"

"You know very well we are in your hands," Lord Rillington said quietly.

"Exactly," he chuckled. "Exactly."

Little did he know that as old Soames, the butler, escorted him up the stairs to his room, I was walking just behind him. I was pleading with Clare. Me, eighth Earl of Rillington, pleading with a chit of a girl.

"Please, the merest touch of cold fingers on his throat."

"No." She shook her head.

"Or a deep groan when he turns out the light."

"Certainly not."

"Let me at least pull the pillow out from under his head when he's asleep."

"No, you cannot." She frowned and, strange though it may seem, I, the ghost of Rillington, was instantly contrite.

"All right, don't be angry. It's only natural for a ghost to haunt, and Wilkinson is as fine an example of a hauntee as I've met in a hundred years. I should have had him crawling under the bed in two minutes flat."

"I've told you before," she persisted, "you must think of some way of raising the thirty-five thousand pounds that Daddy needs."

"My dear child," I protested, "we never worried ourselves about money in my day. My steward provided all I needed. I remember . . ."

I stopped, suddenly struck by a thought.

"Well, what is it you remember?" Clare demanded.

"Treasure," I said. "I seem to remember my grandfather buried a lot of old family plate back in the Civil War."

"Gosh!" Clare clapped her hands. "Are you certain?"

"Almost. Keep quiet for a moment and let me think. It was around 1647. The rebels, old Noll Comwell's Ironsides, were about to attack the castle and Grandfather, so they said, very sensibly decided to hide all our silver plate

and family jewels. Trouble was he got himself killed in the
ensuing battle and no one knew where he had hidden it."

"Didn't you try to find it when . . . ?" She paused.
"When you were alive?"

I shrugged. "Both my father and I had several attempts,
but we finally gave up. There was no proof the Roundheads hadn't found it and, besides, Father married a very
rich heiress who brought along her own plate and jewels.
Your great-grandfather, by the way, gambled it all away
back in 1860."

"But is the treasure still here?" Clare asked. "Have you
found it since your . . . ?"

"Murder? Frankly, I haven't bothered to look. I mean,
a pile of old silver plate is of little use to me. But I suppose
if it *is* still here, I shouldn't have much difficulty in finding
it. I can pass through walls and sink down through paved
floors. Yes, I'll have a look round."

"Please hurry," pleaded Clare. "There isn't a lot of
time, Father is signing the papers this week-end."

"Is he?" I shouted, and the windows rattled. "Why
didn't you say so before? Now, where would old Firebrand Harry have been likely to have hidden his loot?"

"Firebrand Harry?" inquired Clare.

"Yes, that's what my grandfather was called during his
lifetime. Everyone was frightened of him, especially the
Roundheads."

"Might it be buried in the dungeons?" Clare suggested.

"Too obvious," I retorted. "The first place the Roundheads would have searched. The slightest sign of recent
digging and they would have reached for the nearest
spade. No, I favour one of the secret rooms."

"Secret . . . rooms." Clare gasped. "You mean there are
actually secret rooms in the castle?"

I laughed. "My dear girl, what with having to hide

98

Catholics in Henry VIII's time, Protestants in Bloody Mary's, Cavaliers in Cromwell's and rebels when Bonny Prince Charlie invaded, I sometimes wonder if there aren't more secret rooms than known ones. The walls are honeycombed with them. Now you had better retire to bed and I will be on my way."

She wanted to argue, but I cut her short by disappearing and sinking through the floor to the room below, which had been Firebrand Harry's bedroom. I slid into the east wall and found it to be solid granite. I tried the west and the south, all to no avail. Then I examined the fireplace, a grand sixteenth-century affair, large enough for a man to walk into without bending his head, and found the wall at the back was made of a single slab of stone. I passed through it and realized at once that I need search no more. A small room, black as a whale's stomach, lay beyond and, thanks to my ability to see in the dark, I was able to make out a large oak chest standing in the middle of the floor. I then examined the wall through which I had passed and discovered it was, in fact, a door which could be opened by turning the right-hand pillar that supported the mantel-piece. A ghost of experience can, if the occasion so demands blow open an ordinary wooden door, make windows rattle, and cause heavy objects to float across a room, but he cannot, not even if he is highly-gifted like me, turn stone pillars. So I went back to Clare.

"Have you found it?"

I nodded. "I think so. You had better get up and go down to the room below this one. Take some kind of portable light with you."

"I'll fetch a torch."

"Good," I said. "You make your way down the stairs while I sink back through the floor."

Clare took some time to find her way and I was growing

a little impatient when she pushed open the door and entered Firebrand Harry's room.

"Now"—I moved to the fireplace—"there is a small room hidden behind the wall here. You must twist the pillar so the wall will slide back. Can you do that?"

"I'll try."

She put down her torch and grasped the pillar in her small hands and twisted. The wall did not move.

"Put your arms round it," I instructed. "Hug it, girl, then push with your feet."

She obeyed. With both arms round the pillar, she pushed, and she used her legs as levers. Then, with much groaning, the fireplace wall began to move open. Breathless from exertion, Clare picked up her torch and directed its beam into the dark interior. There she saw the chest, some four feet wide, bound with iron bands and with a large keyhole without a key.

Clare was properly appreciative. "You are the cleverest ghost that ever was or ever will be."

I nodded my agreement before pointing out the obvious.

"The chest is too heavy for you to move, so you had better summon your father and say you have accidentally stumbled across a secret room which contains a large chest. It might be good policy not to mention me. A treasure-finding ghost is a rare phenomenon. Now run along and I will remain invisible to watch developments."

When Clare and her parents entered the room they were all carrying torches, for, I am pleased to say, this part of the castle had not been wired for the new-fangled electricity. The earl was the first to gasp his astonishment when he saw the gaping hole in the fireplace wall.

"The child's right. Look, my dear, a secret room and a chest. Good heavens, suppose the old legend is true. . . .

Hold my torch, Clare, while I pull the chest out into the room."

This he found to be no easy task, for over the years rising damp had made the chest stick to the floor. Also it was very heavy, but at last he had it out and standing in the centre of the room.

He felt it all over and examined the lock while I fumed with impatience. Surely the fool realized that he must produce a lever and prise the lid open? Presently this idea slowly penetrated that part of his head he called a brain.

"We must prise the lid open," he said brightly. "Stay here and I'll go down to the workshop. Won't be a moment."

"You see, I was right," Clare stated with justifiable pride. "I said I had found the treasure."

"There's no proof as yet that the chest contains treasure," her mother answered with infuriating common sense. "We must wait until your father returns. I can't imagine how you came to find this room nor how you managed to open it."

"Oh, I just used my intelligence," Clare retorted airily. "I thought the treasure must be hidden somewhere in Old Firebrand Harry's room."

"Whose room?"

"Firebrand Harry's. That is what they called the ghost's . . . I mean, what they called the sixth earl during his lifetime. Everyone knows that."

"Well, I didn't." The countess looked up as her husband entered carrying a stout iron lever. "Charles, did you know the sixth earl was called Firebrand Harry?"

"No, but never mind that now. Let me get to grips with this chest. Stand aside."

He inserted the thin edge of the lever between the lid

and the chest, then pushed downwards. There was the sound of splintering wood and then, with a loud "crack", the lid flew open. All three moved forward with their torches to cluster round the chest, so I had to rise up and hover above them to see what was inside. Firebrand Harry must have been in a great hurry when he packed that chest; a pile of silver plates and goblets galore had been slung in any-old-how and a few necklaces and bracelets were piled on top. The earl lifted each item out and laid the entire collection reverently on the floor.

The silver was black, the jewellery looked extremely grimy, but once cleaned they would be as good as new. I experienced the feeling of satisfaction that comes only to a ghost who has done a worthwhile job.

"I'll pack all this stuff in the safe tonight," said the earl, "and tomorrow, first thing, I'll get a jeweller up from the town to value it." He turned a smiling face to his wife and daughter. "I don't want to raise your hopes unduly, but I think it quite possible we may be able to pack off Mr. Wilkinson with a flea in his ear."

I retired feeling happier than I had since that ill-fated day when Sir Hulbert Makepiece had run his rapier through my heart in the long gallery.

The jeweller arrived at eleven o'clock next morning and was taken at once to the earl's study, where the treasure was laid out for his examination. He was a little bald man, who bristled like a dog that has spotted a rabbit, when his eyes rested on the silver plate.

He unfastened his black bag, took out a magnifying glass, and examined each piece with mounting interest.

"Fine example of fifteenth-century craftsmanship, my lord," he said, "not perfect, but very good."

"And the necklaces," the earl inquired, "the bracelets? What about them?"

The jeweller took up a diamond necklace and studied each stone carefully.

"Not so good, my lord. Some of the stones are imitation. Not unusual with period pieces, I fear. You see, during the Civil War many of the King's supporters had to sell their possessions to raise money for the royal cause. Your ancestor temporized by parting with some of the stones and replacing them by near-perfect imitations. This, of course, has detracted from the overall value of the necklaces, also I fear"—he picked up a bracelet, then a pair of ear pendants—"most of the set pieces. Still"—he put down his magnifying glass—"you should be able to realize a conservative sum of . . ."

He was interrupted by the arrival of Mr. Wilkinson. The big man took in the scene, raked the desk top with a burning glance, then set his lips into a thin line.

"I didn't hear you knock," the earl remarked coldly.

Mr. Wilkinson ignored the implied rebuke.

"What," he asked, pointing to the treasure laid out on the desk, "is all this?"

Lady Rillington could not disguise her jubilation.

"This, Mr. Wilkinson, is the means by which we hope to pay off our debts."

"Really," Mr. Wilkinson sneered, "I was not aware junk could demand such a high price these days."

"Do not be deceived by appearances," the earl remarked dryly. "You were about to tell us, Mr. Smith, before we were interrupted, your opinion of the value of this collection."

"It is only a rough estimate," the jeweller admitted, "but I should say, if the sale were well-advertised, you might reasonably expect a return of say—twenty thousand pounds."

"Is that all?" the earl inquired.

"As I explained, some of the stones are imitations, but their antique value is worth considering. It would depend on who bids, of course. You might get a few thousand more."

"Well," the earl remarked, "twenty thousand will keep the Inland Revenue people quiet for a bit. Then we can throw the castle open to visitors and charge twenty-five pence a head as entrance fee. It will take some time, but we'll manage."

Clare clapped her hands for joy, Lady Rillington positively beamed, and I, invisible, did a little jig of delight. Then Mr. Wilkinson spoke.

"I fear, Lord Rillington, you have overlooked one small, but very important detail. Treasure Trove."

The earl's smile froze. "What are you talking about?"

"Treasure Trove. The government in their wisdom have decreed that all bullion, gold, silver plate, found in the earth or in a private place, belongs to the Crown. The usual practice is to send it to the British Museum, who will, perhaps, reimburse you to a third of its marketable value. So you cannot expect to receive a sum of more than eight or ten thousand pounds. Even this may be subject to income tax."

Mr. Smith, the jeweller, broke the shocked silence.

"I fear the gentleman is correct, my lord. Failure to report the discovery of hidden treasure is a misdemeanour and can be punished by law."

"Then there is no more to be said." The earl sank wearily into a chair. "So much for a wild dream."

"How fortunate," Mr. Wilkinson's voice was like oil flowing over velvet, "my generous offer still stands. Tell you what I'll do, Rillington, I'll add two thousand pounds to the purchase price for your rights in the treasure trove. More than it's worth, I'm sure, despite your man's estimate, but then, my heart was always too large. I can't help giving my money away."

"I think you'd better go," warned Clare, looking anxiously round the room. "Honestly, you must."

Her fears were well-founded, for so great was my rage, it took all my self-control not to wrap cold fingers round the fellow's throat and shake him until his eyes popped out.

"Very well." He grinned his satisfaction. "I'll leave you alone with your—ah, disappointment. May I suggest we meet in your study just before dinner, Rillington, when you can sign the deed of sale and I will hand over my cheque."

"Whatever you say," replied the earl with a deep sigh.

Mr. Wilkinson went out and Clare burst into tears. As for me, I tore up to the battlements, where I allowed my rage to mingle with the wind.

Later, my fury spent, I gravitated towards the earl's study. They were all there; Clare and her mother were seated in deep armchairs, the base-born Wilkinson was perched on the edge of the desk, and the earl was standing by the fireplace. A large document was spread out on the desk top and I saw the words DEED OF SALE, which again fanned the flame of rage within me.

"Before we get down to business," said Wilkinson, "I should like to explain exactly why I am so eager to obtain possession of this castle. I will confess it is not because I love old buildings, nor entirely because I want to make more money, although I fully expect to do so. No, Lord Rillington, high and mighty Lord Rillington, there is another more personal reason."

"I am sure you are going to tell us," remarked the earl with a yawn.

"Yes, indeed," Mr. Wilkinson nodded, "yes, I am going to tell you. You may possibly laugh, you who consider yourselves so well-born. It may interest you to know I am descended from a house which was as noble as yours, even if it did not bear a high-flown title."

The earl smiled. "I cannot remember a Wilkinson numbered among the landed noble families. But, of course, if you say so . . ."

"Wilkinson is but half of my name." The little eyes narrowed. "My grandfather, for reasons of his own, decided to drop the latter half and hide his real identity. Today, I intend to rectify that lapse." He drew himself upright. "Lord Rillington, it is fitting that as an ancestor of mine put an end to one Rillington, I should dispossess another. My true name, sir, is Makepiece—Sir Harold Wilkinson-Makepiece, the last of a noble line."

Clare cried out, "Don't say any more, please."

But the fool would not be silent.

"Makepiece, a family as old as yours and certainly superior."

I gave one echoing shout of joy; the door flew open, three pictures fell from the wall, and I was visible for all to see. Never have I seen such fear, such amazement, on living faces. Lady Rillington stared at me with open mouth, the earl said: "Great Scott," and Mr. Wilkinson, or perhaps I should say Sir Harold Wilkinson-Makepiece, resembled a stranded fish that cannot understand where the sea went. Clare, as usual, tried to appeal to my better nature.

"You mustn't hurt him."

"He's mine," I said, "all mine."

"Who is this fellow?" Wilkinson-Makepiece tried to bluster. "I can assure you, I'm not easily frightened."

I smiled. "Are you certain?" I asked, as I advanced towards him.

He backed away, skirted the desk, then made a bolt for

the door. With another joyful shout I was after him. I chased him along corridors, up stairs, into empty rooms. I smiled at him from mirrors and glared at him through windows. Once I allowed my head to float alongside his, an easy trick when you know how. Finally, I cornered him in the long gallery. He was huddled in a corner, not far from the spot where I was murdered. His teeth were chattering, his face was the colour of an unwashed shroud, and he was breathing very heavily. I stood before him in all my glory, my form and face flowing with a soft green light. When I spoke, my voice boomed like thunder.

"Last of the base-born house of Makepiece, the time has come for you to pay a debt of honour. Your infamous ancestor owed me three thousand pounds on the day he foully murdered me, and it is right that you, as his representative, should settle the account with my descendant, the sixteenth earl."

"Of course." He nodded vigorously. "Anything you say."

"Kindly address me as 'My lord'. I do not encourage familiarities from inferiors."

"Of course, my lord, so sorry, my lord."

"However"—I became thoughtful, for I never had a head for figures—"three thousand pounds two hundred and fifty years ago is worth at least twenty times that sum today. I think sixty thousand would be nearer the mark. You are skilled in drawing up documents, a worthy talent for a base-born Makepiece; you must prepare one more. A deed of sale which states you are buying my Lord Rillington's rights in his treasure trove for sixty thousand pounds. Not the castle, you understand, just the treasure."

"Sixty thousand pounds!" I thought his hair would turn white. "But I won't get back a tenth of that sum."

"Of course," I went on, "you need not pay, I cannot

make you. But in that event I shall be compelled to stay close to you—for ever. When you sit down to eat, I shall be there; perhaps my head will be next to your plate, smiling, wishing you a good appetite. Then, at night I am sure you will welcome me in bed, my cold feet next to yours, my dead fingers gently caressing your throat, my icy nose . . ."

"I'll pay," he screamed, "I'll draw up the deed, anything."

"Indeed," I sighed. "Pity, I was so looking forward to our setting up house together. You are certain? I mean, you won't have misgivings afterwards, instruct your bank to stop payment or anything silly?"

"No, no. I give you my word."

"Well, if you insist. By the way, the present earl may try to refuse your generous gift, it will be up to you to make sure he accepts. Should you fail"—I smiled—"I shall look forward to our long and intimate relationship. Now let us return. I shall be invisible, but, rest assured, I shall be at your side."

"Look here, Wilkinson-Makepiece," the earl protested, "I cannot possibly accept what amounts to a sixty-thousand-pound gift."

"Please"—the fellow was babbling, and with good reason, I had my hand on the back of his neck—"you must accept. You will be doing me a great great favour. Please do me the great kindness of accepting my cheque."

I have never seen such a change in a man, and when the earl at last graciously accepted his cheque and handed over a signed transfer of the treasure, Wilkinson-Makepiece displayed a degree of gratitude of which I had thought him incapable. Of course, the fact that I removed my cold fingers from the back of his neck at the moment of transfer may have contributed to the look of profound relief that lit up his pale features, but I do like to think that even a base-born Makepiece has a better side to his nature, if one only tried to look for it.

"That ghastly apparition," said the earl, "I do hope . . ."

"Please don't mention it." Wilkinson-Makepiece shuddered. "I am not going to think about it—ever."

It was a pity that he had to leave at once—he drove away in one of those horseless carriages at break-neck speed—for I am certain he would have afforded me some little innocent amusement if he had stayed.

"I suppose you will be leaving us now?" said Clare, when I saw her alone some little while later.

"Perhaps," I replied. "I have grown used to the old place, but, frankly, now there is no longer a Makepiece to look for, I am rather at a loss for an occupation."

"Daddy is going to open the castle to visitors," she announced, "and he was saying what a help it would be if you would only show yourself once in a while. There's nothing like a ghost to attract tourists, especially the Americans."

"That is certainly a thought," I said.

You will be pleased to know the earl is quite rich now. He has raised the entrance price to fifty new pence and the place is packed from sunrise to sunset. I make a point of taking a stroll through the castle twice a day and, apart from a few screaming women, I am much appreciated. Ah, here comes a loud-mouthed, base-born American. "I am telling the world," he is declaiming, "there ain't no such thing as a ghost. It's just some jerk dressed up."

I am going to have a wonderful time with him.

Through the Veil

Sir Arthur Conan Doyle

He was a great shock-headed, freckle-faced Borderer, the
lineal descendant of a cattle-thieving clan in Liddesdale. In
spite of his ancestry he was as solid and sober a citizen as
one would wish to see, a town councillor of Melrose, an
elder of the Church, and the chairman of the local branch
of the Young Men's Christian Association. Brown was his
name—and you saw it printed up as "Brown and Handi-
side" over the great grocery stores in the High Street. His
wife, Maggie Brown, was an Armstrong before her marriage, and came from an old farming stock in the wilds of
Teviothead. She was small, swarthy, and dark-eyed, with
a strangely nervous temperament for a Scotch woman. No
greater contrast could be found than the big tawny man
and the dark little woman, but both were of the soil as far
back as any memory could extend.

One day—it was the first anniversary of their wedding
—they had driven over together to see the excavations of
the Roman Fort at Newstead. It was not a particularly
picturesque spot. From the northern bank of the Tweed,
just where the river forms a loop, there extends a gentle
slope of arable land. Across it run the trenches of the excavators, with here and there an exposure of old stonework
to show the foundations of the ancient walls. It had been
a huge place, for the camp was fifty acres in extent, and
the fort fifteen. However, it was all made easy for them

since Mr. Brown knew the farmer to whom the land belonged. Under his guidance they spent a long summer evening inspecting the trenches, the pits, the ramparts, and all the strange variety of objects which were waiting to be transported to the Edinburgh Museum of Antiquities. The buckle of a woman's belt had been dug up that very day, and the farmer was discoursing upon it when his eyes fell upon Mrs. Brown's face.

"Your good leddy's tired," said he. "Maybe you'd best rest a wee before we gang further."

Brown looked at his wife. She was certainly very pale, and her dark eyes were bright and wild.

"What is it, Maggie? I've wearied you. I'm thinkin' it's time we went back."

"No, no, John, let us go on. It's wonderful! It's like a dreamland place. It all seems so close and so near to me. How long were the Romans here, Mr. Cunningham?"

"A fair time, mam. If you saw the kitchen midden-pits you would guess it took a long time to fill them."

"And why did they leave?"

"Well, mam, by all accounts they left because they had to. The folk round could thole them no longer, so they just up and burned the fort aboot their lugs. You can see the fire marks on the stanes."

The woman gave a quick little shudder. "A wild night —a fearsome night," said she. "The sky must have been red that night—and these grey stones, they may have been red also."

"Aye, I think they were red," said her husband. "It's a queer thing, Maggie, and it may be your words that have done it; but I seem to see that business aboot as clear as ever I saw anything in my life. The light shone on the water."

"Aye, the light shone on the water. And the smoke

gripped you by the throat. And all the savages were yell-ing."

The old farmer began to laugh. "The leddy will be writin' a story aboot the old fort," said he. "I've shown many a one ower it, but I never heard it put so clear afore. Some folk have the gift."

They had strolled along the edge of the foss, and a pit yawned upon the right of them.

"That pit was fourteen foot deep," said the farmer. "What d'ye think we dug oot from the bottom o't? Weel, it was just the skeleton of a man wi' a spear by his side. I'm thinkin' he was grippin' it when he died. Now, how cam' a man wi' a spear doon a hole fourteen foot deep. He wasna' buried there, for they aye burned their dead. What make ye o' that, mam?"

"He sprang doon to get clear of the savages," said the woman.

"Weel, it's likely enough, and a' the professors from Edinburgh couldna gie a better reason. I wish you were aye here, mam, to answer a' oor deeficulties sae readily. Now, here's the altar that we foond last week. There's an inscreeption. They tell me it's Latin, and it means that the men o' this fort give thanks to God for their safety."

They examined the old worn stone. There was a large deeply-cut "VV" upon the top of it.

"What does 'VV' stand for?" asked Brown.

"Naebody kens," the guide answered.

"*Valeria Victrix*," said the lady softly. Her face was paler than ever, her eyes far away, as one who peers down the dim aisles of over-arching centuries.

"What's that?" asked her husband sharply.

She started as one who wakes from sleep. "What were we talking about?" she asked.

"About this 'VV' upon the stone."

"No doubt it was just the name of the Legion which put the altar up."

"Aye, but you gave some special name."

"Did I? How absurd! How should I ken what the name was?"

"You said something—'*Victrix*,' I think."

"I suppose I was guessing. It gives me the queerest feeling, this place, as if I were not myself, but someone else."

"Aye, it's an uncanny place," said her husband, looking round with an expression almost of fear in his bold grey eyes. "I feel it mysel'. I think we'll just be wishin' you good evenin', Mr. Cunningham, and get back to Melrose before the dark sets in."

Neither of them could shake off the strange impression which had been left upon them by their visit to the excavations. It was as if some miasma had risen from those damp trenches and passed into their blood. All the evening they were silent and thoughtful, but such remarks as they did make showed that the same subject was in the minds of each. Brown had a restless night, in which he dreamed a strange connected dream, so vivid that he woke sweating and shivering like a frightened horse. He tried to convey it all to his wife as they sat together at breakfast in the morning.

"It was the clearest thing, Maggie," said he. "Nothing that has ever come to me in my waking life has been more clear than that. I feel as if these hands were sticky with blood."

"Tell me of it—tell me slow," said she.

"When it began, I was oot on a braeside. I was laying flat on the ground. It was rough, and there were clumps of heather. All round me was just darkness, but I could hear the rustle and the breathin' of men. There seemed a great multitude on every side of me, but I could see no one. There was a low chink of steel sometimes, and then a number of voices would whisper 'Hush!' I had a ragged club in my hand, and it had spikes o' iron near the end of it. My heart was beatin' quickly, and I felt that a moment of great danger and excitement was at hand. Once I dropped my club, and again from all round me the voices in the darkness cried, 'Hush!' I put oot my hand, and it touched the foot of another man lying in front of me. There was someone at my very elbow on either side. But they said nothin'.

"Then we all began to move. The whole braeside seemed to be crawlin' downwards. There was a river at the bottom and a high-arched wooden bridge. Beyond the bridge were many lights—torches on a wall. The creepin' men all flowed towards the bridge. There had been no sound of any kind, just a velvet stillness. And then there was a cry in the darkness, the cry of a man who has been stabbed suddenly to the hairt. That one cry swelled out for a moment, and then the roar of a thoosand furious voices. I was runnin'. Everyone was runnin'. A bright red light shone out, and the river was a scarlet streak. I could see my companions now. They were more like devils than men, wild figures clad in skins, with their hair and beards streamin'. They were all mad with rage, jumpin' as they ran, their mouths open, their arms wavin', the red light beatin' on their faces. I ran, too, and yelled out curses like the rest. Then I heard a great cracklin' of wood, and I knew that the palisades were doon. There was a loud whistlin' in my ears, and I was aware that arrows were flyin' past me. I got to the bottom of a dyke, and I saw a hand stretched doon from above. I took it, and was dragged to the top. We looked doon, and there were silver men beneath us holdin' up their spears. Some of our folk sprang on to the spears. Then we others followed, and we killed the soldiers before they could draw the spears oot again. They shouted loud in some foreign tongue, but no mercy was shown them. We went ower them like a wave, and trampled them doon into the mud, for they were few, and there was no end to our numbers.

"I found myself among buildings, and one of them was on fire. I saw the flames spoutin' through the roof. I ran on, and then I was alone among the buildings. Someone ran across in front o' me. It was a woman. I caught her by the arm, and I took her chin and turned her face so as the light of the fire would strike it. Whom think you that it was, Maggie?"

His wife moistened her dry lips. "It was I," she said.

He looked at her in surprise. "That's a good guess," said he. "Yes, it was just you. Not merely like you, you understand. It was you—you yourself. I saw the same soul in your frightened eyes. You looked white and bonny and wonderful in the firelight. I had just one thought in my head—to get you awa' with me; to keep you all to mysel' in my own home somewhere beyond the hills. You clawed at my face with your nails. I heaved you over my shoulder, and I tried to find a way oot of the light of the burning hoose and back into the darkness.

"Then came the thing that I mind best of all. You're ill, Maggie. Shall I stop? My God! you have the very look on your face that you had last night in my dream. You screamed. He came runnin' in the firelight. His head was bare; his hair was black and curled; hc had a naked sword in his hand, short and broad, little more than a dagger. He stabbed at me, but he tripped and fell. I held you with one hand, and with the other——"

His wife had sprung to her feet with writhing features.

"Marcus!" she cried. "My beautiful Marcus! Oh, you

brute! you brute! you brute!" There was a clatter of tea-cups as she fell forward senseless upon the table.

They never talk about that strange isolated incident in their married life. For an instant the curtain of the past had swung aside, and some strange glimpse of a forgotten life had come to them. But it closed down, never to open again. They live their narrow round—he in his shop, she in her household—and yet new and wider horizons have vaguely formed themselves around them since that summer evening by the crumbling Roman fort.

The Doll's Ghost

Marion Crawford

It was a terrible accident, and for one moment the splendid machinery of Cranston House got out of gear and stood still. The butler emerged from the retirement in which he spent his elegant leisure, two grooms of the chambers appeared simultaneously from opposite directions, there were actually housemaids on the grand staircase, and those who remember the facts most exactly assert that Mrs. Pringle herself positively stood upon the landing. Mrs. Pringle was the housekeeper. As for the head nurse, the under nurse, and the nursery-maid, their feelings cannot be described.

The Lady Gwendolen Lancaster-Douglas-Scroop, youngest daughter of the ninth Duke of Cranston, and aged six years and three months, picked herself up quite alone, and sat down on the third step of the grand staircase in Cranston House.

"Oh!" ejaculated the butler, and he disappeared again.

"Ah!" responded the grooms of the chambers, as they also went away.

"It's only that doll," Mrs. Pringle was distinctly heard to say, in a tone of contempt.

The under nurse heard her say it. Then the three nurses gathered round Lady Gwendolen and patted her, and gave her unhealthy things out of their pockets, and hurried her out of Cranston House as fast as they could, lest it should be found out upstairs that they had allowed the Lady Gwendolen Lancaster-Douglas-Scroop to tumble down the grand staircase with her doll in her arms. And as the doll was badly broken, the nursery-maid carried it, with the pieces, wrapped up in Lady Gwendolen's little cloak. It was not far to Hyde Park, and when they had reached a quiet place they took means to find out that Lady Gwendolen had no bruises. For the carpet was very thick and soft, and there was thick stuff under it to make it softer.

Lady Gwendolen Douglas-Scroop sometimes yelled, but she never cried. It was because she had yelled that the nurse had allowed her to go downstairs alone with Nina, the doll, under one arm, while she steadied herself with her other hand on the balustrade, and trod upon the polished marble steps beyond the edge of the carpet. So she had fallen, and Nina had come to grief. . . .

Mr. Bernard Puckler and his little daughter lived in a little house in a little alley, which led out off a quiet little street not very far from Belgrave Square. He was the great doll doctor, and his extensive practice lay in the most aristocratic quarter. He mended dolls of all sizes and ages, boy dolls and girl dolls, baby dolls in long clothes, and grown-up dolls in fashionable gowns, talking dolls and dumb dolls, those that shut their eyes when they lay down, and those whose eyes had to be shut for them by means of a mysterious wire. His daughter Else was only just over twelve years old, but she was already very clever at mending dolls' clothes, and at doing their hair, which is harder than you might think, though the dolls sit quite still while it is being done.

Mr. Puckler had originally been a German, but he had dissolved his nationality in the ocean of London many years ago, like a great many foreigners. He still had one or two German friends, however, who came on Saturday evenings and smoked with him and played picquet or "skat" with him for farthing points, and called him "Herr Doctor", which seemed to please Mr. Puckler very much.

He looked older than he was, for his beard was rather long and ragged, his hair was grizzled and thin, and he wore horn-rimmed spectacles.

As for Else, she was a thin, pale child, very quiet and neat, with dark eyes and brown hair that was plaited down her back and tied with a bit of black ribbon. She mended the dolls' clothes and took the dolls back to their homes when they were quite strong again.

The house was a little one, but too big for the two people who lived in it. There was a small sitting-room on the street, and the workshop was at the back, and there were three rooms upstairs. But the father and daughter lived most of their time in the workshop, because they were generally at work, even in the evenings.

Mr. Puckler laid Nina on the table and looked at her a long time, till the tears began to fill his eyes behind the horn-rimmed spectacles. He was a very susceptible man, and he often fell in love with the dolls he mended, and found it hard to part with them when they had smiled at him for a few days. They were real little people to him, with characters and thoughts and feelings of their own, and he was very tender with them all. But some attracted him especially from the first, and when they were brought to him maimed and injured, their state seemed so pitiful to him that the tears came easily. You must remember that he had lived among dolls during a great part of his life, and understood them.

"How do you know that they feel nothing?" he went on to say to Else. "You must be gentle with them. It costs nothing to be kind to the little beings, and perhaps it makes a difference to them."

And Else understood him, because she was a child, and she knew that she was more to him than all the dolls.

He fell in love with Nina at first sight, perhaps because her beautiful brown glass eyes were something like Else's own, and he loved Else first and best, with all his heart. And, besides, it was a very sorrowful case. Nina had evidently not been long in the world, for her complexion was perfect, her hair was smooth where it should be smooth, and curly where it should be curly, and her silk clothes were perfectly new. But across her face was that frightful gash, like a sabre-cut, deep and shadowy within, but clean and sharp at the edges. When he tenderly pressed her head to close the gaping wound, the edges made a fine, grating sound, that was painful to hear, and the lids of the dark eyes quivered and trembled as though Nina were suffering dreadfully.

"Poor Nina!" he exclaimed sorrowfully. "But I shall not hurt you much, though you will take a long time to get strong."

He always asked the names of the broken dolls when they were brought to him, and sometimes the people knew what the children called them, and told him. He liked "Nina" for a name. Altogether and in every way she pleased him more than any doll he had seen for many years, and he felt drawn to her, and made up his mind to make her perfectly strong and sound, no matter how much labour it might cost him.

Mr. Puckler worked patiently a little at a time, and Else watched him. She could do nothing for poor Nina, whose clothes needed no mending. The longer the doll doctor worked the more fond he became of the yellow hair and the beautiful brown glass eyes. He sometimes forgot all the other dolls that were waiting to be mended, lying side by side on a shelf, and sat for an hour gazing at Nina's face, while he racked his ingenuity for some new invention by which to hide even the smallest trace of the terrible accident.

She was wonderfully mended. Even he was obliged to admit that; but the scar was still visible to his keen eyes, a very fine line right across the face, downwards from right to left. Yet all the conditions had been most favourable for a cure, since the cement had set quite hard at the first attempt and the weather had been fine and dry, which makes a great difference in a dolls' hospital.

At last he knew that he could do no more, and the under nurse had already come twice to see whether the job was finished, as she coarsely expressed it.

"Nina is not quite strong yet," Mr. Puckler had answered each time, for he could not make up his mind to face the parting.

And now he sat before the square deal table at which he worked, and Nina lay before him for the last time with a big brown-paper box beside her. It stood there like her coffin, waiting for her, he thought. He must put her into it, and lay tissue paper over her dear face, and then put on the lid, and at the thought of tying the string his sight was dim with tears again. He was never to look into the glassy depths of the beautiful brown eyes any more, nor to hear the little wooden voice say "Pa-pa" and "Ma-ma". It was a very painful moment.

In the vain hope of gaining time before the separation, he took up the little sticky bottles of cement and glue and gum and colour, looking at each one in turn, and then at Nina's face. And all his small tools lay there, neatly arranged in a row, but he knew that he could not use them again for Nina. She was quite strong at last, and in a country where there should be no cruel children to hurt her she might live a hundred years, with only that almost imperceptible line across her face, to tell of the fearful thing that had befallen her on the marble steps of Cranston House.

Suddenly Mr. Puckler's heart was quite full, and he rose abruptly from his seat and turned away.

"Else," he said unsteadily, "you must do it for me. I cannot bear to see her go into the box."

So he went and stood at the window with his back turned, while Else did what he had not the heart to do.

"Is it done?" he asked, not turning round. "Then take her away, my dear. Put on your hat, and take her to Cranston House quickly, and when you are gone I will turn round."

Else was used to her father's queer ways with the dolls, and though she had never seen him so much moved by a parting, she was not much surprised.

"Come back quickly," he said, when he heard her hand on the latch. "It is growing late, and I should not send you at this hour. But I cannot bear to look forward to it any more."

When Else was gone, he left the window and sat down in his place before the table again, to wait for the child to come back. He touched the place where Nina had lain, very gently, and he recalled the softly-tinted pink face, and the glass eyes, and the ringlets of yellow hair, till he could almost see them.

The evenings were long, for it was late in the spring. But it began to grow dark soon, and Mr. Puckler wondered why Else did not come back. She had been gone an hour and a half, and that was much longer than he had expected, for it was barely half a mile from Belgrave Square to Cranston House. He reflected that the child might have been kept waiting, but as the twilight deepened he grew anxious, and walked up and down in the dim workshop, no longer thinking of Nina, but of Else, his own living child, whom he loved.

An indefinable, disquieting sensation came upon him by fine degrees, a chilliness and a faint stirring of his thin hair, joined with a wish to be in any company rather than to be alone much longer. It was the beginning of fear.

He told himself in strong German-English that he was a foolish old man, and he began to feel about for the matches in the dusk. He knew just where they should be, for he always kept them in the same place, close to the little tin box that held bits of sealing-wax of various colours, for some kinds of mending. But somehow he could not find the matches in the gloom.

Something had happened to Else, he was sure, and as his fear increased, he felt as though it might be allayed if he could get a light and see what time it was. Then he called himself a foolish old man again, and the sound of his own voice startled him in the dark. He could not find the matches.

The window was grey still; he might see what time it was if he went close to it, and he could go and get matches out of the cupboard afterwards. He stood back from the table, to get out of the way of the chair, and began to cross the board floor.

Something was following him in the dark. There was a small pattering, as of tiny feet upon the boards. He stopped and listened, and the roots of his hair tingled. It was nothing and he was a foolish old man. He made two steps more, and he was sure that he heard the little pattering again. He turned his back to the window, leaning against the sash so that the panes began to crack, and he faced the dark. Everything was quite still, and it smelt of paste and cement and wood-filings as usual.

"Is that you, Else?" he asked, and he was surprised by the fear in his voice.

There was no answer in the room, and he held up his watch and tried to make out what time it was by the grey dusk that was just not darkness. So far as he could see, it was within two or three minutes of ten o'clock. He had been a long time alone. He was shocked, and frightened for Else, out in London, so late, and he almost ran across the room to the door. As he fumbled for the latch, he distinctly heard the running of the little feet after him.

"Mice!" he exclaimed feebly, just as he got the door open.

He shut it quickly behind him, and felt as though some cold thing had settled on his back and were writhing upon him. The passage was quite dark, but he found his hat and was out in the alley in a moment, breathing more freely, and surprised to find how much light there still was in the open air. He could see the pavement clearly under his feet, and far off in the street to which the alley led he could hear the laughter and calls of children, playing some game out of doors. He wondered how he could have been so nervous, and for an instant he thought of going back into the house to wait quietly for Else. But instantly he felt that nervous fright of something stealing over him again. In any case it was better to walk up to Cranston House and ask the servants about the child. One of the women had perhaps taken a fancy to her, and was even now giving her tea and cake.

He walked quickly to Belgrave Square, and then up the broad streets, listening as he went, whenever there was no other sound, for the tiny footsteps. But he heard nothing, and was laughing at himself when he rang the servants' bell at the big house. Of course, the child must be there.

The person who opened the door was quite an inferior person—for it was a back door—but affected the manners of the front, and stared at Mr. Puckler superciliously.

No little girl had been seen, and he knew "nothing about no dolls".

"She is my little girl," said Mr. Puckler tremulously, for all his anxiety was returning tenfold, "and I am afraid something has happened."

The inferior person said rudely that "nothing could have happened to her in that house, because she had not been there, which was a jolly good reason why"; and Mr. Puckler was obliged to admit that the man ought to know, as it was his business to keep the door and let people in. He wished to be allowed to speak to the under nurse, who knew him; but the man was ruder than ever, and finally shut the door in his face.

When the doll doctor was alone in the street, he steadied himself by the railing, for he felt as though he were breaking in two, just as some dolls break, in the middle of the backbone.

Presently he knew that he must be doing something to find Else, and that gave him strength. He began to walk as quickly as he could through the streets, following every highway and byway which his little girl might have taken on her errand. He also asked several policemen in vain if they had seen her, and most of them answered him kindly, for they saw that he was a sober man and in his right senses, and some of them had little girls of their own.

It was one o'clock in the morning when he went up to his own door again, worn out and hopeless and broken-hearted. As he turned the key in the lock, his heart stood still, for he knew that he was awake and not dreaming, and that he really heard those tiny footsteps pattering to meet him inside the house along the passage.

But he was too unhappy to be much frightened any more, and his heart went on again with a dull regular pain, that found its way all through him with every pulse. So he went in, and hung up his hat in the dark, and found the matches in the cupboard and the candlestick in its place in the corner.

Mr Puckler was so much overcome and so completely worn out that he sat down in his chair before the work-table and almost fainted, as his face dropped forward upon his folded hands. Beside him the solitary candle burned steadily with a low flame in the still warm air.

"Else! Else!" he moaned against his yellow knuckles. And that was all he could say, and it was no relief to him. On the contrary, the very sound of the name was a new and sharp pain that pierced his ears and his head and his very soul. For every time he repeated the name it meant that little Else was dead, somewhere out in the streets of London in the dark.

He was so terribly hurt that he did not even feel something pulling gently at the skirt of his old coat, so gently that it was like the nibbling of a tiny mouse. He might have thought that it was really a mouse if he had noticed it.

"Else! Else!" he groaned, right against his hands.

Then a cool breath stirred his thin hair, and the low flame of the one candle dropped down almost to a mere spark, not flickering as though a draught were going to blow it out, but just dropping down as if it were tired out. Mr. Puckler felt his hands stiffening with fright under his face; and there was a faint rustling sound, like some small silk thing blown in a gentle breeze. He sat up straight, stark and scared, and a small wooden voice spoke in the stillness.

"Pa-pa," it said, with a break between the syllables.

Mr. Puckler stood up in a single jump, and his chair fell over backwards with a smashing noise upon the wooden floor. The candle had almost gone out.

It was Nina's doll-voice that had spoken, and he should have known it among the voices of a hundred other dolls. And yet there was something more in it, a little human ring, with a pitiful cry and a call for help, and the wail of a hurt child. Mr. Puckler stood up, stark and stiff, and tried to look round, but at first he could not, for he seemed to be frozen from head to foot.

Then he made a great effort, and he raised one hand to each of his temples, and pressed his own head round as he would have turned a doll's. The candle was burning so low that it might as well have been out altogether, for any light it gave, and the room seemed quite dark at first. Then he saw something. He would not have believed that he could be more frightened than he had been just before that. But he was, and his knees shook, for he saw the doll standing in the middle of the floor, shining with a faint and ghostly radiance, her beautiful glassy brown eyes fixed on his. And across her face the very thin line of the break he had mended shone as though it were drawn in light with a fine point of white flame.

Yet there was something more in the eyes, too; there was something human, like Else's own, but as if only the doll saw him through them, and not Else. And there was enough of Else to bring back all his pain and to make him forget his fear.

"Else! My little Else!" he cried aloud.

The small ghost moved, and its doll-arm slowly rose and fell with a stiff, mechanical motion.

"Pa-pa," it said.

It seemed this time that there was even more of Else's tone echoing somewhere between the wooden notes that reached his ears so distinctly and yet so far away. Else was calling him, he was sure.

His face was perfectly white in the gloom, but his knees did not shake any more, and he felt that he was less frightened.

"Yes, child! But where? Where?" he asked. "Where are you, Else!"

"Pa-pa!"

The syllables died away in the quiet room.

There was a low rustling of silk, the glassy brown eyes turned slowly away, and Mr. Puckler heard the pitter-patter of the small feet in the bronze kid slippers as the figure ran straight to the door. Then the candle burned high again, the room was full of light, and he was alone.

Mr. Puckler passed his hand over his eyes and looked about him. He could see everything quite clearly, and he felt that he must have been dreaming, though he was standing instead of sitting down, as he should have been if he had just waked up. The candle burned brightly now. There were the dolls to be mended, lying in a row with their toes up. The third one had lost her right shoe, and Else was making one. He knew that, and he was certainly not dreaming now. He had not been dreaming when he had come in from his fruitless search and had heard the doll's footsteps running to the door. He had not fallen asleep in his chair. How could he possibly have fallen asleep when his heart was breaking? He had been awake all the time.

He steadied himself, set the fallen chair upon its legs, and said to himself again very emphatically that he was a foolish old man. He ought to be out in the streets looking for his child, asking questions, and inquiring at the police stations, where all accidents were reported as soon as they were known, or at the hospitals.

"Pa-pa!"

The longing, wailing, pitiful little wooden cry rang from the passage, outside the door, and Mr. Puckler stood for an instant with white face, transfixed and rooted to the spot. A moment later his hand was on the latch. Then he was in the passage, with the light streaming from the open door behind him.

Quite at the other end he saw the little phantom shining clearly in the shadow, and the right hand seemed to beckon to him as the arm rose and fell once more. He knew all at once that it had not come to frighten him but to lead him, and when it disappeared, and he walked boldly towards the door, he knew that it was in the street outside, waiting for him. He forgot that he was tired and had eaten no supper, and had walked many miles, for a sudden hope ran through and through him, like a golden stream of life.

And sure enough, at the corner of the alley, and at the corner of the street, and out in Belgrave Square, he saw the small ghost flitting before him. Sometimes it was only a shadow, where there was other light, but then the glare of the lamps made a pale green sheen on its little Mother Hubbard frock of silk; and sometimes, where the streets were dark and silent, the whole figure shone out brightly, with its yellow curls and rosy neck. It seemed to trot along like a tiny child, and Mr. Puckler could hear the pattering of the bronze kid slippers on the pavement as it ran. But it went very fast, and he could only just keep up with it, tearing along with his hat on the back of his head and his thin hair blown by the night breeze, and his horn-rimmed spectacles firmly set upon his broad nose.

On and on he went, and he had no idea where he was. He did not even care, for he knew certainly that he was going the right way.

Then at last, in a wide, quiet street, he was standing

before a big, sober-looking door that had two lamps on each side of it, and a polished brass bell-handle, which he pulled.

And just inside, when the door was opened, in the bright light, there was the little shadow, and the pale green sheen of the little silk dress, and once more the small cry came to his ears, less pitiful, more longing.

"Pa-pa!"

The shadow turned suddenly bright, and out of the brightness the beautiful brown glass eyes were turned up happily to his, while the rosy mouth smiled so divinely that the phantom doll looked almost like a little angel just then.

"A little girl was brought in soon after ten o'clock," said the quiet voice of the hospital doorkeeper. "I think they thought she was only stunned. She was holding a big brown-paper box against her, and they could not get it out of her arms. She had a long plait of brown hair that hung down as they carried her."

"She is my little girl," said Mr. Puckler, but he hardly heard his own voice.

He leaned over Else's face in the gentle light of the children's ward, and when he had stood there a minute the beautiful brown eyes opened and looked up to his.

"Pa-pa!" cried Else softly, "I knew you would come!"

Then Mr. Puckler did not know what he did or said for a moment, and what he felt was worth all the fear and terror and despair that had almost killed him that night. But by and by Else was telling her story, and the nurse let her speak, for there were only two other children in the room, who were getting well and were sound asleep.

"They were big boys with bad faces," said Else, "and they tried to get Nina away from me, but I held on and fought as well as I could till one of them hit me with something, and I don't remember any more, for I tumbled down and I suppose the boys ran away, and somebody found me there. But I'm afraid Nina is all smashed."

"Here is the box," said the nurse. "We could not take it out of her arms till she came to herself. Would you like to see if the doll is broken?"

And she undid the string cleverly, but Nina was all smashed to pieces. Only the gentle light of the children's ward made a pale green sheen in the folds of the little Mother Hubbard frock.

A Long Day Without Water

Joan Aiken

This story is all about tears—tears locked inside a heart, heart lost in a river, river shut inside a house, house in a village that didn't want it. Better get out your handkerchiefs then, for it sounds like a whole sky full of cloud coming along, doesn't it? And yet the ending, when we get there, isn't solid sad.

So listen.

Our village is called Appleby under Scar, and there's a river, the Skirwith Beck, that runs through the middle of it. Or did. Ran down the middle of the village green, chuckling and muttering among its rocks; clean-washed gravelbeds in summer on either side; in winter, of course, it was up to chest high, brown and foamy like the best oatmeal stout. In summer, days together, the children would be playing there with dams, and stepping-stones, making castles on the sandbanks, picking up quartz stones, white, purple, and pink, all sparkling. A beautiful stream, the Skirwith Beck, the best kind. You can keep your willowy, muddy, winding rivers.

And the village green, on either side, was common land, villagers used to pasture their geese and donkeys there; lots of people used to have an old moke for when they wanted to go up on the fell and bring down a load of peat.

Summer evenings, half the village would be out on the

green, enjoying the sunshine. There was a young fellow, Johnny Rigby, who had a little farm; hardly more than a smallholding, but he worked it hard and made a living from it; he was one of three brothers. Anyway this Johnny Rigby was a rare lad for playing the fiddle and composing songs; he used to play his fiddle on the green, and the girls used to dance. Or everybody would gather round to listen if he'd made up a new song.

I can remember one of his to this day; kind of a catch, or round, it was.

> *Standing corn, running river*
> *Singing wind, laughing plover*
> *Running fox, standing grain*
> *Leaping salmon, weeping rain*
> *Shining sun, singing lark*
> *Running roe, listening dark,*
> *Laughing river, standing corn*
> *Happy village where I was born.*

You see? It went round and round; pretty tune it had, still goes round and round in my head.

Johnny Rigby was friendly with a girl called Martha; nothing definite yet, but when he'd made up a new song, Martha would generally be the one that sat nearest to hear him sing it, and the first to get it by heart: Martha Dyson, pink cheeks and black hair, and bright, dark eyes that saw farther than most. Folk were pretty certain they'd get wed by and by.

Well, somewhere in among those long summer evenings of singing and chat on the Skirwith bank, some little chaps in glasses drove up to the village in a big Bentley car, and they were busy for days together, pottering about taking samples of soil, poking instruments into the ground, weighing and measuring, peering about them through spyglasses, even getting down into the Skirwith Beck and taking samples of gravel from underneath *that*.

Nobody bothered about them. We're peaceable folk in these parts; if chaps don't worry us, we won't worry them. They used to eat their dinners in the Falcon pub, and we'd give them a civil good-day, but no more; we don't get thick with strangers all in a hurry round here; we give ourselves time to look them over first. And we had hardly given ourselves more than a couple of weeks to do that, when they were gone again, and then time went by and we forgot them.

But two or three months later—the hay was in and the harvest was half through—we heard what they'd been up to, and it was this.

It seems some big chemical firm—United Kingdom Alloys, the name was—had got wind there was a layer of mineral right under our village green, something quite uncommon and out of the way. Demetrium, it was called, a kind of nickel, Tom Thorpe told me it was, but that's as maybe. And the long and the short of it was, they wanted permission to dig up the green, or, in their language, opencast mine it, to a depth of fifteen feet.

Well! You can guess that stirred up a lot of talk in the village.

A few folk were dead against it, old Thunders Barstow for one. He was the sexton, and got his nickname from his habit of shouting "The Lord shall send his thunders upon you", when he didn't approve of something.

"What'll happen?" he said. "They'll come here, wi' all their load of heavy digging equipment, they'll wreck the road from here to Paxton, carting yon stuff away, they'll make a right shambles o' the green; I shouldn't wonder if half the houses didn't tumble down because they'll undermine the foundations; they'll spoil the beck wi' their gravel and refuse, tha can say good-bye to t'trout and salmon, and then what? When they've got what they come for, they'll be off, leaving the place a fair wilderness."

Of course United Kingdom Alloys promised and swore they would do no such thing. Every care would be taken of amenities, they said, in a letter on stiff, crackly paper, the dug-out area would be filled in again and landscaped, all debris taken away, any damage made good, and so forth.

"Landscaped!" snorted old Thunders. "What about our chestnuts? Tha cannot tweak up a two-hundred-year-old chestnut tree and set it back again as if it was a snowdrop bulb, sithee!"

Well, United Kingdom Alloys did admit they'd have to chop down the chestnuts—twenty of them, there were, all round the edge of the green—but they said they'd plant others, *mature trees*, they said, in another letter on ever stiffer, cracklier paper, as soon as the work was completed.

"After all," said Sam Oakroyd, "there's no brass wi'out muck. And tha can see they mean to play fair by us."

Brass, of course, was the nub of the business. U.K.A. were offering a right handsome sum for the use of our land—a figure that made most folk's eyes pop out on stalks when they heard it, though of course you had to remember it was going to be split up among the twenty people who owned the grazing rights on the green. And that was the hitch—everyone whose cottage faced on to the green had a say in the matter, and the firm couldn't so much as set a trowel into the ground till the whole twenty had agreed, as well as the Ministry of Town and Country Planning.

Well, the Ministry agreed—no argument there—and

bit by bit everyone else did, as they realized what advantage it would bring them. Tom Thorpe could get a new farm truck, the Oakroyds would be able to send their daughter to music college, widow Kirby could get a modern stove put in her cottage, young Sally Gateshead could buy herself a hunter, the Bateses would be able to achieve their dearest wish, which was a colour telly, and the Sidebothams had set their hearts on a holiday in Madeira. One person who didn't agree was old Thunders Barstow, but his cottage didn't front on the green, so he had no say in the matter. And a lot of people thought old Thunders was a bit touched, anyway.

But just when everything seemed swimming along merrily and in a fair way to be fixed up, the whole scheme came to a stop, because of one other person.

That person was Johnny Rigby.

His two brothers had signed on the dotted line quick enough. Old man Rigby had died without making a will, and his farm had been split in three; there was just enough land for each brother, but you had to work hard to make it pay, and the two elder Rigbys, who shared the old man's house, although they weren't bone idle, weren't all that wild keen on work; they were fair tickled at the prospect of a nest egg from United Kingdom Alloys. Each brother owned grazing rights on the green, as Johnny had his own cottage, left him by his gran, and each had to agree before the company could start work.

But Johnny wouldn't, and he was the last person in the village to make a stand.

He said it would spoil the place. He said no matter what was done afterwards, in the way of landscaping, Appleby would never be the same again. I think there were quite a few others agreed with him in their hearts, but they were overborne by their husbands—or wives—or children—

who could see the benefits of hard cash, and were happy to let the future take care of itself.

Everybody argued with Johnny and tried to persuade him to change his mind. And as he wouldn't, the arguments grew more and more hot-tempered. People don't mince words in our parts.

"Tha stupid young milksop!" shouted old Sam Oakroyd. "Tha'rt holding up progress and keeping good brass out o' folk's pockets, all for the sake of a moonshiny notion. A few trees and a bit o' rough pasture! Grass can be sown again, can't it?"

"And what about the river?" said Johnny. "Can they put that back the way it was, after it's been taken out of its bed and run through a concrete pipe-line?"

Johnny had fished and paddled and swum in the beck since he was out of his pram; he knew every rock and rowan tree along it, from Skipley to Paxton-le-Pool.

"Aye, they'll put it back—they said so, didn't they? Come on, lad, don't be daft—just stop fussing and sign." Old Oakroyd had the letter of acceptance, with everybody's names on it.

But Johnny wouldn't.

So there was a lot of ill-feeling against him. The Sidebothams said flat out that he must be mental, to refuse good cash, and ought to be committed to Skipley Home for Defectives. Tom Thorpe threatened to punch his head, several times his front windows were smashed, and I even heard someone let fly at him with a shotgun one night, as he came home on his motor-bike from Paxton. There was no legal way he could be forced to change his mind, see; he had a right to his own point of view. His own brothers wouldn't speak to him; they were the angriest of the lot. The only person who stood by him was Martha Dyson.

"How are we going to get that thick-skulled brother o'

yours to change his mind?" Tom Thorpe said to Wilfred and Michael Rigby in the pub one night.

"I dare say he'll come round in time," Wilfred said.

"Time! That firm won't keep their offer open for ever. There's big deposits of demetrium in Brazil, I read in the paper."

"Then why the devil can't they *go* to Brazil for the stuff, 'stead o' scraping up our green to get tuppence-haporth out of it?' grumbled old Thunders.

"This is cheaper and handier for them, you silly old man."

"Cheaper! Cheaper. The Lord shall call his thunders down on this pennypinching generation—aye, he shall give their flocks to hot thunderbolts," declared the old man, who loved every stone of Appleby, and hated the thought of change.

Taking no notice of old Thunders, Wilfred Rigby said:

"The only way to get John to change his mind is by public boycott. He's always been a kind of a friendly, popular chap, with his fiddling and his songs; he'd feel it hard if nobody spoke to him, if nobody listened to his songs any more. That'd bring him round, I reckon."

"Bring him round? It'd break his heart," said old Thunders angrily. But no one took any notice of *him*.

So that was what they did. Nobody in the village would speak to Johnny. If he went into the pub, or the post-office, folk turned their backs; if he strolled up to a group on the green, they all walked away.

Well, it's bitter hard for anybody in the world to have a thing like that happen to them—to be thrust out and given the cut by your own kin and neighbours—but for a song-writer it's worst of all. See, if you think about it, a song-writer needs folk to sing his songs *to*, he doesn't just make them up to sing into the empty air. It's like electricity: no connection, no current. Without friends to listen to his songs, and dance to his tunes, Johnny was like a fish without water to swim in, a bird without air to fly in; there just wasn't any point to him.

When it got too cold, in autumn-time, for musical evenings on the village green, Johnny'd been in the habit of holding kind of open-house every Thursday evening. He hadn't much furniture in his cottage, for all the spare cash he had went on fertilizer and stuff for his land, but that made all the more room for friends. He had an old piano that had been his gran's, and anyone who liked could drop in for a bit o' singing. If they brought a bottle of beer with them, all the better. Past winters, the house used to be chockfull every Thursday, and people dancing in his patch of front garden too. He'd leave the door open, so the light would shine across the green, and you could hear the sound of fiddle and singing clear over the chuckle of the Skirwith Beck.

But not this autumn.

The first Thursday when it was too rainy and dark to linger outside, Johnny left his door open. It was pouring wet, and the sound of the beck was like a train running over points in the distance. The light from the door shone out, yellow, on the rain. Martha was away, staying with her auntie in London, expected back next day. So Johnny was alone. He'd written a new song, and he played the tune over softly on the piano, and louder on the fiddle; but nobody came. An hour went by, still nobody came. Johnny went outside in the wet and looked this way and that; no sign of anybody coming. But there was a light, and noise, from the Falcon pub, across the green, so he walked over. As he got closer he could hear voices singing and someone bashing the old pub piano; Mrs. Ellie Side-botham, it was, he saw when he got outside the window;

her playing was enough to give you sinus trouble. But all the village seemed to be in there, singing and enjoying themselves.

Johnny pushed open the door and went in.

A dead silence fell.

Johnny nodded to Mr. Baker, who kept the pub, and said he'd have a pint of bitter. Mr. Baker couldn't refuse to serve him, so he did, but he didn't speak. Then Johnny took his drink and went over to the piano and pulled a bit of sheet music out of his pocket.

"I've written a new song, Mrs. Sidebotham," he said. "Like to play it for me?"

Ellie Sidebotham was a silly, flustered kind of woman; put you in mind of a moulting pullet. She didn't know how to refuse, so she started to play the tune, making a right botch of it.

And Johnny turned and faced the room and began to sing.

> *It's a long walk in the dark*
> *On the blind side of the moon*
> *And it's a long day without water*
> *When the river's gone——*

But before he had sung any more than that, the bar had emptied. Folk just put down their drinks and left.

Ellie Sidebotham shuffled her way off the piano stool. "I—I must be going too," she said, and scuttled off.

Johnny looked round at the emptiness. He said, "It seems I'm not welcome here," and he walked out.

Wherever he went from the pub, he didn't go home till daylight; some folk said he just walked up and down the village green all night, thinking. In the morning he did go home, but that night's tramping up and down in the wet had done for him; big, strong chap as he was, he came down with a raging pneumonia, and when Martha got back from her auntie's in London and went along to see how he was, she found him tossing and turning on his bed with a temperature of a hundred and six. She ran to the pub and phoned for an ambulance to take him to hospital, but the Skirwith Beck was flooded and they had to take the long way round, and by the time they got there, Johnny was in a coma from which he didn't recover.

Folk felt pretty bad after his death, as you can guess.

There was a big turn-out for the funeral; the whole village came along, done up in black, looking respectful.

Appleby church stands on a kind of knoll above the village, opposite Martha's cottage. The knoll is an island when the beck's in spate, and it was in spate that day; it had rained solid ever since Johnny died. The footbridge was under water, so the only way to get to the graveyard was to row across. The vicar, Mr. Haxley, was waiting on the other side. When all the mourners got to the river-bank, Martha Dyson came out from her cottage and faced them.

"You lot can just go home again," she said. "You didn't want my Johnny, and *you*'re not wanted here. And if you want my opinion of you, you can have it—you're a lot of cowardly murderers, and you broke Johnny's heart among you, and I hope you're proud of yourselves!"

Not a soul had owt to say. They turned round, looking as shamed as dogs that have been caught sheep-worrying, and walked away through the rain. Martha Dyson and old Thunders began rowing the coffin across to the church. But the current was fierce, he was an old man, and she only a bit of a lass; a huge eddy of flood-water and branches came down on them and capsized the boat. Martha was a good swimmer, but she had her hands full with getting the old man to the bank; the vicar helped pull him out, and the first thing was to get the pair of them dry and tended. By the time folk came to look for the boat and the coffin, neither could be found. The boat finally turned up, stove-in, down at Paxton-le-Pool. But the coffin with Johnny's body in it they never found, though the police dragged the Skirwith all the way to where it joins the Ouse.

Well, you know how tales start up; it wasn't long before folk were saying the heart in Johnny's body had been so heavy with grief that it sank the boat.

But that wasn't the end of the matter, as you shall hear.

Of course, even if they pulled long faces, there were plenty of folk in the village who were relieved at Johnny's death, because now there was nothing to stand in the way of the United Kingdom Alloy scheme. His land went to his two brothers, and they had already signed the form. So within two weeks the green was covered with bull-dozers and those big grabbing machines that look like nought in the world but prehistoric monsters, and they'd cut down the chestnuts, and the grass on Appleby green was a thing of the past.

Some folk were even mean enough to say wasn't it a good thing that Johnny and Martha hadn't got wed yet —they'd fixed to get married at Christmas, it came out— because if she'd been his widow, instead of only his intended, she'd have owned the grazing rights and been able to withhold her permission. And there's no doubt she would have. She was very bitter against the village. Very bitter indeed, she was.

Those Rigby brothers must have felt guilty right down to their socks, for, believe it or not, when the U.K.A. paid over the fee for use of land—which, fair play, they did pretty promptly, though it turned out to be only half what they'd said; the other half, they explained, would be paid on completion of the operation—Wilfred Rigby went along to see Martha Dyson. They hadn't spoken since the funeral.

Martha's cottage, up the dale, opposite the church, had been her family home from way back. Martha's grandmother had been a celebrated witch, or wise woman, in her day, could charm warts and lay curses and make prophecies; some folk said that Martha could too. Her mother and father had died in the bad flood of '68, and she lived on her own, kept bees, and sold the honey in Paxton; did quite well out of it. She was feeding her bees with sugar-syrup when Wilfred came along. The beck ran right past her gate, and there were two queer old carved swans on the gateposts, asleep with their heads under their wings—at least, they were said to be swans, but you could make them into pretty well anything you chose.

Wilfred had to clear his throat several times and finally shout quite loud to attract Martha's attention; the beck was brawling away, still extra-high, and from the village there was a continual grinding and roaring from the earth-moving machinery, and every now and then the ground would tremble as they dumped a big load of topsoil, or split a rock. By now, naturally, the whole village was a sea of slurry, and the road down to Paxton just a rutted, muddy watercourse.

"Well," said Martha, hearing at last and turning round, "what do *you* want?"

Wilfred—awkward and fumbling enough—went into an explanation of how—if by this time Martha had been married to Johnny—and if Johnny hadn't died—and if he'd agreed to the U.K.A. scheme—Martha would have come in for a bit of the brass. At last she understood him.

"You're offering me money?"

Wilfred shuffled his feet and brought out that, yes, he was.

"Why?"

He looked more uncomfortable still. He didn't like to admit that he was scared stiff of Martha's anger and wanted to soothe her down. He shuffled his feet again in the wet grass, and said:

"We thought—Mike and I—that you might like to go on a bit of a holiday. Or—or the vicar was suggesting that as poor Johnny hasn't got a gravestone, we might wish to put up a memorial tablet to him. Maybe you'd like to use some of the money for that?"

Martha's eyes fairly blazed at him.

"You can just take your dirty money away from here, Wilfred Rigby, back to the mucky hole you've made of Appleby," she said. "I've got some brass of my own, that my gran left me, and I intend to put up my own memorial to Johnny. And I'd advise you not to try—there's some hypocrisy that even the wind and weather can't abide. Any tablet *you* put up would crack in the first frost, it would get struck by lightning or washed away by a flood."

"You're a hard, unforgiving woman, Martha Dyson," said Wilfred.

"I've cause," she snapped.

At that moment there was an extra loud crashing rumble from the village. And then Wilfred and Martha saw a queer and frightening thing. The Skirwith Beck, rushing down its rocky way, did a kind of sudden lurch sideways in its bed—just as a startled horse will shy at something ahead of it—the water lurched and rocked, and then, quick as I'm speaking, sank away out of sight, down into the ground.

"My lord! The beck! What's come to it!" Wilfred gasped.

"It's gone," said Martha sombrely. "Due to you and your money-grabbing mates it's gone. And I can tell you this, Wilfred Rigby—I shan't forgive you or anybody else in Appleby till it comes back again."

And with that she turned her back on him and wouldn't speak any more and he was glad enough to hurry away.

Well, you can guess there was plenty more talk in the village about the lost beck. Some said it was due to natural causes—the vibrations from the heavy digging had likely cracked open an underground cavern, and the water had sunk through into it. But there were plenty believed it was the weight of Johnny Rigby's heavy heart that had sunk the river, as it had sunk the rowboat. And there were a few that thought Martha Dyson had done it, out of revenge against the village that had killed her Johnny. Martha never spoke to a soul in Appleby these days— except old Thunders—she bought her groceries in Paxton when she went with the honey.

Meanwhile the digging went on. Appleby looked like some place in a war-zone that's had half a dozen battles fought in it, back and forth. And the beck never came back. Trees in gardens began to die, because their roots weren't getting enough water.

And Martha built her memorial to Johnny Rigby. She had a grand architect from London come down for the job, and a builder from York. It was a queer-looking thing enough when it was done—a little house in the church-yard, all made of stone, with carvings on the outside all over—ears of wheat, birds, foxes, deer, fish, leaves, and what looked like ripples of water twining in and among and through all these things. It had a right unchancy feel about it—when you looked at it close you could have sworn the stone was moving, like grass waving or water running. There was a door at one end, and over the lintel

Martha got the architect to put the two swans from her gateposts, with their heads under their wings.

On the side was carved the name John Rigby, and underneath some words:

Thou art cast out of thy grave like an abominable branch...

For the waters of Nimrim shall be desolate; for the hay is withered away, the grass faileth, there is no green thing...

Woe to the multitude of many people, which make a noise like the noise of the seas...

And behold at eveningtide trouble; and before the morning he is not. This is the portion of them that spoil us, and the lot of them that rob us. Isaiah, 14, 15, 17.

The vicar wasn't best pleased when he saw the words that had been carved, but Martha said they were Bible words, and by that time the architect and the builders had left, so in the end they were allowed to stay. There were a lot of complaints in the village about the tomb itself—folk said it was an outrage, and should be taken away. But the vicar put a stop to that.

Pretty soon there was a new tale in the village about this tomb.

The Bates family had a boy who wasn't quite right in the head. Simple Steve, or Silly Steve, he was called; the other children wouldn't play with him because he hardly ever spoke, but only made patterns on the ground with leaves and twigs and stones. It was a queer tale enough about *him*, and a sad one. Mrs. Bates had had two boys, and was set on a girl for her next; when Steve was born, another boy, she wouldn't speak to him, kept him shut away in a back bedroom, and fed him only slops till he was six or seven. Lots of folk didn't even know he existed till the school attendance officer, doing a check, discovered that Steve ought to have been going to school for a couple of years and couldn't even speak. There was a fuss, threats of prosecution, but in the end it died down. Steve was sent to school, but he didn't learn much. The teacher was very angry about it all and said he wasn't really simple; if he'd been cared for and spoken to properly from the start it would have been all right; but it was too late now. Well, there you are; that's the kind of thing you find even in families that seem quite normal and above-board.

Simple Steve used to spend quite a lot of time in the graveyard, playing his pattern-games on the flat tombstones. Old Thunders didn't mind him; in fact the two got on quite well; they could make themselves understood to each other in a kind of sign language. Steve used to help cut the grass and clip the hedges. The old man would whistle as he worked and Steve, though he could hardly talk, could hum a tune; Old Thunders taught him some of Johnny Rigby's tunes. But there was one corner of the graveyard Steve would never go near, and that was where Johnny Rigby's memorial stood; he explained to the old man that he was afraid of the tomb because the beck was all shut up inside that little house, and one day it was going to break out and flood all over the village. By and by somehow this tale got round, and although they knew it was nonsense, a lot of folk half believed it, specially the children.

Martha had the key of the door; she had said, if ever Johnny's coffin was found, it should be put in; so nobody could get in. It used to be a dare-game for the braver kids, on a bright sunshiny afternoon, to go and listen at the keyhole. They'd come away quaking and giggling, declaring they could hear the beck running inside—like when you put your ear to a shell. Not one of them would have had the nerve to go near the place at night.

By this time the winter was nearly over. Frost and snow

hadn't stopped the U.K.A.—they'd been digging away like badgers all through. There had been one or two mishaps—a few people fell into the diggings at night and broke legs or arms; the works were taken a bit too near the Rigby brothers' house and it collapsed, but they weren't killed, and the U.K.A. swore they'd pay compensation. Also they cut through the village water-supply and sewage system, but the Public Health lot made them put the sewer right pretty quick, before they had a typhoid epidemic on their hands. The Rigbys weren't so lucky; they hadn't got their compensation by the time the U.K.A. people left, nor had Thorpe, for his collapsed barn, nor the Bateses for their garden which had sunk down ten feet, nor widow Kirby, who'd had twelve ton of subsoil accidentally dumped on hers. And there were various other troubles of the kind, but people reckoned the company would pay up for these things at the same time as they paid the second half of the fee for use of land.

Well, the excavators left, and took their machinery with them, leaving the place like the crater of a volcano; and folk were beginning to wonder when the landscapers would be along with their turf, and mature trees, and whatnot, to make good the devastation, fill in the excavated area, and carry out all their promises.

It was at this point that we read in the papers about the United Kingdom Alloy company going bankrupt.

Over-extended its resources, was the phrase used in court when the case was heard. They'd had irons in too many fires, borrowed cash here to pay for operations there which turned out less successful than they'd hoped; and the outcome of the matter was they'd gone into liquidation, paid sixpence in the pound to their creditors, and the head of the firm had disappeared, thought to have absconded to Brazil to escape all the trouble he'd left behind him.

And as for our mature trees, topsoil, turf, compensation, and the Skirwith Beck, we could whistle for them.

You'd hardly believe what happened next.

Martha Dyson still wasn't speaking to anyone in the village. People said she was so bitter, even the birds and the wild animals kept away from her garden. But one day a deputation from the village went to call on her: Mrs. Kirby, Mrs. Bates, Tom Thorpe, and the Sidebothams. They stood inside Martha's gate looking nervous till she came out and asked them what they wanted. They all hummed and ha'd and looked at one another, until at last Ellie Sidebotham burst out with it.

"We've come to ask you to take the curse off!"

"Curse, what curse?" Martha says.

"The curse you put on the village! We've no water-supply, the trees and plants are all dying, the green's just a hole full of shingle—there's no end to the trouble. Oh, Miss Dyson, do please take it off. We're scared to think what might happen if it gets any worse!"

At that Martha laughed, a short, scornful laugh.

"You poor fools, *I* didn't put any curse on you," she said. "It was your own short-sighted greed put you in this mess, and you'll just have to get yourselves out of it again as best you can."

"But you said to Will Rigby that until the Skirwith Beck came back . . ."

"I said I shouldn't forgive you until then, and it's true, I shan't. Now go away and leave me in peace," Martha said.

"Then you're a hard, heartless woman, Martha Dyson!" squeaked Ellie Sidebotham. "And with all your show of mourning Johnny Rigby, I don't believe you've ever shed a tear for him."

White-faced and dry-eyed, Martha glared at her. Then she said:

"Get out of my garden. And you can tell the rest of them, down at the village, that if anyone else comes here without being asked, I *shall* get out my grandmother's book of curses."

They cleared out pretty quick at that, and went back to the village, muttering. As for Martha, she sat down on her doorstep, sick with sadness, and shivering, shivering cold. For it was true, since Johnny's death, she hadn't been able to cry; not a tear had left her eyes.

Well, the people of Appleby saw they'd get no help from Martha, and they found they'd get none, either, from the Ministry of Town and Country Planning, which said it might be able to do something for them in a couple of years but not sooner. So they realized they'd have to help themselves, and they clubbed together and started a fund for Village Beautification. The Bateses reckoned they could do without their colour TV another year, Sally Gateshead sold the new hunter, the Sidebothams fixed to go to Blackpool instead of Madeira. And so on. Furthermore they arranged a rota of working parties to start getting the green back into shape. The trouble was, fetching down enough topsoil from the fells to fill in the hole; that was going to take a lot of men a lot of time. However, they'd hardly got started when the cold came on, very severe.

Up to then it had been an unusually mild winter, for our part. But in late March, after a specially warm spell, there was a sudden real blizzard. First it thundered, then it hailed, then the snow came down solid white, out of a black sky. And the snow went right on for twenty-four hours, till all you could see of Appleby were a few humps, for roofs of houses, and the church spire on its knoll. The shallow crater in the middle of the village was filled with snow, and looked decenter than it had for many a week.

There were no trees above the snow; what hadn't been chopped had all fallen during the winter.

We're well used to snow, of course; so folk who hadn't beasts to tend stayed in and kept snug. At least there was plenty of firewood: chestnut wood. But in the middle of the night following the storm all of a sudden there came the loudest noise you can imagine; some thought it was the H-bomb, others that the top of Skipley Fell had come loose and slid down in an avalanche.

Well, it was a kind of avalanche, they discovered in the morning. The bottom of the crater that had been Appleby green had fallen in, due to the weight of snow piled in it, and the crater was now a whole lot deeper; but before they had time to discover how much deeper, it filled up with water. For the sudden cold had turned to a sudden thaw; the snow was melting as fast as it had come.

That morning Martha was looking over her bee-hives, to make sure they'd taken no hurt in the snow, when she saw a black procession of men going up to the church, carrying something shoulder-high.

Mr. Haxley the vicar came over and tapped on Martha's gate. His face was solemn, and he looked as if he didn't know how to begin what he had to say. But she got there first.

"They've found him?" she said.

"Yes, my dear. I've come to ask for the key."

Seemingly, all that rock and snow and rubble, crashing down through the bottom of the crater, must have filled up the underground chamber again, or blocked the entrance, and in doing so it had washed up the coffin of Johnny Rigby from where it had been lodged somewhere underground. It was found beached on the edge of the pool that had been Appleby green.

Martha gave the key to Mr. Haxley. But the men found

they didn't need it, for the end of the empty tomb, and the tree that stood nearest to it, had both been struck by lightning in the storm the night before. The end wall of the tomb had fallen away, and the door was all charred.

The men of the village, who had carried Johnny's coffin up, laid it inside the tomb while the vicar read the funeral service, and then they rebuilt the wall and set in a new door. But they couldn't find the two stone swans, which seemed to have been clean destroyed. All that time, Martha watched them from her garden gateway. When they were leaving, she made them a kind of bow, to signify she was grateful for what they'd done. And when they'd gone, she sat down on her doorstep, threw her apron over her head, and cried as if a dam had burst inside her.

But that day wasn't over for Martha yet. After a while, as she sat there grieving, but more gently now, she heard a sound by her. She pulled the apron off her face and found the little Bates lad, Simple Steve, sitting on the step next her, quiet-like, making one of his patterns with sticks and leaves.

"Hallo!" she said, fair astonished, for no kid from the village ever set foot inside her garden.

He gave her a nod, and the kind of grunt that was all he'd do for hallo. And went on with his pattern. It was a peaceful kind of thing to watch, and presently she got to helping him, handing him bits of stuff, and showing him where he could make the pattern better.

Steve began humming to himself, as he often did.

"Where did you learn that?" asked Martha, startled. For the tune was one of Johnny's.

Steve nodded his head, sideways, towards the church-yard over the way, meaning, probably, that old Thunders had taught it him.

Martha took up the tune with him, singing the words.

A Long Day Without Water

It's a long walk in the dark
On the blind side of the moon
And it's a long day without water
When the river's gone
And it's hard listening to no voice
When you're all alone.

Steve learned the words from her, after his fashion, and he began singing them too.

"You sing well, Steve," she told him.

At that, Steve's face did a thing it had never done before. It smiled. Then he pointed past Martha. She turned, and saw that an old tail-less black cat, Mrs. Kirby's Tib, had come into the garden. And that wasn't all. There were rabbits, and a stray ewe, a young fox, even a roe-deer, which had all pushed their way through the hedge.

"Mercy, what's come over the creatures?" said Martha, more and more amazed.

"They know the beck's coming," said Steve, nodding. "I did, too."

She understood what he meant then. In the bad flood of '68, only Martha's cottage and the church knoll stood above water-level.

"I'd best warn them," she said. "You stay here, Steve."

And she walked quickly down to Appleby, where half the village was out, gazing at the pool that had been Appleby green. They gawped when they saw Martha, as you can guess.

"I've come to tell you the beck's coming down," she said. "You'd best—you'd best come up to my place."

They didn't hang about. In our parts we know how, when the snow melts up on the high fells, a little trickle of water can turn to a raging torrent in ten minutes. Tom Thorpe went round, shouting them out of their houses, and they were up at Martha's, carrying all they could, almost as quick as I'm telling it. And only just in time, too, for the Skirwith Beck came thundering down the dale only a few minutes after, as if it was carrying the troubles and quarrels of the whole village on its back.

They had to stay up at Martha's for three hours, while the water raged through the village. She made them cups of tea and so forth, while the women helped, and they all shared out what food they'd brought up with them. Then the water went down—it's fast come, fast go, up here—and they went back to look at the damage.

Well, it wasn't too bad. The houses are solid-built, they were all right; of course there was a lot of mud and wet that would want cleaning out. Everybody set to, right off, scrubbing and lighting fires and airing. But the wonderful thing was that in its wild spate the beck had fetched down enough peat and loam and topsoil from the high fell to cover the ugly stony crater the United Kingdom Alloy Company had left behind them. There was still a small, deep, round pool in the middle; the beck had made a new course for itself, ran in one side and out the other.

Two swans were swimming about on the pool. No one knew where they had come from.

It was all hard work, after that, for months on. Getting the dirt evenly spread, making a new pathway round the green, paving it with flat stones, and sowing grass. Whatever was done, Martha Dyson was there, helping. With the Beautification Fund they bought young chestnut trees from a nursery and set them round the way the others had been.

"Reckon they ought to see our grandchildren's grandchildren out," Tom Thorpe said.

Young Steve Bates went to live with Martha. He just wouldn't leave her house, when the others went back after the flood. Mrs. Bates raised no objections and Martha said she'd like to adopt him. He did better with his book-learning, after, though he'd never make Skipley Grammar. But he started learning the fiddle, and he was fair handy at that.

Well, Johnny Rigby was right in one thing he said. He'd said that, no matter what happened afterwards, Appleby would never be the same again. And it isn't. But maybe in some ways it's better.

The Demon King

J. B. Priestley

Among the company assembled for Mr. Tom Burt's
Grand Annual Pantomime at the old Theatre Royal,
Bruddersford, there was a good deal of disagreement.
They were not quite "the jolly, friendly party" they pretended to be—through the good offices of "Thespian"—
to the readers of *The Bruddersford Herald* and *Weekly
Herald Budget*. The Principal Boy told her husband and
about fifty-five other people that she could work with
anybody, was famous for being able to work with anybody, but that nevertheless the management had gone and
engaged, as Principal Girl, the one woman in the profession who made it almost impossible for anybody to work
with anybody. The Principal Girl told her friend, the
Second Boy, that the Principal Boy and the Second Girl
were spoiling everything and might easily ruin the show.
The Fairy Queen went about pointing out that she did
not want to make trouble, being notoriously easy-going,
but that sooner or later the Second Girl would hear a few
things that she would not like. Johnny Wingfield had
been heard to declare that some people did not realize even
yet that what audiences wanted from a panto was some
good fast comedy work by the chief comedian, who had
to have all the scope he required. Dippy and Doppy, the
broker's men, hinted that even if there were two stages,
Johnny Wingfield would want them both all the time.
    But they were all agreed on one point, namely, that

there was not a better demon in provincial panto than
Mr. Kirk Ireton, who had been engaged by Mr. Tom Burt
for this particular show. The pantomime was *Jack and Jill*,
and those people who are puzzled to know what demons
have to do with Jack and Jill, those innocent water-
fetchers, should pay a visit to the nearest pantomime,
which will teach them a lot they did not know about fairy
tales. Kirk Ireton was not merely a demon, but the Demon
King, and when the curtain first went up, you saw him on
a darkened stage standing in front of a little chorus of
attendant demons, made up of local baritones at ten shil-
lings a night. Ireton looked the part, for he was tall and
rather satanically featured and was known to be very
clever with his make-up; and what was more important,
he sounded the part too, for he had a tremendous bass
voice, of most demonish quality. He had played Mephisto-
pheles in *Faust* many times with a good touring opera company. He was, indeed, a man with a fine future behind
him. If it had not been for one weakness, pantomime would
never have seen him. The trouble was that for years now
he had been in the habit of "lifting the elbow" too much.
That was how they all put it. Nobody said that he drank
too much, but all agreed that he lifted the elbow. And the
problem now was—would there be trouble because of this
elbow-lifting?

He had rehearsed with enthusiasm, sending his great
voice to the back of the empty, forlorn gallery in the two
numbers allotted to him, but at the later rehearsals there
had been ominous signs of elbow-lifting.

"Going to be all right, Mr. Ireton?" the stage-manager
inquired anxiously.

Ireton raised his formidable and satanic eyebrows. "Of
course it is," he replied, somewhat hoarsely. "What's
worrying you, old man?"

The other explained hastily that he wasn't worried. "You'll go well here," he went on. "They'll eat those two numbers of yours. Very musical in these parts. But you know Bruddersford, of course. You've played here before."

"I have," replied Ireton grimly. "And I loathe the dam' place. Bores me stiff. Nothing to do in it."

This was not reassuring. The stage-manager knew only too well Mr. Ireton was already finding something to do in the town, and his enthusiastic description of the local golf courses had no effect. Ireton loathed golf too, it seemed. All very ominous.

They were opening on Boxing Day night. By the afternoon, it was known that Kirk Ireton had been observed lifting the elbow very determinedly in the smoke-room of "The Cooper's Arms", near the theatre. One of the stage-hands had seen him: "And by gow, he wor lapping it up an' all," said this gentleman, no bad judge of anybody's power of suction. From there, it appeared, he had vanished, along with several other riotous persons, two of them thought to be Leeds men—and in Bruddersford they know what Leeds men are.

The curtain was due to rise at seven-fifteen sharp. Most members of the company arrived at the theatre very early. Kirk Ireton was not one of them. He was still absent at six-thirty, though he had to wear an elaborate make-up, with glittering tinselled eyelids and all the rest of it, and had to be on the stage when the curtain rose. A messenger was dispatched to his lodgings, which were not far from the theatre. Even before the messenger returned, to say that Mr. Ireton had not been in since noon, the stage-manager was desperately coaching one of the local baritones, the best of a stiff and stupid lot, in the part of the Demon King. At six-forty-five, no Ireton; at seven, no Ireton. It was hopeless.

"All right, that fellow's done for himself now," said the great Mr. Burt, who had come to give his Grand Annual his blessing. "He doesn't get another engagement from me as long as he lives. What's this local chap like?"

The stage-manager groaned and wiped his brow. "Like nothing on earth except a bow-legged baritone from a Wesleyan choir."

"He'll have to manage somehow. You'll have to cut the part."

"Cut it, Mr. Burt! I've slaughtered it, and what's left of it, he'll slaughter."

Mr. Tom Burt, like the sensible manager he was, believed in a pantomime opening in the old-fashioned way, with a mysterious dark scene among the supernaturals. Here it was a cavern in the hill beneath the Magic Well, and in these dismal recesses the Demon King and his attendants were to be discovered waving their crimson cloaks and plotting evil in good, round chest-notes. Then the Demon King would sing his number (which had nothing whatever to do with Jack and Jill or demonology either), the Fairy Queen would appear, accompanied by a white spotlight, there would be a little dialogue between them, and then a short duet.

The cavern scene was all set, the five attendant demons were in their places, while the sixth, now acting as King, was receiving a few last instructions from the stage-manager, and the orchestra, beyond the curtain, were coming to the end of the overture, when suddenly, from nowhere, there appeared on the dimly-lighted stage a tall and terrifically imposing figure.

"My God! There's Ireton," cried the stage-manager, and bustled across, leaving the temporary Demon King, abandoned, a pitiful makeshift now. The new arrival was coolly taking his pace in the centre. He looked superb.

The costume, a skin-tight crimson affair touched with a baleful green, was far better than the one provided by the management. And the make-up was better still. The face had a greenish phosphorescent glow, and its eyes flashed between glittering lids. When he first caught sight of that face, the stage-manager felt a sudden idiotic tremor of fear, but being a stage-manager first and a human being afterwards (as all stage-managers have to be), he did not feel that tremor long, for it was soon chased away by a sense of elation. It flashed across his mind that Ireton must have gone running off to Leeds or somewhere in search of this stupendous costume and make-up. Good old Ireton! He had given them all a fright, but it had been worth it.

"All right, Ireton?" said the stage-manager quickly.

"All right," replied the Demon King, with a magnificent, careless gesture.

"Well, you get back in the chorus then," said the stage-manager to the Wesleyan baritone.

"That'll do me champion," said the gentleman, with a sigh of relief. He was not ambitious.

"All ready?"

The violins began playing a shivery sort of music, and up the curtain went. The six attendant demons, led by the Wesleyan, who was in good voice now that he felt such a sense of relief, told the audience who they were and hailed their monarch in appropriate form. The Demon King, towering above them, dominating the scene superbly, replied in a voice of astonishing strength and richness. Then he sang the number allotted to him. It had nothing to do with Jack and Jill and very little to do with demons, being a rather commonplace bass song about sailors and shipwrecks and storms, with thunder and lightning effects supplied by the theatre. Undoubtedly this was the same song that had been rehearsed; the words were the same; the music was the same. Yet it all seemed different. It was really sinister. As you listened, you saw the great waves breaking over the doomed ships, and the pitiful little white faces disappearing in the dark flood. Somehow, the storm was much stormier. There was one great clap of thunder and flash of lightning that made all the attendant demons, the conductor of the orchestra, and a number of people in the wings, nearly jump out of their skins.

"And how the devil did you do that?" said the stage-manager, after running round to the other wing.

"That's what I said to 'Orace 'ere," said the man in charge of the two sheets of tin and the cannon ball.

"Didn't touch a thing that time, did we, mate?" said Horace.

"If you ask me, somebody let off a firework, one o' them big Chinese crackers, for that one," his mate continued. "Somebody monkeying about, that's what it is."

And now a white spotlight had found its way on to the stage, and there, shining in its pure ray, was Miss Dulcie Farrar, the Fairy Queen, who was busy waving a silver wand. She was also busy controlling her emotions, for somehow she felt unaccountably nervous. Opening night is opening night, of course, but Miss Farrar had been playing Fairy Queens for the last ten years (and Principal Girls for the ten years before them), and there was nothing in this part to worry her. She rapidly came to the conclusion that it was Mr. Ireton's sudden reappearance, after she had made up her mind that he was not turning up, that had made her feel so shaky, and this caused her to feel rather resentful. Moreover, as an experienced Fairy Queen who had had trouble with demons before, she was convinced that he was about to take more than his share of the stage. Just because he had hit upon such a good make-up! And it *was* a good make-up, there could be no question about that. That greenish face, those glittering eyes—really, it was awful. Overdoing it, she called it. After all, a panto *was* a panto.

Miss Farrar, still waving her wand, moved a step or two nearer, and cried:

> "*I know your horrid plot, you evil thing,*
> *And I defy you, though you are the Demon King.*"

"What, you?" he roared, contemptuously, pointing a long forefinger at her.

Miss Farrar should have replied: "Yes, I, the Queen of Fairyland," but for a minute she could not get out a word. As that horribly long forefinger shot out at her, she had felt a sudden sharp pain and had then found herself unable to move. She stood there, her wand held out at a ridiculous angle, motionless, silent, her mouth wide open. But her mind was active enough. "Is it a stroke?" it was asking feverishly. "Like Uncle Edgar had that time at Greenwich. Oo, it must be. Oo, whatever shall I do? Oo. Oo. Ooooo."

"Ho-ho-ho-ho-ho." The Demon King's sinister baying mirth resounded through the theatre.

"Ha-ha-ha-ha-ha." This was from the Wesleyan and his friends, and was a very poor chorus of laughs, dubious, almost apologetic. It suggested that the Wesleyan and his friends were out of their depth, the depth of respectable Bruddersfordian demons.

Their king now made a quick little gesture with one hand, and Miss Farrar found herself able to move and speak again. Indeed, the next second, she was not sure that she had ever been *unable* to speak and move. That horrible minute had vanished like a tiny bad dream. She defied him again, and this time nothing happened beyond an ex-

change of bad lines of lame verse. There were not many of
these, however, for there was the duet to be fitted in, and
the whole scene had to be played in as short a time as
possible. The duet, in which the two supernaturals only
defied one another all over again, was early Verdi by way
of the local musical director.

After singing a few bars each, they had a rest while the
musical director exercised his fourteen instrumentalists in
a most imposing operatic passage. It was during this halt
that Miss Farrar, who was now quite close to her fellow-
duettist, whispered: "You're in great voice, tonight, Mr.
Ireton. Wish I was. Too nervous. Don't know why, but
I am. Wish I could get it out like you."

She received, as a reply, a flash of those glittering eyes (it
really was an astonishing make-up) and a curious little
signal with the long forefinger. There was no time for
more, for now the voice part began again.

Nobody in the theatre was more surprised by what happened then than the Fairy Queen herself. She could not
believe that the marvellously rich soprano voice that came
pealing and soaring belonged to her. It was tremendous.
Covent Garden would have acclaimed it. Never before, in
all her twenty years of hard vocalism, had Miss Dulcie
Farrar sung like that, though she had always felt that
somewhere inside her there was a voice of that quality only
waiting the proper signal to emerge and then astonish the
world. Now, in some fantastic fashion, it had received that
signal.

Not that the Fairy Queen overshadowed her supernatural colleague. There was no overshadowing *him*. He
trolled in a diapason bass, and with a fine fury of gesture.
The pair of them turned that stolen and botched duet into
a work of art and significance. You could hear Heaven
and Hell at battle in it. The curtain came down on a good

rattle of applause. They are very fond of music in Bruddersford, but unfortunately the people who attend the first night of the pantomime are not the people who are most fond of music, otherwise there would have been a furore.

"Great stuff that," said Mr. Tom Burt, who was on the spot. "Never mind, Jim. Let 'em take a curtain. Go on, you two, take the curtain." And when they had both bowed their acknowledgements, Miss Farrar excited and trembling, the Demon King cool and amused, almost contemptuous, Mr. Burt continued: "That would have stopped the show in some places, absolutely stopped the show. But the trouble here is, they won't applaud, won't get going easily."

"That's true, Mr. Burt," Miss Farrar observed. "They take a lot of warming up here. I wish they didn't. Don't you, Mr. Ireton?"

"Easy to warm them," said the tall crimson figure.

"Well, if anything could, that ought to have done," the lady remarked.

"That's so," said Mr. Burt condescendingly. "You were great, Ireton. But they won't let themselves go."

"Yes, they will." The Demon King, who appeared to be taking his part very seriously, for he had not yet dropped into his ordinary tones, flicked his long fingers in the air, roughly in the direction of the auditorium, gave a short laugh, turned away, and then somehow completely vanished, though it was not difficult to do that in those crowded wings.

Half an hour later, Mr. Burt, his manager, and the stage-manager, all decided that something must have gone wrong with Bruddersford. Liquor must have been flowing like water in the town. That was the only explanation.

J. B. Priestley

"Either they're all drunk or I am," cried the stage-manager.

"I've been giving 'em pantomimes here for five-and-twenty years," said Mr. Burt, "and I've never known it happen before."

"Well, nobody can say they're not enjoying it."

"Enjoying it! They're enjoying it too much. They're going daft. Honestly, I don't like it. It's too much of a good thing."

The stage-manager looked at his watch. "It's holding up the show, that's certain. God knows when we're going to get through at this rate. If they're going to behave like this every night, we'll have to cut an hour out of it."

"Listen to 'em now," said Mr. Burt. "And that's one of the oldest gags in the show. Listen to 'em. Nay, dash it, they must be all half-seas over."

What had happened? Why—this: that the audience had suddenly decided to let itself go in a fashion never known in Bruddersford before. The Bruddersfordians are notoriously difficult to please, not so much because their taste is so exquisite but rather because, having paid out money, they insist upon having their money's worth, and usually arrive at a place of entertainment in a gloomy and suspicious frame of mind. Really tough managers like to open a new show in Bruddersford, knowing very well that if it will go there, it will go anywhere. But for the last half-hour of this pantomime there had been more laughter and applause than the Theatre Royal had known for the past six months. Every entrance produced a storm of welcome. The smallest and stalest gags set the whole house screaming, roaring, and rocking. Every song was determinedly encored. If the people had been specially brought out of jail for the performance, they could not have been more easily pleased.

166

"Here," said Johnny Wingfield, as he made an exit as a Dame pursued by a cow, "this is frightening me. What's the matter with 'em? Is this a new way of giving the bird?"

"Don't ask me," said the Principal Boy. "I wasn't surprised they gave me such a nice welcome when I went on, because I've always been a favourite here, as Mr. Burt'll tell you, but the way they're carrying on now, making such a fuss over nothing, it's simply ridiculous. Slowing up the show, too."

After another quarter of an hour of this monstrous enthusiasm, this delirium, Mr. Burt could be heard grumbling to the Principal Girl, with whom he was standing in that close proximity which Principal Girls somehow invite. "I'll tell you what it is, Alice," Mr. Burt was saying. "If this goes on much longer, I'll make a speech from the stage, asking 'em to draw it mild. Never known 'em to behave like this. And it's a funny thing, I was only saying to somebody—now who was it I said that to?—anyhow, I was only saying to somebody that I wished this audience would let themselves go a bit more. Well, now I wish they wouldn't. And that's that."

There was a chuckle, not loud, but rich, and distinctly audible.

"Here," cried Mr. Burt. "Who's that? What's the joke?"

It was obviously nobody in their immediate vicinity. "It sounded like Kirk Ireton," said the Principal Girl, "judging by the voice." But Ireton was nowhere to be seen. Indeed, one or two people who had been looking for him, both in his dressing-room and behind, had not been able to find him. But he would not be on again for another hour, and nobody had time to discover whether Ireton was drinking again or not. The odd thing was, though, that the audience lost its wild enthusiasm just as suddenly as it had found it, and long before the interval it had turned itself into the familiar stolid Bruddersford crowd, grimly waiting for its money's worth. The pantomime went on its way exactly as rehearsed, until it came to the time when the demons had to put in another appearance.

Jack, having found the magic water and tumbled down the hill, had to wander into the mysterious cavern and there rest awhile. At least, he declared that he would rest, but being played by a large and shapely female, and probably having that restless feminine temperament, what he did do was to sing a popular song with immense gusto. At the end of that song, when Jack once more declared that he would rest, the Demon King had to make a sudden appearance through a trapdoor. And it was reported from below, where a spring-board was in readiness, that no Demon King had arrived to be shot on to the stage.

"Now where—oh, where—the devil has Ireton got to?" moaned the stage-manager, sending people right and left, up and down, to find him.

The moment arrived, Jack spoke his and her cue, and the stage-manager was making frantic signals to her from the wings.

"Ouh-wer," screamed Jack, and produced the most realistic bit of business in the whole pantomime. For the stage directions read *Shows fright*, and Jack undoubtedly did show fright, as well he (or she) might, for no sooner was the cue spoken than there came a horrible green flash, followed by a crimson glare, and standing before her, having apparently arrived from nowhere, was the Demon King. Jack was now in the power of the Demon King and would remain in those evil clutches until rescued by Jill and the Fairy Queen. And it seemed as if the Principal Boy had suddenly developed a capacity for acting (of which nobody had ever suspected her before), or else that she was thoroughly frightened, for now she behaved like a large rabbit in tights. That unrehearsed appearance of the Demon King seemed to have upset her, and now and then she sent uneasy glances into the wings.

It had been decided, after a great deal of talk and drinks round, to introduce a rather novel dancing scene into this pantomime, in the form of a sort of infernal ballet. The Demon King, in order to show his power and to impress his captive, would command his subjects to dance—that is, after he himself had indulged in a little singing, assisted by his faithful six. They talk of that scene yet in Bruddersford. It was only witnessed in its full glory on this one night, but that was enough, for it passed into civic history, and local landlords, were often called in to settle bets about it in the pubs. First, the Demon King sang his second number, assisted by the Wesleyan and his friends. He made a glorious job of it, and after a fumbled opening and a sudden glare from him, the Wesleyan six made a glorious job of it too. Then the Demon King had to call for his dancing subjects, who were made up of the troupe of girls known as Tom Burt's Happy Yorkshire Lasses, daintily but demonishly tricked out in red and green. While the Happy Yorkshire Lasses pranced in the foreground, the six attendants were supposed to make a few rhythmical movements in the background, enough to suggest that, if they wanted to dance, they could dance, a suggestion that the stage-manager and the producer knew to be entirely false. The six, in fact, could not dance and would not try very hard, being not only wooden but also stubborn Bruddersford baritones.

But now, the Happy Yorkshire Lasses having tripped a measure, the Demon King sprang to his full height, which seemed to be about seven feet two inches, swept an arm along the Wesleyan six, and commanded them harshly to dance. And they did dance, they danced like men possessed. The King himself beat time for them, flashing an eye at the conductor now and again to quicken that gentleman's baton, and his faithful six, all with the most grotesque and puzzled expressions on their faces, cut the most amazing capers, bounding high into the air, tumbling over one another, flinging their arms and legs about in an ecstasy, and all in time to the music. The sweat shone on their faces; their eyes rolled forlornly; but still they did not stop, but went on in crazier and crazier fashion, like genuine demons at play.

"All dance!" roared the Demon King, cracking his long fingers like a whip, and it seemed as if something had inspired the fourteen cynical men in the orchestral pit, for they played like madmen grown tuneful, and on came the Happy Yorkshire Lasses again, to fling themselves into the wild sport, not as if they were doing something they had rehearsed a hundred times, but as if they, too, were inspired. They joined the orgy of the bounding six, and now, instead of there being only eighteen Happy Lasses in red and green, there seemed to be dozens and dozens of them. The very stage seemed to get bigger and bigger, to give space to all these whirling figures of demoniac revelry. And as they all went spinning, leaping, cavorting crazily, the audience, shaken at last out of its stolidity, cheered them on, and all was one wild insanity.

Yet when it was done, when the King cried, "Stop!" and all was over, it was as if it had never been, as if everybody had dreamed it, so that nobody was ready to swear that it had really happened. The Wesleyan and the other five all felt a certain faintness, but each was convinced that he had imagined all that wild activity while he was making a few sedate movements in the background. Nobody could be quite certain about anything. The pantomime went on its way; Jack was rescued by Jill and the Fairy Queen (who was now complaining of neuralgia); and the Demon King allowed himself to be foiled, after which he quietly disappeared again. They were looking for him when the whole thing was over except for that grand entry of all the characters at the very end. It was his business to march in with the Fairy Queen, the pair of them dividing between them all the applause for the supernaturals. Miss Farrar, feeling very miserable with her neuralgia, delayed her entrance for him, but as he was not to be found, she climbed the little ladder at the back alone, to march solemnly down the steps towards the audience. And the extraordinary thing was that when she was actually making her entrance, at the top of those steps, she discovered that she was not alone, that her fellow-supernatural was there too, and that he must have slipped away to freshen his make-up. He was more demonish than ever.

As they walked down between the files of Happy Yorkshire Lasses, now armed to the teeth with tinsel spears and shields, Miss Farrar whispered: "Wish I'd arranged for a bouquet. You never get anything here."

"You'd like some flowers?" said the fantastic figure at her elbow.

"Think I would! So would everybody else."

"Quite easy," he remarked, bowing slowly to the footlights. He took her hand and led her to one side, and it is a fact—as Miss Farrar will tell you, within half an hour of your making her acquaintance—that the moment their hands met, her neuralgia completely vanished. And now came the time for the bouquets. Miss Farrar knew what they would be; there would be one for the Principal Girl, bought by the management, and one for the Principal Boy, bought by herself.

"Oo, look!" cried the Second Boy. "My gosh!—Bruddersford's gone mad."

The space between the orchestral pit and the front row of stalls had been turned into a hothouse. The conductor was so busy passing up bouquets that he was no longer visible. There were dozens of bouquets, and all of them beautiful. It was monstrous. Somebody must have spent a fortune on flowers. Up they came, while everybody cheered, and every woman with a part had at least two or three. Miss Farrar, pink and wide-eyed above a mass of orchids, turned to her colleague among the supernaturals, only to find that once again he had quietly disappeared. Down came the curtain for the last time, but everybody remained standing there, with arms filled with expensive flowers, chattering excitedly. Then suddenly somebody cried, "Oo!" and dropped her flowers, and others cried, "Oo!" and dropped *their* flowers, until at last everybody who had had a bouquet had dropped it and cried, "Oo!"

"Hot," cried the Principal Girl, blowing on her fingers, "hot as anything, weren't they? Burnt me properly. That's a nice trick."

"Oo, look!" said the Second Boy, once more. "Look at 'em all. Withering away." And they were, every one of them, all shedding their colour and bloom, curling, writhing, withering away. . . .

"Message come through for you, sir, an hour since," said the doorkeeper to the manager, "only I couldn't get at yer. From the Leeds Infirmary, it is. Says Mr. Ireton was knocked down in Boar Lane by a car this afternoon, but he'll be all right tomorrow. Didn't know who he was at first, so couldn't let anybody know."

The manager stared at him, made a number of strange

noises, then fled, signing various imaginary temperance pledges as he went.

"And another thing," said the stage-hand to the stage-manager. "That's where I saw the bloke last. He was there one minute and next minute he wasn't. And look at the place. All scorched."

"That's right," said his mate, "and what's more, just you take a whiff—that's all, just take a whiff. Oo's started using brimstone in the the-ater? Not me nor you neither. But I've a good idea who it is."

Faithful Jenny Dove

Eleanor Farjeon

Alack the day, alack the day
When my true love went away!
They killed my true love over sea,
And when they killed him they killed me.

I

When Robert Green, my true love, went to the Wars,
there was but one ghost in our village of Maltby. Now
there are two.

Let me tell you. Jenny Dove is my name, and when I
was sixteen years old they called me the prettiest girl in
Maltby, though that is not for me to say. At all events,
Robert Green, my true love, thought so; but then no
doubt there was never a girl with a sweetheart who could
not say the same; but then it was not only Robert Green;
there were others; though for me there was only Robert.
And when we had been plighted three short months, he
went to the Wars.

But I go a little too fast. I ought first to tell you of the
Young Squire of Bride's Lane. We could not have told
you in Maltby how far back his legend went; for all we
knew, he had always been there. Many people had seen
him, so they said, but none agreed about his manner of
dress—one said he wore a coat of mail, one said he wore a
ruff, another a frilled shirt—so there was no judging when

he had lived. But all agreed that they had heard him weeping at break of day beside the churchyard gate at the end of the lane by which all the Ladies of Maltby arrive to be married; and as the sun came up and touched him where he leaned against the gate, he sank upon his knees beside it and melted away. For the Young Squire was a morning ghost, and that's perhaps why the details of him were hard to swear to—the black night throws them up, but seen in daylight, a ghostly ruff or a shirt-frill may be all one. I had never seen the Squire myself, never in my life.

But the day my true love left me, I rose early and met him, at his request, by the church porch, for he had a fancy to stand at the altar with me and make a vow of constancy, as binding on us both as marriage might be. We would have liked very well to be married, but our mothers would not hear of it, though I wanted but four years, and he but two, of twenty. So he thought of this vow instead, and as I said: "If love itself is not stronger than marriage, Robert, what use is it at all?"

"Yes, Jenny," he said, "marriage lasts only as long as life, but love lasts after death."

I thought this very true, as well as very poetical. Robert was indeed a poet, and had written me some beautiful lines for Saint Valentine, and also when my linnet died.

Well, as I say, we met in the early morning in the church porch, before anybody was stirring, and as ill luck would have it the church door was locked. This dashed us very much, and we could not wake the verger, who was in charge of the key, because he was my own uncle, and particularly against Robert on account of his age, which indeed he could not help, and time would remedy.

I could only just keep back my tears for disappointment, and Robert looked serious, but was too manly to weep.

"What shall we do?" I asked, relying on his strength and wisdom.

"We will pledge ourselves beside some other cross," he answered thoughtfully, and glanced over the churchyard with its monuments.

But at this I shuddered. "Oh no! Not one of *those!*"

"Then come and stand with me by Eleanor's Cross," said he, and that pleased me better. Just outside the village was one of Queen Eleanor's Crosses where her coffin had rested, I forget how many hundred years ago. It was a husband's tribute to a faithful wife, and well suited to our purpose. The quickest way was by the Bride's Lane, and as we crossed the churchyard to leave by that wicket the sun was just rising. On reaching it we both looked up together and said in one breath, I, "Do not weep, Robert!" and he, "Jenny, you must not weep!" But neither of us was weeping in the least and the sun shone bright into the lane, where Robert and I looked too late to see anything. But we had both heard the weeping. I took it for an omen, if Robert did not, but I said nothing; and we walked down the Bride's Lane to the cross-roads where Eleanor's Cross stood on a grassy mound. There we took our oath, and what better words could we find than Robert's own:

"Marriage lasts only as long as life, but love lasts after death."

We each repeated these words, and then I added a promise of my own.

"Robert," I said, "until you return to me I will come every morning at daybreak to this Cross to watch for you; and here, where we now part, we will meet again."

"My faithful Jenny!" said he, and kissed me tenderly, and then I confess I melted into tears; but he said quickly, "Smile, Jenny, smile! You'll smile when we meet, let me leave you smiling."

So I managed to smile till he was out of sight. It was difficult, but it is wonderful what you can do.

The Wars lasted two whole years, and then the soldiers began to come back. During the first year I had had three letters from Robert, my true love, which were a great comfort to me. In the first one he said among other things, "How often I think of my faithful Jenny, smiling by Eleanor's Cross, as I last saw her. I have begun a ballad about you, or rather it is put into your mouth, as it were —the first bit goes:

> *Alack the day, alack the day*
> *When my true love went away!*
> *If he should die I will not wive*
> *With any other man alive.*
>
> *I stood there smiling in the light,*
> *The day my true love went to fight—*

but I cannot get any further with it. I would like to put in your white bonnet with the pink rose under the brim, and your pink frock with white frills, as I always see you. I think it will come out pretty if I can manage it."

In the second letter he said: "I cannot get on with the ballad, there is so much to do, but no doubt I will finish it one day."

In the third letter, which began: "My faithful, smiling Jenny, do you still go every morning to the Cross?" he did not speak of the ballad.

Of course I told him I did so, rain or fine, wind, sleet or snow, and all the village knew of it, and sometimes one or another who was out even came by to watch me, and the lads and girls teased me, though not unkindly, but my mother called me a silly. He did not answer this letter at all.

Then, as I say, there was peace and the men began to

come home, but not all of them, of course; and news took a long time coming, so there was much anxiety first, even when joy and not grief was to follow. But it is very strange how much hope there can be with anxiety, and every morning when I went to sit by the Cross, I was quite sure it was the day I would see Robert, my true love, come home from the Wars. And every day I came away, in spite of my heavy heart, I felt that there was always to-morrow to wait for.

And so another year went by.

Long before it was over they began to come and talk to me, sometimes kind and sometimes scolding. My mother said I was a fool to be wasting my chances, the girls told me to give it up, some of the boys came wooing on their own, and even my best friend, Mary Poole, talked gravely to me.

"Jenny," said she, "the War's been over for a year, and all the men that we know of are home again, and for a whole year before that even Robert's mother had no news of him. Jenny, you cannot go on waiting by the Cross all your life."

"Oh, Mary!" I said. "I promised I would."

"How long had you and Robert loved each other?" said she. "Scarcely three months—and how old are you now? Only nineteen. Why, you may live another sixty years!"

"That would be a long marriage," I said, "but not very long for love. Oh, Mary!" I said to her. "You do not know what true love is."

"I do, Jenny," said she.

"Who is it?" I asked.

But she was silent.

"And can you, then, Mary," I said, "bid me not to go to the Cross?"

She bent her head and went away without answering.

Then my mother went to his mother, and his mother came to me.

"Jenny," said she, "you're a good faithful girl, as so pretty a girl need seldom be. I'll own I mistrusted you when you were younger, for looks like yours might catch a lord. But I'll say now, if Robert came home I'd give him to you with my blessing. But he won't come home, Jenny; and I'll give you my blessing the day you go to church with another."

"I'll wait to go there with Robert," I said.

Then for a little they left me in peace.

Just a year after the ending of the Wars, I went to the Cross as usual. It was a lovely spring morning, and the larks were going up, and the grass round Eleanor's Cross was blue with speedwell, and it was easy to be full of hope; so when, as I sat there, a soldier came limping up the road, it did not surprise me in the least. I sprang up and looked towards him, smiling with all my heart. However, it was not Robert, my true love.

He was a much older man, about thirty years old, greatly hurt by the Wars, as well as lame. He came slowly to the Cross and stood before me, looking me up and down. I waited for him to speak, but the words seemed hard to him.

"So you're here then, missy," he said at last.

"Yes," I said.

"Jenny Dove, are ye?"

I said "Yes", again.

"I've a message for ye," he said.

"Tell it to me," I said.

" 'Tis written," he said.

"Oh, is it a letter?" I said.

"Nay," he said, " 'tis the end of a song."

Then he handed me an old bit of paper, very soiled, and on it was written these four lines:

Alack the day, alack the day
When my true love went away!
They killed my true love over sea,
And when they killed him they killed me.

The writing was very bad, but of course it was Robert's. So I smiled at the lame soldier in the light. On my stone in the churchyard they have cut the words:
JENNY DOVE
WHO DIED OF LOVE

II

The morning after my burial, I rose early as usual. During my short illness I had been obliged to miss a few sunrises at Eleanor's Cross; it could not be helped. But after this I did not miss one; or yes, just one—and even then, in a way, I did not; but that will come later.

It was scarcely a week since I had met the lame soldier by the Cross, and if any morning could have been lovelier than that one, this was. I was in good time, so I took the long way over the Glebe Farm and through the village. The Glebe meadows were full of flowers. It is a beautiful thing to walk through flowers. No, I do not mean to walk among them, but to walk through them. They pass through your feet, and for a moment your feet and the flowers are one. Some of their sweetness is left in your feet from the daisies and primroses, and if your steps are happy, no doubt some of your joy remains with the flowers. In the copse I found a bed of violets, and lay on it so that I was filled from top to toe. I found it was so with all things. Trees and hedges and houses can all be a part of you; indeed, wherever you are, you become for that time the thing you

pass through; nothing is lovelier than a bird flying through your heart.

It was the same with people. You could be closer to them than when you were alive. It was a pleasure to run among the school-children as they came out of school. I walked with my friends when they did not know it, and every day I sat in the same chair with my mother. If a person is sad you can carry a shadow away from her heart as you pass through her, and if you are happy you can leave your own light there.

In buildings, too, and things that grow, you feel whatever life has left there. I always knew when joy or pain had filled the hands that laid the stones and raised the rafters, what the lives had been of those they sheltered afterwards; I always knew where men had quarrelled in the market, and where lovers had met in the woods. But now and then as I went about I lit upon something I could not understand—something sweeter than life, that had been left beneath a tree or in a flower. If it was a mood, it seemed finer than any mood shed from the bodies of things and creatures. Whenever I discovered it my spirit grew twice as happy as it had been, yet who or what had left it there I could not imagine.

I was glad to be a morning ghost, for it was only during my little vigil by the Cross that I could be seen, and then not by everybody; after that I was free for the day and not visible at all, so that I could go where I pleased and startle no one. The night-ghosts are less fortunate, for, as I once said, the dark shows them up so, and it is a sad thing to be feared. Besides, for some reason which I do not know, most of the night-ghosts have sorrows. I had none. My only duty was to sit for half an hour in the morning by the Cross, smiling as the sun came up. This was all due to Robert, my true love. Thanks to him, I was a smiling ghost. None of us can escape a little duty, and mine could not have been lighter. Early as it was, a waggoner passed sometimes, and in the fine weather, if I looked down the west road, I would often see Mary Poole crossing the pastures to turn out the cows. Many ghosts long for nothing but to be laid, but I did not wish to be; why should I? I had never while I lived had such delight in the world. I knew that had I died and Robert lived, I should have haunted the Cross only till he came home, and then I should have rested quiet in my grave. But now that could not happen, for Robert was dead, and I would always haunt the Cross. I took to saying the little verse the soldier gave me, every morning as the sun rose. I had little enough to do, and it seemed in keeping to repeat it:

> *Alack the day, alack the day*
> *When my true love went away!*
> *They killed my true love over sea,*
> *And when they killed him they killed me.*

Besides, it was quite true. But I never stopped smiling as I said it. Many of the villagers said they had seen me, and one or two of them really had. And Mary Poole once heard me. I found her standing by the Cross one morning when I arrived. She was looking up the road and did not see me, so I sat down behind her, and when the sun came up I said my piece. She turned and looked at me, and grew pale, and said nothing. So I sat smiling at her till it was time to fade.

The only thing was that sometimes I felt lonely. You would think this was not possible, seeing that any moment I could become part of a beech-tree, or a young lamb, or a crop of barley, or the busy road, or Gaffer Vine's warm chimney-corner. Still, it was so. I would have been glad of someone to talk to.

One morning in July I was a little late. I cannot think how I came to oversleep myself, but when I stood beside my headstone plaiting my hair, I saw by the sky that I would not have time to go by the Glebe and the village, where I loved to pass through the rooms of my sleeping friends. So I ran as quick as I could to the little wicket that opened on the Bride's Lane, a way I had not taken since I died. As I hurried down the lane I saw the Young Squire hurrying up it. It is a funny thing, but I had quite forgotten him till now.

They are all wrong about his dress. He wears a green jerkin and his face is most beautiful. He is twenty years old.

When he saw me coming he waved his hand, and cried: "Jenny Dove, who died for love?"

"Yes, Young Squire," I said, "but I am in such haste— please do not keep me now."

"Ah, Jenny, thou'rt a young ghost yet!" said he. "How could I keep thee? Pass, child, pass—but meet me at seven in the Withybed."

So we ran straight through each other—but, oh dear, the confusion of it! I never felt anything like it. For when you mingle with a solid body it is different; you seem to become a part of that thing, rather than it becomes part of you. But when you mingle with a ghost like yourself there is no telling which is which. For one instant I felt quite lost, I did not know where or who I was, or if what I had been would ever come out of that wilderness. And when I'd slipped through, I was indeed not certain how much of me was left behind, and how much of him I had carried away. I was only just in time at the Cross that morning, and the half-hour went very slow.

When it was over, I went back to the churchyard to watch the clock, and at last it wanted but fifteen minutes to seven. So I thought I would go to the Withybed and finish waiting there, and I did, and as I reached it I saw the Young Squire coming too; we were both ahead of time.

We sat down together in the willow-herb and looked at each other.

"Pretty Jenny," said he, "I have not seen thee these three months, not once since they laid thee in thy green grave. But I have heard of thee, and often found thy traces in the fields and spinneys."

"Do *I* leave traces, Young Squire?" I asked.

"Wherever thou goest," he answered.

"And do you, too?"

"I too, wherever I go. Why, Jenny, what dost thou think? That bodies can leave their spiritual signs, and spirits cannot? Ah, Jenny, it's the spirit's spirit leaves the sign of angels on the earth—or of fallen angels."

I considered this for a while, and then a thought struck me. "Please move a little, Young Squire," I said.

He did so, and I instantly sat where he had sat. In the willow-herb, whose rosy sprays had stood within his heart, I recognized the delicate trace which had so puzzled and enchanted me wherever I had found it.

"*You* do not leave the sign of fallen angels," I said, and held my hand out to him smiling. He laid his own on it, and I could not tell which was which.

"Jenny," said he, "these three months I have found thy smiles left wherever the spring was sweetest, and I have tried to find thee all day long. For day-ghosts are rare, and I have had some hundred lonely years. I knew it was thy task to smile at dawn by Eleanor's Cross; but unfortunately I must weep by the Bride's Wicket at precisely the same hour, and hasten to the Cross as I might at the end of my task, thou wert always gone. Let us not lose each other again, Jenny."

I told him we would not, and we agreed to meet in the

Withybed each day at seven. It promised great happiness for both of us.

So ten years passed by, and we were as happy as we thought to be. For if one alone can take joy in the world's beauty, how much more can two together! And the joy was not of the living, who fears death tomorrow; the joy was endless, that fear was not for us.

Ghosts, I must tell you, seldom ask questions. What was, matters so little, what is, so much; only our small daily tasks bound us for a few minutes to the lives we had left, and when those were finished we had no cares for our own, or curiosity for the other's past. Our working hours being the same, just what each did was never seen by the other, and, as I say, we were not curious to ask.

However, a few years after our first meeting it happened one Sunday that we went to church together, for it was the day I had died, and I wished to sit with my mother in her pew. And when the service was ended, and the church empty, we wandered through it looking at this and that, and by the old tomb where the Crusader and his Lady lay, the Young Squire halted, looking very kindly on the almost faceless figure. Suddenly he laughed.

"Jenny," he said, "lie there upon my Lady's effigy."

So I did as he asked, enveloping the stone form with my own and felt strangely as he stood over me, looking down at me with the look I loved most.

"Yes," he said, "thou art fairer than she was."

"Oh, did you know her?" I asked.

"I died for love of her," he said. "I was Squire in her father's house, and we loved in secret, and my love was my passion, but hers was her pleasure. Then this knight came back from the East, and wooed her, and she was willing; and she summoned me to one last meeting, and as she lay in my arms told me with light words that this was the end.

And I cried out that there might be an end to a woman's love, but there was none to her faithlessness, and left her. And the day she was to be married I sat and wept beside the wicket through which she must pass, and as the sun came up I swore to haunt that spot until one woman should prove faithful; and then I slew myself, where she and this knight found me later on. Cannot our pain make fools of us, Jenny? And so we die for love, which we should live for." He smiled at me, and we went out of the church together; and as we crossed the graveyard he stopped beside my grave and read the stone.

"You also died for love," said the Young Squire. "To whom were *you* faithless, Jenny Dove?"

Oh, do you know how a shadow crosses a sunny field? Would you think such a shadow could fall on a smiling ghost, as I was? Yet it did. All of a sudden I feared to tell the Young Squire my story; I feared to tell him I was faithful to Robert Green, my true love, killed in the Wars. For then, you see——

I hung my head.

My Young Squire laughed at me, and said as he often did: "Oh, Jenny, thou'rt a young ghost yet! So young, thou canst still feel shame! And I'm so old that I can no longer feel bitterness. Smile, Jenny, smile!"

But if you will believe me, when he said this the tears ran down my face, and he looked at me in surprise, for he had never seen me weep before. Then suddenly he gaily laughed again, and ran in on me and stood over me, and surrounded me, so that once more I did not know myself from him, or my tears from his laughter, but in that wonderful confusion I heard his voice, merry, sweet and teasing—

"Pretty Jenny! Smiling Jenny! Faithless Jenny!" he said, did my Young Squire.

When I heard him call me "faithless" I laughed too, and ran out of him, and he after me. It was a great game, the chase, the slipping through, the capture, that could be no capture unless I wished—until such time as I did wish and stood quite still. We played that game often after this. And often he teased me for my story, and asked me what I did by Eleanor's Cross, and for what sin to love I was condemned to smile—he teased me for the pleasure of making me hang my head. But I did not weep again; why need I, seeing I had resolved never to tell him my story?

Then the tenth year passed by, and I went on a spring morning to Eleanor's Cross and sat and watched the road. And just before the sun came up, along the road, as it might have been ten years ago, came a limping soldier of thirty years old. But this time it was Robert Green, my true love, home from the Wars.

III

As soon as he saw me he cried: "Jenny! Jenny! Faithful Jenny!" and came limping to the Cross. He held out his trembling hands that seemed afraid to touch me.

"Jenny, to find you here!" he said. "My Jenny, you have not changed a hair—but you're prettier, surely! And see, 'tis the pink gown and the white bonnet, as of old! And see, you're smiling still! To find you here where I left you, smiling still!" He buried his face in his hands. "Oh, say a word to me, my love," he sobbed.

But I could not speak.

He mastered himself and looked at me earnestly.

"Jenny, I've startled ye," he said. "Yes, thoughtless that I am. You believe me dead, because I was so long a-coming —and maybe you had my message that I wrote on the battlefield when I truly thought I was dying, and gave my wounded comrade to bring to you, if he should be luckier than me. Did you have it, Jenny?"

I nodded.

"My little love! It might have broken your heart."

"It did, Robert." They were my first words to him.

"Oh, cruel—but I'll mend it for ye, Jenny. But do not look at me so strange, see, it is myself in very faith, feel this hand, Jenny, indeed I am no ghost."

"But I am, Robert."

He looked at me as though he did not understand, then opened his arms and flung them about me, and then, poor man, he threw himself upon the ground by Eleanor's Cross with his face in the grass.

The sun came up just then, so I said my lines:

> *Alack the day, alack the day*
> *When my true love went away!*
> *They killed my true love over sea,*
> *And when they killed him they killed me.*

He lifted his face from the grass. "God help me!" said Robert Green, my true love.

"Robert," I said, "do not grieve so, there is less to grieve for than you might fancy."

"Yes, that's true," said he, "for do you remember our vow? Marriage lasts only as long as life, but love lasts after death. I need not ask ye if ye remember it, my pretty love; have ye not kept faith after death itself? Ah, Jenny, if ever a woman was faithful, you are she!"

As he said these words the shadow fell upon me, the shadow I had felt five years ago. Suddenly it seemed to me that I could smile no more. And looking over Robert's head where he knelt in the grass at my feet, trying, poor soul, to kiss them, I saw the Young Squire standing with sorrow in his eyes.

"Alas!" I cried, "what has brought you here now, when you should be at your weeping?"

"Jenny," said the Young Squire, "when I came up the Bride's Lane this morning, I felt I had no cause to weep; I leaned on the wicket, and no tears came; I could not understand it; I ran to find thee—and how do I find thee! See, with thy true love at thy feet, praising thee as the only faithful woman among women! Ah, Jenny, how hast thou deceived me!—God help me, I fear I am laid!"

He turned and fled away, and oh, if a ghost's heart could have cracked, mine would have then.

But Robert, who had not heard him, but only my question—love giving him eyes and ears for me, which no others had; yet giving him none for other ghosts than me—Robert with worshipping eyes also answered me.

"What brings me here, but you?" he said. "And as for weeping, I'll be at that no more. See, Jenny, death need matter nothing to us; I'll keep troth with you by the Cross each morning till I die. Even if I may not touch you, I can see you and speak with you, and that half-hour of love's sweet looks and words will carry me through each day. Smile, Jenny, smile, for love lasts after death!"

But I could not smile, for even for him I saw no happiness.

"Dear Robert," I said gently, "that's a vain dream. Have you forgotten to what I pledged myself when thirteen years ago we parted here? I vowed to watch each dawn beside the Cross till you returned again. Your death and my death could not break my vow—but see, my dear, you have returned, and I shall watch no more. God help me!" I sighed, "I fear—I fear I am laid."

"Jenny! You will not leave me—you will come again!"

"It will not be in my power, Robert," I said. "In a few minutes, this, my last vigil, will be ended, and I must go."

"Is there no hope?" cried Robert. "Of what use was it to come home to you, only to lose you? Oh, Jenny, is there no way?"

I thought and thought; and then, at the end of the west road, I saw Mary Poole passing to turn out the cows. Robert's back was towards her and she went without his seeing her. I thought suddenly there might be hope.

"Robert," I said, "were you true to me all these years?"

"As true as your own self," he said reproachfully. "How can you ask?"

"It might have changed things if you had not been," I said. "I am not certain—but, Robert, if you had been faithless, I might still have been allowed to lie unquiet in my grave; I might still have come each morning to the Cross, where we pledged our love; and for the sake of that broken pledge, I might have said at sunrise:

> *Alack the day, alack the day*
> *When my true love went away!*
> *My love a faithless love was he,*
> *And when he broke his faith, broke me.*

They are not such pretty lines as yours, dear Robert, but they might have served—if you had been a little faithless."

"But I was not," said Robert obstinately.

"But you might be," I said quickly.

"Never!" he vowed.

"Robert, listen," I said. "I have only a moment now. Listen with all your heart. Life is life, and death is death. You will find that death can end no love that has ever been, and that love is one and also many, and none the less true for that. Well, this is for after death. But life must be lived, not wasted. While I am a memory you still have powers to be used till you become a memory, too. And there are those you might use them with, Robert, those that need them, as you will need—theirs. Indeed, there are many powers in life that cannot be used alone. And as we find beauty, as fair and sweet not only in one flower, so we may find love as true and pure not only in one woman. Dear Robert, my time's short—promise me one last thing."

"Anything, Jenny!"

"Do not show yourself in the village today—let no one know you're home until tomorrow. And come at daybreak to the Cross again."

"Will you be here?" he asked.

"I'll try to be," I said; and then I faded.

I did not know how it would be at all—for me, for Robert, for Mary, or the Young Squire. But all that day I was so restless, it seemed to me I could not lie quiet in my grave that night, and if it was so with me, might it not be so with him? But I had no means of knowing, for I saw him nowhere.

Next morning, to my joy, I rose as usual. I knew I was being given one more chance. I dressed my hair my prettiest, and pulled out my frills, and tucked the rose under my bonnet-brim just where it showed its best. Then full of hope, I sped, not to Eleanor's Cross, but to Mary Poole's bedroom.

She was still asleep. I saw how tired and sad she looked, and older than her thirty years. Oh dear, dear me! I sat down by her mirror, and pulled the little curls round my ears, and tied my sash again. Then I waked her. She did not know why she stopped to gather six sweet violets and one dewy leaf from the bed by the path where they grew blue each spring. She did not know why, when she came to the end of the west road, instead of going straight across to the pastures she turned up it to Eleanor's Cross. But she knew —she knew who it was that waited there. She knew as well as I.

"Robert!" she cried, and went as white as a ghost.

He looked up quickly, but quicker still I had entered Mary Poole, who was my best friend, and stayed there, looking my prettiest and kindest at him.

"Mary!" he stammered—"I thought it would be Jenny."

Her eyes filled with tears, and she said, "Our Jenny died."

He came to her and took her hand. Oh, then I looked at Robert Green, my true love, with all my love, through Mary's tears. She never would have looked so, had she known it. Suddenly Robert took her in his arms and kissed her. How could he help it?

Then I slipped through her, through his arms, and him, so that neither saw me, and I looked at her and him; and she looked no more than one and twenty, and prettier than she had been at that age, and he looked not much older, and very tender. For, as I said, you leave what is in you with those you pass through.

I did not wait to see more—this was the one day I spoke of, when I neglected my task. I ran as fast as I could up the Bride's Lane, and there, oh joy! was my Young Squire, by the wicket, weeping his heart out.

He had just finished as I came up.

"Jenny-all-smiles!" he cried. "Why art thou smiling so? Tell me, why am I here and not resting in my grave? And why art not thou?"

"Oh, Young Squire," I said, "how can I rest in my grave when Robert Green, my true love, is false to me. And how can you in yours, when I am false to him?"

I heard him say, "Pretty Jenny! Smiling Jenny! Faithless Jenny!" and then began the game of catch.

Mary and Robert have six blooming children and a little farm. It is a happy life. Sometimes they come of a morning to chat with me during my vigil, when I've nothing to do till the sun comes up, and I say my piece:

Alack the day, alack the day
When my true love went away!
My love a faithless love was he,
And when he broke his faith, broke me.

As I said, we all have our duties, and none could be lighter than mine. Then I am free to go to the Withybed. It is a happy life.

The Twilight Road

H. F. Brinsmead

Four little girls scrawled and scattered along a white sand ribbon of road that ran towards darkness.

It was blurred with time, frayed at its edges, where water had washed over it or growth impinged; for it was the old, convict-built mountain trail. Only a few Old-timers, now, or the loner, self-sufficient children of the Candlebark Country, could find the place where it turned aside from the used highway; only they knew where it shrugged away over the soft-shouldered foothills, then up and up, over a cold stream, ever upward bound, pushing into the dark forest, quickly smothering into the coming night.

The old road etched with its faint finger the monkey-puzzle mountains, the ragged ridges—the poorlands of the sandstone country that followed the candlebarks—at last to lose itself among lush volcanic peaks, sombre with white ash, sassafras pungent and damp, and the abrasive trunks of tree ferns.

The four little girls knew the Old Road well. They, who could find where wild violets spawned, and crayfish shadowed the stones of streams, had eyes for the wraith-like trail, built long ago by the chain-gangs, before the days of Starlight the Bushranger, and the coaches of Cobb and Co. It was their secret place; their place of twilight.

"Look! There's a snake!" Hazel, the second eldest, brought them to a halt as she started backwards.

"It's only a black stick!" said Celia.

"It moved! I *saw* it——!"

Susan broke in. "It *did* move!" She peered at the black question mark on the white sand.

"Silly!" scoffed Celia. "It's only a crooked stick!"

She stooped and put out her hand to pick it up. Her curlicue back showed a row of cotton-reels beneath her summer dress. Then when her hand almost touched it, the black stick straightened. It flowed from its crooked shape and slid away over the sand, and so to the rocky wastes, by clumps of old-man's-beard and the hard foliage of geebung bushes.

Celia gasped with shock, shuddering and half-sobbing. Oh, the fright of it! The others comforted her.

"Never mind, Celi—never mind."

"It's all right now, Celi—it's gone, all gone."

"Mind you——" said Hazel, "I *said* it was a snake! I *told* you——!"

Susan nudged her urgently.

"Come, let's go home, do let's."

"Yes." Celia wiped her eyes. "I want to go home."

"Steffy?" Susan looked around them, for the fourth child.

"Steffany! Wherever has she gone?"

The three girls called their sister, looking up and down the road—to the right, where it traced back towards the highway—to the left, where it clambered out of the sandstone poorlands, blurring into the labyrinth of the rainforest.

"She must have gone home already, of course," said Hazel. "She's such a scary-cat, she must have run off as soon as she saw the snake!"

"Most likely." Susan nodded. "Oh, isn't she naughty! I wonder why we didn't see her?"

"Because we were looking at the snake, of course! Do come!"

The girls ran off—three of them, at least—down towards the farmhouse at the edge of the candlebark country, where a light burned in a window, pale in the evening.

But the youngest—Steffany—ran light-footed, up into the distance, where the Old Road tunnelled into the deepsea gloom, suffused with a sulphurous glow beneath the heavy leaves of the rain-forest.

Here the whistling grew clearer.

It was a tiny sound of a whistle that she had heard, walking with her sisters back where the road was clear and white. Then it had been faint and uncertain, no more than a ghost of a memory of a song. But it had called to her, pleading about her ears—a faint, far sound of a whistled tune. . . .

The child ran between walls of living growth, her face set in a tight mask of fear. As she moved through the void, she knew not what horrors could lurk in the forest's half-seen depths, at this strange hour. Swinging overhead, the sky was a narrow swathe of luminous silk, a gibbous moon woven into its texture, and faintly watermarked with the odd star or two. The air was heavy and cloying with silence—except for her own footfalls, and the fitful piping tune.

Now the close trees gave way for a small space, to a narrow shelf, where a spring stream indented the mountain-side before the last, steep crest. Here, all that was left of the road was a milestone; it was half-buried in long grass.

A fire glowed jewel-bright in the dusk. A figure was
seated by the stone, shapeless and bulky. A man. His
clothes were ragged. His eyes caught the red light of the
fire. His lips were pursed. His fingers held to them a
battered penny whistle.

Beside the man's fire was his meagre swag and a thin,
black dog had taken possession of it with familiar pre-
sumption; it lay gazing into the flames, muzzle on paws,
pensive, only its eyes reflecting the same red gleams
of light that flickered from the fire into those of his
master.

The child stopped short for a moment, then timidly
drew closer to the pair.

At sight of her the man made a quick movement, as

though for flight, his hand above his head in a defensive gesture. Then, seeing her alone, his figure half-relaxed; only his eyes were still wary and irrational, with their red gleam.

Steffany saw now that, beneath the rough husk of his unkempt poverty, he was no more than a boy. The dog crept close to him, cowering against his legs. Fear drained away from the child, leaving only fascination and a deep pity; she did not know why.

"Please——" she said awkwardly. "I—I—heard you playing."

"You alone?" He spoke in a rasping whisper.

She nodded, eyes round with wonder.

"Are you followed?"

"Oh, no—no, truly. Please, don't be afraid. There's only me."

She drew closer still; then, taking her courage, sat down on the milestone.

"Would you play for me again?" she asked softly. "I'd like to know your tune."

"Sure and I daren't play it, girleen. Only a small, little bit of an ave I played—and look how it's brought you! No more, not a note dare I pipe. They'd hear it for sure and they'd be after coming for me."

"Coming for you? Who'd come for you?"

Terror seemed to grip his ravaged face.

"Och, the Redcoats, dear love you. I've not had the heart to play me whistle since I found it, mind—not until this night."

"But what Redcoats? And why would they come for you?"

He looked around furtively, put his lips close to her ear and whispered: "I've broken loose, then! It was for the dog here I done it, not for meself, I swear be the Finn! Had it not been for the dog's sake I'd have borne the lash and whatever, so I would!"

"Tell me about it," said the child. "I'll never harm you, cross my heart and spit my death."

Hesitantly he began, gaining confidence until his words dropped with a rhythm into the lap of the dusk, all in a strange brogue that she could not remember having heard before.

"In the road gangs I was, you'll understand. Shipped for life, I was, because of me father's coat of green. He wore the green, d'you see. So it was here in the chain-gang I fetched up, aworkin' on the road buildin', down to Taberag Ridge. The overseer was a great man for the whip, I'm telling you. Ah, a cruel man of iron, and no mistake. It's that cold in the winter-time, girleen, when there's snow on the wind. It's then that the hunger seems to eat into you, and the bruises ache bad. But—you'll be for lookin' at this dog now. A stray, he was. Left behind by a bullock train. Well, he took up with us convicts; and he stuck by us, so he did. Fed himself on rabbits and such—and me, too, sometimes. He slept with us at night to keep us warm. He'd lick our sores for us. This dog, see, he's a proper Christian and 'tis meself will swear to it.

"So it's when the overseer takes to him with the lash, girleen——" (Here the boy put his hand over his eyes, and the dog looked up lovingly, as though he heard and understood every word, and suffered with his master.)

"It's then—and may the holy angels forgive me—that a kind of red anger came into me brain, like. It took hold of me. I could not fight against it." His voice broke. Then in a moment he went on.

"I struck him down," he whispered.

"I wrested the lash from his hands. It was as though I

had the strength of ten—as though possessed of devils I was, may the Gentle Mother help me.

"And I lashed the man.

"Ah, I gave him one for poor Jake Donegal, that died in the winter of the cough. And I lashed him for Ted Barnaby, that had gangrene of his leg iron. I lashed him for the heathen black that he rode down for a Sunday's sport. But most of all—I lashed him for this dog here. You'll maybe think it no reason. But I could not help it, as I tell you. I lashed him for this innocent creature, that is a friend to man with every hair of his body—so I did."

The boy covered his face, and the firelight seemed a place of dark tragedy. Then slowly, he took away his hands.

"So——" he whispered. "So—then—I stopped. Because—he was dead, see. I'd killed him."

The child drew away and tried to look into his face, in the flickering firelight. The boy said:

"I wrenched out of me leg iron. It was loose with the starvation, no doubt. And—then I took to the ridges. I went up all the time—always up. And so I came here. Now I'm spent. But if they catch me 'twill be me for the Hanging Tree on Taberag Ridge."

At first the child had no words to lighten the burden on the conscience of the ragged boy. But she placed her warm arm across his back, where every bone made the bars of a cage, as though in protection. After a while she said, "Don't be afraid. Whatever happens—don't be afraid. You did what you had to do. See—I am not afraid of you. The dog and I, we love you."

"If the soldiers take me," he said, "I'll remember that. Yes, I'll remember that."

Then he thrust into her pinafore his queer, rusted penny whistle.

"Keep it," he said. "Maybe some day it will be you who'll play—and I who'll hear, and come."

Quite suddenly, darkness gathered, and a drowsiness took hold of her. Tides of sleep came swirling like smoke before her eyes. . . .

They found her—the search-party—high on the mountains, just as the dawn was breaking.

"But, Steffy," asked her father. "How did you light a fire? Did you have matches, then? Tell us how you came to be lost, my girl. Tell us how you endured through the night."

She shook her head. It seemed only full of a confused dreaming.

A queer, rusted whistle was in her pocket. A quaint, old-fashioned penny whistle, the like of which had not been seen around for many a year.

Even when she was grown, Steffany kept the whistle, as a curio; a souvenir of the time in childhood, when she wandered off alone, at dusk, on the Old Convicts' Road.

But she never played it, of course. It was too rusted. And so old, there was no one to teach her how to bring forth its tune.

Fiddler, Play Fast, Play Faster

Ruth Sawyer

It is a strange island and an enchanted one—our Isle of Man. It took many a thousand years and more before mankind discovered it, it being well known that the spirits of water, of earth, of air and fire did put on it an enchantment, hiding it with a blue flame of mist, so that it could not be seen by mortal eye. The mist was made out of the heat of a great fire and the salt vapour of the sea and it covered the island like a bank of clouds. Then one day the fire was let out, the sea grew quiet, and lo, the island stood out in all its height of mountains and ruggedness of coast, its green of fens and rushing of waterfalls. Sailors passing saw it. And from that day forth men came to it and much of its enchantment was lost.

But not all. Let you know that at all seasons of the year there are spirits abroad on the Isle, working their charms and making their mischief. And there is on the coast, overhanging the sea, a great cavern reaching below the earth, out of which the Devil comes when it pleases him, to walk where he will upon the Isle. A wise Manxman does not go far without a scrap of iron or a lump of salt in his pocket; and if it is night, likely, he will have stuck in his cap a sprig of rowan and a sprig of wormwood, feather from a seagull's wing and skin from a conger eel. For these keep away evil spirits; and who upon the Isle would meet with evil, or who would give himself foolishly into its power?

So it is that in the south upon the ramparts of Castle Rushen the cannon are mounted on stone crosses above the ramparts; and when a south Manxman knocks at his neighbour's door he does not cry out: "Are you within?" But rather he asks: "Are there any sinners inside?" For evil is a fearsome thing, and who would have traffic with it?

I am long beginning my tale, but some there may be who know little of our Isle and a story-teller cannot always bring his listeners by the straightest road to the story he has to tell. This one is of the south, where the mists hang the heaviest, where the huts are built of turf and thatched with broom, where the cattle are small and the goats many, and where a farmer will tell you he has had his herd brought to fold by the fenodyree—a goblin that is half goat, half boy. But that is another tale.

Let me begin with an old Manx saying—it tunes the story well: "When a poor man helps another, God in His Heaven laughs with delight." This shows you that the men of Man are kind to one another, and God is not far from them even when the Devil walks abroad.

Count a hundred years, and as many more as you like, and you will come to the time of my story. Beyond Castletown in the sheading of Kirk Christ Rushen lived, then, a lump of lad named Billy Nell Kewley. He could draw as sweet music from the fiddle as any fiddler of Man. When the Christmas-time began, he was first abroad with his fiddle. Up the glens and over the fens, fiddling for this neighbour and that as the night ran out, calling the hour and crying the weather, that those snug on their beds of chaff would know before the day broke what kind of day it would be making. Before Yule he started his fiddling, playing half out of the night and half into the day, playing this and playing that, carrying with him, carefully in his cap, the sprig of rowan and the sprig of wormwood, with the iron and salt in the pocket of his brown woollen breeches. And there you have Billy Nell Kewley on the Eve of Saint Fingan.

Now over Castletown on a high building of cliff rises Castle Rushen. Beyond stands the oldest monastery on the Isle, in ruin these hundreds of years, Rushen Abbey, with its hundred treens of land. It was through the Forest of Rushen Billy Nell was coming on Saint Thomas's Eve, down the Glen to the Quiggan hut, playing the tune "Andisop" and whistling a running of notes to go with it. He broke the whistle, ready to call the hour: "Two of the morning," and the weather: "Cold—with a mist over all," when he heard the running of feet behind him in the dark.

Quick as a falcon he reached for the sprig in his cap. It was gone; the pushing through the green boughs of the forest had torn it. He quickened his own feet. Could it be a buggan after him—an ugly, evil one, a fiend of Man who cursed mortals and bore malice against them, who would bring a body to perdition and then laugh at him? Billy Nell's feet went fast—went faster.

But his ear, dropping behind him, picked up the sound of other feet; they were going fast—and faster. Could it be the fenodyree—the hairy one? That would be not so terrible. The fenodyree played pranks, but he, having once loved a human maid, did not bring evil to humans. And he lived, if the ancient ones could be believed, in Glen Rushen.

And then a voice spoke out of the blackness. "Stop, I command!"

What power lay in that voice! It brought the feet of Billy Nell to a stop—for all he wanted them to go on, expected them to keep running. Afterwards he was remembering the salt and iron in his pocket he might have thrown between himself and what followed so closely after him out of the mist. But he did nothing but stop—stop and say to himself: "Billy Nell Kewley, could it be the Noid ny Hanmey who commands—the Enemy of the Soul?" And he stood stock still in the darkness too frightened to shiver, for it was the Devil himself he was thinking of.

He who spoke appeared, carrying with him a kind of reddish light that came from everywhere and nowhere, a light the colour of fever, or heat lightning, or of the very pit of Hell. But when Billy Nell looked he saw as fine a gentleman as ever had come to Man—fine and tall, grave and stern, well clothed in knee breeches and silver buckles and lace and such finery. He spoke with grace and grimness: "Billy Nell Kewley of Castletown, I have heard you are a monstrous good fiddler. No one better, so they say."

"I play fair, sir," said Billy Nell modestly.

"I would have you play for me. Look!" He dipped into a pocket of his breeches and drawing out a hand so white, so tapering, it might have been a lady's, he showed Billy Nell gold pieces. And in the reddish light that came from everywhere and nowhere Billy saw the strange marking on them. "You shall have as many of these as you can carry away with you if you will fiddle for me and my company three nights from tonight," said the fine one.

"And where shall I fiddle?" asked Billy Nell Kewley.

"I will send a messenger for you, Billy Nell; half-way up the Glen he will meet you. This side of midnight he will meet you."

"I will come," said the fiddler, for he had never heard of so much gold—to be his for a night's fiddling. And being not half so fearful he began to shiver. At that moment a cock crew far away, a bough brushed his eyes, the mist hung about him like a cloak, and he was alone. Then he ran, ran to Quiggan's hut, calling the hour: "Three of the clock," crying the weather: "Cold with a heavy mist."

The next day he counted, did Billy Nell Kewley, counted the days up to three and found that the night he was to fiddle for all the gold he could carry with him was Christmas Eve. A kind of terror took hold of him. What manner of spirit was the Enemy of the Soul? Could he be anything he chose to be—a devil in Hell or a fine gentleman on Earth? He ran about asking everyone, and everyone gave him a different answer. He went to the monks of the Abbey and found them working in their gardens, their black cowls thrown back from their faces, their bare feet treading the brown earth.

The Abbot came, and dour enough he looked. "Shall I go, your reverence? Shall I fiddle for one I know not? Is it good gold he is giving me?" asked Billy Nell.

"I cannot answer any one of those questions," said the Abbot. "That night alone can give the answers: Is the gold good or cursed? Is the man noble or is he the Devil? But go. Carry salt, carry iron and bollan bane. Play a dance and watch. Play another—and watch. Then play a Christmas hymn and see!"

This side of midnight, Christmas Eve, Billy Nell Kewley climbed the Glen, his fiddle wrapped in a lamb's fleece to keep out the wet. Mist, now blue, now red, hung over the blackness, so thick he had to feel his way along the track with his feet, stumbling.

He passed where Castle Rushen should have stood. He passed on, was caught up and carried as by the mist and in it. He felt his feet leave the track, he felt them gain it again. And then the mist rolled back like clouds after a storm and before him he saw such a splendid sight as no lump of lad had ever beheld before. A castle, with court-yard and corridors, with piazzas and high roofings, spread before him all a-glowing with light. Windows wide and doorways wide, and streaming with the light came laughter. And there was his host more splendid than all, with velvet and satin, silver and jewels. About him moved what Billy Nell took to be high-born lords and ladies, come from overseas no doubt, for never had he seen their like on Man.

In the middle of the great hall he stood, unwrapping his fiddle, sweetening the strings, rosining the bow, limbering his fingers. The laughter died. His host shouted:

"Fiddler, play fast—play faster!"

In all his life and never again did Billy Nell play as he played that night. The music of his fiddle made the music of a hundred fiddles. About him whirled the dancers like crazy rainbows: blue and orange, purple and yellow, green and red all mixed together until his head swam with the colour. And yet the sound of the dancers' feet was the sound of the grass growing or the corn ripening or the holly reddening—which is to say no sound at all. Only there was the sound of his playing, and above the sound of his host shouting, always shouting:

"Fiddler, play fast—play faster!"

Ever faster—ever faster! It was as with a mighty wind Billy Nell played now, drawing the wild, mad music from his fiddle. He played tunes he had never heard before, tunes which cried and shrieked and howled and sighed and sobbed and cried out in pain.

"Play fast—play faster!"

He saw one standing by the door—a monk in black cowl, barefooted, a monk who looked at him with deep sad eyes and held two fingers of his hand to his lips as if to hush the music.

Then, and not till then, did Billy Nell Kewley remember what the Abbot had told him. But the monk—how came he here? And then he remembered that, too. A tale so old it had grown ragged with the telling, so that only a scrap here and there was left: how long ago, on the blessed Christmas Eve, a monk had slept through the Midnight Mass to the Virgin and to the new-born Child, and how, at compline on Christmas Day, he was missing and never seen again. The ancient ones said that the Devil had taken him away, that Enemy of All Souls, had stolen his soul because he had slept over Mass.

Terror left Billy Nell. He swept his bow so fast over the strings of his fiddle that his eyes could not follow it.

"Fiddler, play fast—play faster!"

"Master, I play faster and faster!" He moved his own body to the mad music, moved it across the hall to the door where stood the monk. He crashed out the last notes; on the floor at the feet of the monk he dropped iron, salt, and bollan bane. Then out of the silence he drew the notes of a Christmas carol—softly, sweetly it rose on the air:

> *Adeste fideles, laeti triumphantes,*
> *Venite, venite in Bethlehem:*
> *Natum videte, Regem angelorum:*
> *Venite adoremus, venite adoremus,*
> *Venite adoremus—Dominum.*

Racked were the ears of Billy Nell at the sounds which surged above the music, groans and wailing, the agony of souls damned. Racked were his eyes with the sights he saw: the servants turned to fleshless skeletons, the lords and ladies to howling demons. And the monk with the black cowl and bare feet sifted down to the grass beneath the vanishing castle—a heap of grey dust. But in the dust shone one small spark of holy light—a monk's soul, freed. And Billy Nell took it in his hand and tossed it high in the wind as one tosses a falcon to the sky for free passage. And he watched it go its skimming way until the sky gathered it in.

Billy Nell Kewley played his way down the Glen, stopping to call the hour: "Three of this blessed Christmas Morning," stopping to cry the weather: "The sky is clear . . . the Christ is born."

Uncle Einar

Ray Bradbury

"It will take only a minute," said Uncle Einar's sweet wife.

"I refuse," he said. "And that takes but a *second*."

"I've worked all morning," she said, holding to her slender back, "and you won't help? It's drumming for a rain."

"Let it rain," he cried, morosely. "I'll not be pierced by lightning just to air your clothes."

"But you're so quick at it."

"Again, I refuse." His vast tarpaulin wings hummed nervously behind his indignant back.

She gave him a slender rope on which were tied four dozen fresh-washed clothes. He turned it in his fingers with distaste. "So it's come to this," he muttered, bitterly. "To this, to this, to this." He almost wept angry and acid tears.

"Don't cry; you'll wet them down again," she said. "Jump up, now, run them about."

"Run them about." His voice was hollow, deep, and terribly wounded. "I say: let it thunder, let it pour!"

"If it was a nice, sunny day I wouldn't ask," she said, reasonably. "All my washing gone for nothing if you don't. They'll hang about the house——"

That *did* it. Above all, he hated clothes flagged and festooned so man had to creep under on the way across a room. He jumped up. His vast green wings boomed. "Only so far as the pasture fence!"

Whirl: up he jumped, his wings chewed and loved the cool air. Before you'd say Uncle Einar Has Green Wings he sailed low across his farmland, trailing the clothes in a vast fluttering loop through the pounding concussion and back-wash of his wings!

"Catch!"

Back from the trip, he sailed the clothes, dry as popcorn, down on a series of clean blankets she'd spread for their landing.

"Thank you!" she cried.

"Gahh!" he shouted, and flew off under the apple tree to brood.

Uncle Einar's beautiful silk-like wings hung like sea-green sails behind him, and whirred and whispered from his shoulders when he sneezed or turned swiftly. He was one of the few in the Family whose talent was visible. All his dark cousins and nephews and brothers hid in small towns across the world, did unseen mental things or things with witch-fingers and white teeth, or blew down the sky like fire-leaves or loped in forests like moon-silvered wolves. They lived comparatively safe from normal humans. Not so a man with great green wings.

Not that he hated his wings. Far from it! In his youth he'd always flown nights, because nights were rare times for winged men! Daylight held dangers, always had, always would; but nights, ah, nights, he had sailed over islands of cloud and seas of summer sky. With no danger to himself. It had been a rich, full soaring, an exhilaration.

But now he could not fly at night.

On his way home to some high mountain pass in Europe after a Homecoming among Family members in Mellin Town, Illinois (some years ago) he had drunk too much rich crimson wine. "I'll be all right," he had told himself, vaguely, as he beat his long way under the morn-

ing stars, over the moon-dreaming country hills beyond
Mellin Town. And then—crack out of the sky——

A high-tension tower.

Like a netted duck! A great sizzle! His face blown black
by a blue sparkler of wire, he fended off the electricity with
a terrific back-jumping percussion of his wings and fell.

His hitting the moonlit meadow under the tower made
a noise like a large telephone book dropped from the
sky.

Early the next morning, his dew-sodden wings shaking
violently, he stood up. It was still dark. There was a faint
bandage of dawn stretched across the east. Soon the bandage would stain and all flight would be restricted. There
was nothing to do but take refuge in the forest and wait
out the day in the deepest thicket until another night gave
his wings a hidden motion in the sky.

In this fashion he met his wife.

During the day, which was warm for November first in
Illinois country, pretty young Brunilla Wexley was out
to udder a lost cow, for she carried a silver pail in one
hand as she sidled through thickets and pleaded cleverly
to the unseen cow to please return home or burst her gut
with unplucked milk. The fact that the cow would have
most certainly come home when her teats really needed
pulling did not concern Brunilla Wexley. It was a sweet
excuse for forest-journeying, thistle-blowing, and flower
chewing; all of which Brunilla was doing as she stumbled
upon Uncle Einar.

Asleep near a bush, he seemed a man under a green
shelter.

"Oh," said Brunilla, with a fever. "A man. In a camp-
tent."

Uncle Einar awoke. The camp-tent spread like a large
green fan behind him.

213

Ray Bradbury

"Oh," said Brunilla, the cow searcher. "A man with wings."

That was how she took it. She was startled, yes, but she had never been hurt in her life, so she wasn't afraid of anyone, and it was a fancy thing to see a winged man and she was proud to meet him. She began to talk. In an hour they were old friends, and in two hours she'd quite forgotten his wings were there. And he somehow confessed how he happened to be in this wood.

"Yes, I noticed you looked banged around," she said. "That right wing looks very bad. You'd best let me take you home and fix it. You won't be able to fly all the way to Europe on it, anyway. And who wants to live in Europe these days?"

He thanked her, but he didn't quite see how he could accept.

"But I live alone," she said. "For, as you see, I'm quite ugly."

He insisted she was not.

"How kind of you," she said. "But I am, there's no fooling myself. My folks are dead, I've a farm, a big one, all to myself, quite far from Mellin Town, and I'm in need of talking company."

But wasn't she afraid of him? he asked.

"Proud and jealous would be more near it," she said. "*May* I?" And she stroked his large green membraned veils with careful envy. He shuddered at the touch and put his tongue between his teeth.

So there was nothing for it but that he come to her house for medicaments and ointments, and my! what a burn across his face, beneath his eyes! "Lucky you weren't blinded," she said. "How'd it happen?"

"Well . . ." he said, and they were at her farm, hardly noticing they'd walked a mile, looking at each other.

214

A day passed, and another, and he thanked her at her door and said he must be going, he much appreciated the ointment, the care, the lodging. It was twilight and between now, six o'clock, and five the next morning, he must cross an ocean and a continent. "Thank you; goodbye," he said, and started to fly off in the dusk and crashed right into a maple tree.

"Oh!" she screamed, and ran to his unconscious body.

When he waked the next hour he knew he'd fly no more in the dark again ever; his delicate night-perception was gone. The winged telepathy that had warned him where towers, trees, houses and hills stood across his path, the fine clear vision and sensibility that guided him through mazes of forest, cliff, and cloud, all were burnt for ever by that strike across his face, that blue electric fry and sizzle.

"How?" he moaned softly. "How can I go to Europe? If I flew by day, I'd be seen and—miserable joke—maybe shot down! Or kept for a zoo perhaps, what a life *that'd* be! Brunilla, tell me, what shall I do?"

"Oh," she whispered, looking at her hands. "We'll think of something. . . ."

They were married.

The Family came for the wedding. In a great autumnal avalanche of maple, sycamore, oak, elm leaf they hissed and rustled, fell in a shower of horse-chestnut, thumped like winter apples on the earth, with an over-all scent of farewell-summer on the wind they made in their rushing. The ceremony was brief as a black candle lit, blown out, and smoke left still on the air. Its briefness, darkness, upside-down and backward quality escaped Brunilla, who only listened to the great tide of Uncle Einar's wings faintly murmuring above them as they finished out the rite. And as for Uncle Einar, the wound across his nose was almost healed and, holding Brunilla's arm, he felt Europe grow faint and melt away in the distance.

He didn't have to see very well to fly straight up, or come straight down. It was only natural that on this night of their wedding he take Brunilla in his arms and fly right up into the sky.

A farmer, five miles over, glanced at a low cloud at midnight, saw faint glows and crackles.

"Heat lightning," he observed, and went to bed.

They didn't come down till morning, with the dew.

The marriage took. She had only to look at him, and it lifted her to think she was the only woman in the world married to a winged man. "Who else could say it?" she asked her mirror. And the answer was: "No one!"

He, on the other hand, found great beauty behind her face, great kindness and understanding. He made some changes in his diet to fit her thinking, and was careful with his wings about the house; knocked porcelains and broken lamps were nerve-scrapers, he stayed away from them. He changed his sleeping habits, since he couldn't fly nights now anyhow. And she in turn fixed chairs so they were comfortable for his wings, put extra padding here or took it out there, and the things she said were the things he loved her for. "We're in our cocoons, all of us. See how ugly I am?" she said. "But one day I'll break out, spread wings as fine and handsome as you."

"You broke out long ago," he said.

She thought it over. "Yes," she had to admit. "I know just which day it was, too. In the woods when I looked for a cow and found a tent!" They laughed and with him holding her she felt so beautiful she knew their marriage had slipped her from her ugliness, like a bright sword from its case.

216

They had children. At first there was fear, all on his part, that they'd be winged.

"Nonsense, I'd love it!" she said. "Keep them out from underfoot."

"Then," he exclaimed, "they'd be in your *hair*!"

"Ow!" she cried.

Four children were born, three boys and a girl who, for their energy, seemed to have wings. They popped up like toadstools in a few years, and on hot summer days asked their father to sit under the apple tree and fan them with his cooling wings and tell them wild starlit tales of island clouds and ocean skies and textures of mist and wind and how a star tastes melting in your mouth, and how to drink cold mountain air, and how it feels to be a pebble dropped from Mt. Everest, turning to a green bloom, flowering your wings just before you strike bottom!

This was his marriage.

And today, six years later, here sat Uncle Einar, here he was, festering under the apple tree, grown impatient and unkind; not because this was his desire, but because after the long wait, he was still unable to fly the wild night sky; his extra sense had never returned. Here he sat despondently, nothing more than a summer sun-parasol, green and discarded, abandoned for the season by the reckless vacationers who once sought the refuge of its translucent shadow. Was he to sit here for ever, afraid to fly by day because someone might see him? Was his only flight to be as a drier of clothes for his wife, or a fanner of children on hot August noons? His one occupation had *always* been flying Family errands, quicker than storms. A boomerang, he'd whickled over hills and valleys and like a thistle, landed. He had always had money; the Family had good use for their winged man! But now? Bitterness! His wings jittered and whisked the air and made a captive thunder.

"Papa," said little Meg.

The children stood looking at his thought-dark face.

"Papa," said Ronald. "Make more thunder!"

"It's a cold March day, there'll soon be rain and plenty of thunder," said Uncle Einar.

"Will you come watch us?" asked Michael.

"Run on, run on! Let Papa brood!"

He was shut of love, the children of love, and the love of children. He thought only of heavens, skies, horizons, infinities, by night or day, lit by star, moon, or sun, cloudy or clear, but always it was skies and heavens and horizons that ran ahead of you for ever when you soared. Yet here he was, sculling the pasture, kept low for fear of being seen.

Misery in a deep well!

"Papa, come watch us; it's March!" cried Meg. "And we're going to the Hill with all the kids from town!"

Uncle Einar grunted. "What hill is that?"

"The Kite Hill, of course!" they all sang together.

Now he looked at them.

Each held a large paper kite, their faces sweating with anticipation and an animal glowing. In their small fingers were balls of white twine. From the kites, coloured red and blue and yellow and green, hung caudal appendages of cotton and silk strips.

"We'll fly our kites!" said Ronald. "Won't you come?"

"No," he said, sadly. "I mustn't be seen by anyone or there'd be trouble."

"You could hide and watch from the woods," said Meg. "We made the kites ourselves. Just because we know how."

"How do you know how?"

"You're our father!" was the instant cry. "That's why!"

He looked at his children for a long while. He sighed. "A kite festival, is it?"

"Yes, sir!"

"I'm going to win," said Meg.

"No, *I'm*!" Michael contradicted.

"Me, *me*!" piped Stephen.

"God up the chimney!" roared Uncle Einar, leaping high with a deafening kettle-drum of wings. "Children! Children, I love you dearly!"

"Father, what's wrong?" said Michael, backing off.

"Nothing, nothing, nothing!" chanted Einar. He flexed his wings to their greatest propulsion and plundering. Whoom! they slammed like cymbals. The children fell flat in the backwash! "I have it, I *have* it; I'm free again! Fire in the flue! Feather on the wind! Brunilla!" Einar called to the house. His wife appeared. "I'm free!" he called, flushed and tall, on his toes. "Listen, Brunilla, I don't need the night any more! I can fly by day! I don't need the night! I'll fly *every* day and *any* day of the year from now on!—but, God, I waste time, talking. Look!"

And as the worried members of his family watched, he seized the cotton tail from one of the little kites, tied it to his belt behind, grabbed the twine ball, held one end in his teeth, gave the other end to his children, and up, up into the air he flew, away into the March wind!

And across the meadows and over the farms his children ran, letting out string to the daylit sky, bubbling and stumbling, and Brunilla stood back in the farmyard and waved and laughed to see what was happening; and her children marched to the far Kite Hill and stood, the four of them, holding the ball of twine in their eager, proud fingers, each tugging and directing and pulling. And the children from Mellin Town came running with *their* small kites to let up on the wind, and they saw the great green kite leap and hover in the sky and exclaimed:

"Oh, oh, what a kite! What a kite! Oh, I wish I'd a kite like that! Where, where did you *get* it!"

"Our father made it!" cried Meg and Michael and Stephen and Ronald, and gave an exultant pull on the twine and the humming, thundering kite in the sky dipped and soared and made a great and magical exclamation mark across a cloud!

The Ghost Ship

Richard Middleton

Fairfield is a little village lying near the Portsmouth Road about half-way between London and the sea. Strangers who find it by accident now and then, call it a pretty, old-fashioned place; we who live in it and call it home don't find anything very pretty about it, but we should be sorry to live anywhere else. Our minds have taken the shape of the inn and the church and the green, I suppose. At all events we never feel comfortable out of Fairfield.

Of course the Cockneys with their vasty houses and noise-ridden streets, can call us rustics if they choose, but for all that Fairfield is a better place to live in than London. Doctor says that when he goes to London his mind is bruised with the weight of the houses, and he was a Cockney born. He had to live there himself when he was a little chap, but he knows better now. You gentlemen may laugh—perhaps some of you come from London way —but it seems to me that a witness like that is worth a gallon of arguments.

Dull? Well, you might find it dull, but I assure you that I've listened to all the London yarns you have spun tonight, and they're absolutely nothing to the things that happen at Fairfield. It's because of our way of thinking and minding our own business. If one of your Londoners were set down on the green of a Saturday night when the ghosts of the lads who died in the war keep tryst with the lasses who lie in the churchyard, he couldn't help being curious and interfering, and then the ghosts would go somewhere where it was quieter. But we just let them come and go and don't make any fuss, and in consequence Fairfield is the ghostliest place in all England. Why, I've seen a headless man sitting on the edge of the well in broad daylight, and the children playing about his feet as if he were their father. Take my word for it, spirits know when they are well off as much as human beings.

Still, I must admit that the thing I'm going to tell you about was queer even for our part of the world, where three packs of ghost-hounds hunt regularly during the season, and blacksmith's great-grandfather is busy all night shoeing the dead gentlemen's horses. Now that's a thing that wouldn't happen in London, because of their interfering ways, but blacksmith he lies up aloft and sleeps as quiet as a lamb. Once when he had a bad head he shouted down to them not to make so much noise, and in the morning he found an old guinea left on the anvil as an apology. He wears it on his watch-chain now. But I must get on with my story; if I start telling you about the queer happenings at Fairfield I'll never stop.

It all came of the great storm in the spring of '97, the year that we had two great storms. This was the first one, and I remember it very well, because I found in the morning that it had lifted the thatch of my pigsty into the widow's garden as clean as a boy's kite. When I looked over the hedge, widow—Tom Lamport's widow that was—was prodding for her nasturtiums with a daisy-grubber. After I had watched her for a little I went down to the "Fox and Grapes" to tell landlord what she said to me. Landlord he laughed, being a married man and at ease with the sex. "Come to that," he said, "the tempest has blowed something into my field. A kind of a ship I think it would be."

I was surprised at that until he explained that it was only a ghost ship and would do no hurt to the turnips. We argued that it had been blown up from the sea at Portsmouth, and then we talked of something else. There were two slates down at the parsonage and a big tree in Lumley's meadow. It was a rare storm.

I reckon the wind had blown our ghosts all over England. They were coming back for days afterwards with foundered horses and as footsore as possible, and they were so glad to get back to Fairfield that some of them walked up the street crying like little children. Squire said that his great-grandfather's great-grandfather hadn't looked so dead-beat since the Battle of Naseby, and he's an educated man.

What with one thing and another, I should think it was a week before we got straight again, and then one afternoon I met the landlord on the green and he had a worried face. "I wish you'd come and have a look at that ship in my field," he said to me; "it seems to me it's leaning real hard on the turnips. I can't bear thinking what the missus will say when she sees it."

I walked down the lane with him, and sure enough there was a ship in the middle of his field, but such a ship as no man had seen on the water for three hundred years, let alone in the middle of a turnip-field. It was all painted black and covered with carvings, and there was a great bay window in the stern for all the world like the Squire's drawing-room. There was a crowd of little black cannon on deck and looking out of her port-holes, and she was anchored at each end to the hard ground. I have seen the wonders of the world on picture-postcards, but I have never seen anything to equal that.

"She seems very solid for a ghost ship," I said, seeing the landlord was bothered.

"I should say it's a betwixt and between," he answered, puzzling over it, "but it's going to spoil a matter of fifty turnips, and missus she'll want it moved." We went up to her and touched the side, and it was as hard as a real ship. "Now there's folks in England would call that very curious," he said.

Now I don't know much about ghost ships, but I should think that that ghost ship weighed a solid two hundred tons, and it seemed to me that she had come to stay, so that I felt sorry for the landlord, who was a married man. "All the horses in Fairfield won't move her out of my turnips," he said, frowning at her.

Just then we heard a noise on her deck and we looked up and saw that a man had come out of her front cabin and was looking down at us very peaceably. He was dressed in a black uniform set out with rusty gold lace, and he had a great cutlass by his side in a brass sheath. "I'm Captain Bartholomew Roberts," he said, in a gentleman's voice, "put in for recruits. I seem to have brought her rather far up the harbour."

"Harbour!" cried landlord; "why, you're fifty miles from the sea."

Captain Roberts didn't turn a hair. "So much as that, is it?" he said coolly. "Well it's of no consequence."

Landlord was a bit upset at this. "I don't want to be un-neighbourly," he said, "but I wish you hadn't brought your ship into my field. You see, my wife sets great store on these turnips."

The captain took a pinch of snuff out of a fine gold box that he pulled out of his pocket, and dusted his fingers with a silk handkerchief in a very genteel fashion. "I'm only here for a few months," he said; "but if a testimony of my esteem would pacify your good lady I should be content," and with the words he loosed a great gold brooch from the neck of his coat and tossed it down to landlord.

Landlord blushed as red as a strawberry. "I'm not denying she's fond of jewellery," he said, "but it's too much for half a sackful of turnips." And indeed it was a handsome brooch.

The captain laughed. "Tut, man," he said, "it's a forced sale, and you deserve a good price. Say no more about it." And nodding good day to us, he turned on his heel and went into the cabin. Landlord walked back up the lane like a man with a weight off his mind. "That tempest has blowed me a bit of luck," he said; "the missus will be main pleased with that brooch. It's better than blacksmith's guinea, any day."

Ninety-seven was Jubilee year, the year of the second Jubilee, you remember, and we had great doings at Fairfield, so that we hadn't much time to bother about the ghost ship, though anyhow it isn't our way to meddle in things that don't concern us. Landlord, he saw his tenant once or twice, when he was hoeing his turnips and passed the time of day, and landlord's wife wore her new brooch to church every Sunday. But we didn't mix much with the ghosts at any time, all except an idiot lad there was in the village, and he didn't know the difference between a man and a ghost, poor innocent! On Jubilee Day, however, somebody told Captain Roberts why the church bells were ringing, and he hoisted a flag and fired off his guns like a loyal Englishman. 'Tis true the guns were shotted, and one of the round shot knocked a hole in Farmer Johnstone's barn, but nobody thought much of that in such a season of rejoicing.

It wasn't till our celebrations were over that we noticed that anything was wrong in Fairfield. 'Twas shoemaker who told me first about it one morning at the "Fox and

Grapes". "You know my great-great-uncle?" he said to me.

"You mean Joshua, the quiet lad," I answered, knowing him well.

"Quiet!" said shoemaker indignantly. "Quiet you call him, coming home at three o'clock every morning as drunk as a magistrate and waking up the whole house with his noise."

"Why, it can't be Joshua!" I said, for I knew him for one of the most respectable young ghosts in the village.

"Joshua it is," said shoemaker; "and one of these nights he'll find himself out in the street, if he isn't careful."

This kind of talk shocked me, I can tell you, for I don't like to hear a man abusing his own family, and I could hardly believe that a steady youngster like Joshua had taken to drink. But just then in came butcher Alwyn in such a temper that he could hardly drink his beer. "The young puppy! the young puppy!" he kept on saying; and it was some time before shoemaker and I found out that he was talking about his ancestor that fell at Senlac.

"Drink?" said shoemaker hopefully, for we all like company in our misfortunes, and butcher nodded grimly.

"The young noodle," he said, emptying his tankard.

Well, after that I kept my ears open, and it was the same story all over the village. There was hardly a young man among all the ghosts of Fairfield who didn't roll home in the small hours of the morning the worse for liquor. I used to wake up in the night and hear them stumble past my house, singing outrageous songs. The worst of it was that we couldn't keep the scandal to ourselves, and the folk at Greenhill began to talk of "sodden Fairfield", and taught their children to sing a song about us:

The Ghost Ship

"Sodden Fairfield, sodden Fairfield, has no use for bread-and-
butter
Rum for breakfast, rum for dinner, rum for tea, and rum for
supper!"

We are easy-going in our village, but we didn't like that.

Of course we soon found out where the young fellows went to get the drink, and landlord was terribly cut up that his tenant should have turned out so badly, but his wife wouldn't hear of parting with the brooch, so that he couldn't give the Captain notice to quit. But as time went on, things grew from bad to worse, and at all hours of the day you would see those young reprobates sleeping it off on the village green. Nearly every afternoon a ghost wagon used to jolt down to the ship with a lading of rum, and though the older ghosts seemed inclined to give the Captain's hospitality the go-by, the youngsters were neither to hold nor to bind.

So one afternoon when I was taking my nap I heard a knock at the door, and there was parson looking very serious, like a man with a job before him that he didn't altogether relish. "I'm going down to talk to the Captain about all this drunkenness in the village, and I want you to come with me," he said straight out.

I can't say that I fancied the visit much myself, and I tried to hint to parson that as, after all, they were only a lot of ghosts, it didn't very much matter.

"Dead or alive, I'm responsible for their good conduct," he said, "and I'm going to do my duty and put a stop to this continued disorder. And you are coming with me, John Simmons." So I went, parson being a persuasive kind of man.

We went down to the ship, and as we approached her, I could see the Captain tasting the air on deck. When he saw parson he took off his hat very politely, and I can tell you that I was relieved to find that he had a proper respect for the cloth. Parson acknowledged his salute and spoke out stoutly enough. "Sir, I should be glad to have a word with you."

"Come on board, sir; come on board," said the Captain, and I could tell by his voice that he knew why we were there. Parson and I climbed up an uneasy kind of ladder, and the Captain took us into the great cabin at the back of the ship, where the bay window was. It was the most wonderful place you ever saw in your life, all full of gold and silver plate, swords with jewelled scabbards, carved oak chairs, and great chests that looked as though they were bursting with guineas. Even parson was surprised, and he did not shake his head very hard when the Captain took down some silver cups and poured us out a drink of rum. I tasted mine, and I don't mind saying that it changed my view of things entirely. There was nothing betwixt and between about that rum, and I felt that it was ridiculous to blame the lads for drinking too much of stuff like that. It seemed to fill my veins with honey and fire.

Parson put the case squarely to the Captain, but I didn't listen much to what he said; I was busy sipping my drink and looking through the window at the fishes swimming to and fro over landlord's turnips. Just then it seemed the most natural thing in the world that they should be there, though afterwards, of course, I could see that that proved it was a ghost ship.

But even then I thought it was queer when I saw a drowned sailor float by in thin air with his hair and beard all full of bubbles. It was the first time I had seen anything quite like that at Fairfield.

All the time I was regarding the wonders of the deep, parson was telling Captain Roberts how there was no peace or rest in the village owing to the curse of drunkenness, and what a bad example the youngsters were setting to the older ghosts. The Captain listened very attentively, and only put in a word now and then about boys being boys and young men sowing their wild oats. But when parson had finished his speech he filled up our silver cups and said to parson, with a flourish, "I should be sorry to cause trouble anywhere where I have been made welcome, and you will be glad to hear that I put to sea tomorrow night. And now you must drink me a prosperous voyage." So we all stood up and drank the toast with honour, and that noble rum was like hot oil in my veins.

After that Captain showed us some of the curiosities he had brought back from foreign parts, and we were greatly amazed, though afterwards I couldn't clearly remember what they were. And then I found myself walking across the turnips with parson, and I was telling him of the glories of the deep that I had seen through the window of the ship. He turned on me severely. "If I were you, John Simmons," he said, "I should go straight home to bed." He has a way of putting things that wouldn't occur to an ordinary man, has parson, and I did as he told me.

Well, next day it came on to blow, and it blew harder and harder, till about eight o'clock at night I heard a noise and looked out into the garden. I dare say you won't believe me, it seems a bit tall even to me, but the wind had lifted the thatch of my pigsty into the widow's garden a second time. I thought I wouldn't wait to hear what widow had to say about it, so I went across the green to the "Fox and Grapes", and the wind was so strong that I danced along on tiptoe like a girl at the fair. When I got to the inn landlord had to help me shut the door; it seemed as though a dozen goats were pushing against it to come in, out of the storm.

"It's a powerful tempest," he said, drawing the beer. "I hear there's a chimney down at Dickory End."

"It's a funny thing how these sailors know about the weather," I answered. "When Captain said he was going tonight I was thinking it would take a capful of wind to carry the ship back to sea, but now here's more than a capful."

"Ah, yes," said landlord, "it's tonight he goes true enough, and, mind you, though he treated me handsome over the rent, I'm not sure it's a loss to the village. I don't hold with gentrice who fetch their drink from London instead of helping local traders to get their living."

"But you haven't got any rum like his," I said, to draw him out.

His neck grew red above his collar, and I was afraid I'd gone too far; but after a while he got his breath with a grunt.

"John Simmons," he said, "if you've come down here this windy night to talk a lot of fool's talk, you've wasted a journey."

Well, of course, then I had to smooth him down with praising his rum, and Heaven forgive me for swearing it was better than Captain's. For the like of that rum no living lips have tasted save mine and parson's. But somehow or other I brought landlord round, and presently we must have a glass of his best to prove its quality.

"Beat that if you can!" he cried, and we both raised our glasses to our mouths, only to stop half-way and look at each other in amaze. For the wind that had been howling outside like an outrageous dog had all of a sudden turned as melodious as the carol-boys of a Christmas Eve.

"Surely that's not my Martha," whispered landlord; Martha being his great-aunt that lived in the loft overhead. We went to the door, and the wind burst it open so that

the handle was driven clean into the plaster of the wall. But we didn't think about that at the time; for over our heads, sailing very comfortably through the windy stars, was the ship that had passed the summer in landlord's field. Her port-holes and her bay-window were blazing with lights, and there was a noise of singing and fiddling on her decks. "He's gone," shouted landlord above the storm, "and he's taken half the village with him!" I could only nod in answer, not having lungs like bellows of leather.

In the morning we were unable to measure the strength of the storm, and over and above my pigsty there was damage enough wrought in the village to keep us busy. True it is that the children had to break down no branches for the firing that autumn, since the wind had strewn the woods with more than they could carry away. Many of our ghosts were scattered abroad, but this time very few came back, all the young men having sailed with Captain; and not only ghosts, for a poor half-witted lad was missing, and we reckoned that he had stowed himself away or perhaps shipped as cabin-boy, not knowing any better.

What with the lamentations of the ghost-girls and the grumblings of families who had lost an ancestor, the village was upset for a while, and the funny thing was that it was the folk who had complained most of the carryings-on of the youngsters, who made most noise now that they were gone. I hadn't any sympathy with shoemaker or butcher, who ran about saying how much they missed their lads, but it made me grieve to hear the poor bereaved girls calling their lovers by name on the village green at night-fall. It didn't seem fair to me that they should have lost their men a second time, after giving up life in order to join them, as like as not. Still, not even a spirit can be sorry for ever, and after a few months we made up our mind that the folk who had sailed in the ship were never coming back, and we didn't talk about it any more.

And then one day, I dare say it would be a couple of years after, when the whole business was quite forgotten, who should come traipsing along the road from Portsmouth but the daft lad who had gone away with the ship, without waiting till he was dead to become a ghost. You never saw such a boy as that in all your life. He had a great rusty cutlass hanging to a string at his waist, and he was tattooed all over in fine colours, so that even his face looked like a girl's sampler. He had a handkerchief in hand full of foreign shells and old-fashioned pieces of small money, very curious, and he walked up to the well outside his mother's house and drew himself a drink as if he had been nowhere in particular.

The worst of it was that he had come back as soft-headed as he went, and try as we might we couldn't get anything reasonable out of him. He talked a lot of gibberish about keel-hauling and walking the plank and crimson murders —things which a decent sailor should know nothing about, so that it seemed to me that for all his manners Captain had been more of a pirate than a gentleman mariner. But to draw sense out of that boy was as hard as picking cherries off a crab-tree. One silly tale he had that he kept on drifting back to, and to hear him you would have thought that it was the only thing that happened to him in his life. "We was at anchor," he would say, "off an island called the Basket of Flowers, and the sailors had caught a lot of parrots and we were teaching them to swear. Up and down the decks, up and down the decks, and the language they used was dreadful. Then we looked up and saw the masts of the Spanish ship outside the harbour. Outside the harbour they were, so we threw the parrots into the sea and sailed out to fight. And all the parrots were drowned in the sea and the language they used was dreadful." That's the sort of boy he was, nothing but silly talk of parrots when we asked him about the fighting. And we never had a chance of teaching him better, for two days after he ran away again, and hasn't been seen since.

That's my story, and I assure you that things like that are happening at Fairfield all the time. The ship has never come back, but somehow as people grow older they seem to think that one of these windy nights she'll come sailing in over the hedges with all the lost ghosts on board. Well, when she comes, she'll be welcome. There's one ghost-lass that has never grown tired of waiting for her lad to return. Every night you'll see her out on the green, straining her poor eyes with looking for the mast-lights among the stars. A faithful lass you'd call her, and I'm thinking you'd be right.

Landlord's field wasn't a penny the worse for the visit, but they do say that since then the turnips that have been grown in it have tasted of rum.

Jimmy Takes Vanishing Lessons

Walter R. Brooks

The school bus picked up Jimmy Crandall every morning at the side road that led up to his aunt's house, and every afternoon it dropped him there again. And so twice a day, on the bus, he passed the entrance to the mysterious road.

It wasn't much of a road any more. It was choked with weeds and blackberry bushes, and the woods on both sides pressed in so closely that the branches met overhead, and it was dark and gloomy even on bright days. The bus driver once pointed it out.

"Folks that go in there after dark," he said, "well, they usually don't ever come out again. There's a haunted house about a quarter of a mile down the road." He paused. "But you ought to know about that, Jimmy. It was your grandfather's house."

Jimmy knew about it, and he knew that it now belonged to his Aunt Mary. But Jimmy's aunt would never talk to him about the house. She said the stories about it were silly nonsense and there were no such things as ghosts. If all the villagers weren't a lot of superstitious idiots, she would be able to rent the house, and then she would have enough money to buy Jimmy some decent clothes and take him to the movies.

Jimmy thought it was all very well to say that there were no such things as ghosts, but how about the people who had tried to live there? Aunt Mary had rented the house three times, but every family had moved out within a week. They said the things that went on there were just too queer. So nobody would live in it any more.

Jimmy thought about the house a lot. If he could only prove that there wasn't a ghost. . . . And one Saturday when his aunt was in the village, Jimmy took the key to the haunted house from its hook on the kitchen door, and started out.

It had seemed like a fine idea when he had first thought of it—to find out for himself. Even in the silence and damp gloom of the old road it still seemed pretty good. Nothing to be scared of, he told himself. Ghosts aren't around in the daytime. But when he came out in the clearing and looked at those blank, dusty windows, he wasn't so sure.

"Oh, come on!" he told himself. And he squared his shoulders and waded through the long grass to the porch.

Then he stopped again. His feet did not seem to want to go up the steps. It took him nearly five minutes to persuade them to move. But when at last they did, they marched right up and across the porch to the front door, and Jimmy set his teeth hard and put the key in the keyhole. It turned with a squeak. He pushed the door open and went in.

That was probably the bravest thing that Jimmy had ever done. He was in a long dark hall with closed doors on both sides, and on the right the stairs went up. He had left the door open behind him, and the light from it showed him that, except for the hat-rack and table and chairs, the hall was empty. And then as he stood there, listening to the bumping of his heart, gradually the light faded, the hall grew darker and darker—as if something

236

huge had come up on the porch behind him and stood there, blocking the doorway. He swung round quickly, but there was nothing there.

He drew a deep breath. It must have been just a cloud passing across the sun. But then the door, all of itself, began to swing shut. And before he could stop it, it closed with a bang. And it was then, as he was pulling frantically at the handle to get out, that Jimmy saw the ghost.

It behaved just as you would expect a ghost to behave. It was a tall, dim, white figure, and it came gliding slowly down the stairs towards him. Jimmy gave a yell, yanked the door open, and tore down the steps.

He didn't stop until he was well down the road. Then he had to get his breath. He sat down on a log. "Boy!" he said. "I've seen a ghost! Golly, was that awful!" Then after a minute, he thought, "What was so awful about it? He was trying to scare me, like that smart Alec who was always jumping out from behind things. Pretty silly business for a grown-up ghost to be doing."

It always makes you mad when someone deliberately tries to scare you. And as Jimmy got over his fright, he began to get angry. And pretty soon he got up and started back. "I must get that key, anyway," he thought, for he had left it in the door.

This time he approached very quietly. He thought he'd just lock the door and go home. But as he tiptoed up the steps he saw it was still open; and as he reached out cautiously for the key, he heard a faint sound. He drew back and peeked around the door jamb, and there was the ghost.

The ghost was going back upstairs, but he wasn't gliding now, he was doing a sort of dance, and every other step he would bend double and shake with laughter.

His thin cackle was the sound Jimmy had heard. Evidently he was enjoying the joke he had played. That made Jimmy madder than ever. He stuck his head farther around the door jamb and yelled "Boo!" at the top of his lungs. The ghost gave a thin shriek and leaped two feet in the air, then collapsed on the stairs.

As soon as Jimmy saw he could scare the ghost even worse than the ghost could scare him, he wasn't afraid any more, and he came right into the hall. The ghost was hanging on to the bannisters and panting. "Oh, my goodness!" he gasped. "Oh, my gracious! Boy, you can't *do* that to me!"

"I did it, didn't I?" said Jimmy. "Now we're even."

"Nothing of the kind," said the ghost crossly. "You seem pretty stupid, even for a boy. Ghosts are supposed to scare people. People aren't supposed to scare ghosts." He got up slowly and glided down and sat on the bottom step. "But look here, boy; this could be pretty serious for me if people got to know about it."

"You mean you don't want me to tell anybody about it?" Jimmy asked.

"Suppose we make a deal," the ghost said. "You keep still about this, and in return I'll—well, let's see; how would you like to know how to vanish?"

"Oh, that would be swell!" Jimmy exclaimed. "But —can you vanish?"

"Sure," said the ghost, and he did. All at once he just wasn't there. Jimmy was alone in the hall.

But his voice went right on. "It would be pretty handy, wouldn't it?" he said persuasively. "You could get into the movies free whenever you wanted to, and if your aunt called you to do something—when you were in the yard, say—well, she wouldn't be able to find you."

"I don't mind helping Aunt Mary," Jimmy said.

"H'm. High-minded, eh?" said the ghost. "Well, then——"

"I wish you'd please reappear," Jimmy interrupted. "It makes me feel funny to talk to somebody who isn't there."

"Sorry, I forgot," said the ghost, and there he was again, sitting on the bottom step. Jimmy could see the step, dimly, right through him. "Good trick, eh? Well, if you don't like vanishing, maybe I could teach you to seep through keyholes. Like this." He floated over to the door and went right through the keyhole, the way water goes down the drain. Then he came back the same way.

"That's useful, too," he said. "Getting into locked rooms and so on. You can go anywhere the wind can."

"No," said Jimmy. "There's only one thing you can do to get me to promise not to tell about scaring you. Go live somewhere else. There's Miller's, up the road. Nobody lives there any more."

"That old shack!" said the ghost, with a nasty laugh. "Doors and windows half off, roof leaky—no thanks! What do you think it's like in a storm, windows banging, rain dripping on you—I guess not! Peace and quiet, that's really what a ghost wants out of life."

"Well, I don't think it's very fair," Jimmy said, "for you to live in a house that doesn't belong to you and keep my aunt from renting it."

"Pooh!" said the ghost. "I'm not stopping her from renting it. I don't take up any room, and it's not my fault if people get scared and leave."

"It certainly is!" Jimmy said angrily. "You don't play fair and I'm not going to make any bargain with you. I'm going to tell everybody how I scared you."

"Oh, you mustn't do that!" The ghost seemed quite disturbed and he vanished and reappeared rapidly several times. "If that got out, every ghost in the country would be in terrible trouble."

So they argued about it. The ghost said if Jimmy wanted money he could learn to vanish; then he could join a circus and get a big salary. Jimmy said he didn't want to be in a circus; he wanted to go to college and learn to be a doctor. He was very firm. And the ghost began to cry. "But this is my *home*, boy," he said. "Thirty years I've lived here and no trouble to anybody, and now you want to throw me out into the cold world! And for what? A little money! That's pretty heartless." And he sobbed, trying to make Jimmy feel cruel.

Jimmy didn't feel cruel at all, for the ghost had certainly driven plenty of other people out into the cold world. But he didn't really think it would do much good for him to tell anybody that he had scared the ghost. Nobody would believe him, and how could he prove it? So after a minute he said, "Well, all right. You teach me to vanish and I won't tell." They settled it that way.

Jimmy didn't say anything to his aunt about what he'd done. But every Saturday he went to the haunted house for his vanishing lesson. It is really quite easy when you know how, and in a couple of weeks he could flicker, and in six weeks the ghost gave him an examination and he got a B plus, which is very good for a human. So he thanked the ghost and shook hands with him and said, "Well, good-bye now. You'll hear from me."

"What do you mean by that?" said the ghost suspiciously. But Jimmy just laughed and ran off home.

That night at supper Jimmy's aunt said, "Well, what have you been doing today?"

"I've been learning to vanish."

His aunt smiled and said, "That must be fun."

"Honestly," said Jimmy. "The ghost up at grand-father's taught me."

"I don't think that's very funny," said his aunt. "And will you please not—why, where are you?" she demanded, for he had vanished.

"Here, Aunt Mary," he said, as he reappeared.

"Merciful heavens!" she exclaimed, and she pushed back her chair and rubbed her eyes hard. Then she looked at him again.

Well it took a lot of explaining and he had to do it twice more before he could persuade her that he really could vanish. She was pretty upset. But at last she calmed down and they had a long talk. Jimmy kept his word and didn't tell her that he had scared the ghost, but he said he had a plan, and at last, though very reluctantly, she agreed to help him.

So the next day she went up to the old house and started to work. She opened the windows and swept and dusted and aired the bedding, and made as much noise as possible. This disturbed the ghost, and pretty soon he came floating into the room where she was sweeping. She was scared all right. She gave a yell and threw the broom at him. As the broom went right through him and he came nearer, waving his arms and groaning, she shrank back.

And Jimmy, who had been standing there invisible all the time, suddenly appeared and jumped at the ghost with a "Boo!" And the ghost fell over in a dead faint.

As soon as Jimmy's aunt saw that, she wasn't frightened any more. She found some smelling salts and held them under the ghost's nose, and when he came to she tried to help him into a chair. Of course she couldn't help him much because her hands went right through him. But at last he sat up and said reproachfully to Jimmy, "You broke your word!"

"I promised not to tell about scaring you," said the boy, "but I didn't promise not to scare you again."

And his aunt said, "You really are a ghost, aren't you? I thought you were just stories people made up. Well, excuse me, but I must get on with my work." And she began sweeping and banging around with her broom harder than ever.

The ghost put his hands to his head. "All this noise," he said. "Couldn't you work more quietly, ma'am?"

"Whose house is this, anyway?" she demanded. "If you don't like it, why don't you move out?"

The ghost sneezed violently several times. "Excuse me," he said. "You're raising so much dust. Where's that boy?" he asked suddenly. For Jimmy had vanished again.

"I'm sure I don't know," she replied. "Probably getting ready to scare you again."

"You ought to have better control of him," said the ghost severely. "If he was my boy, I'd take a hairbrush to him."

"You have my permission," she said, and she reached right through the ghost and pulled the chair cushion out from under him and began banging the dust out of it. "What's more," she went on, as he got up and glided wearily to another chair, "Jimmy and I are going to sleep here nights from now on, and I don't think it would be very smart of you to try any tricks."

"Ha, ha," said the ghost nastily. "He who laughs last——"

"Ha, ha, yourself," said Jimmy's voice from close behind him. "And that's me, laughing last."

The ghost muttered and vanished.

Jimmy's aunt put cotton in her ears and slept that night in the best bedroom with the light lit. The ghost screamed for a while down in the cellar, but nothing happened, so he came upstairs. He thought he would appear to her as two glaring, fiery eyes, which was one of his best tricks, but first he wanted to be sure where Jimmy was. But he couldn't find him. He hunted all over the house, and though he was invisible himself, he got more and more nervous. He kept imagining that at any moment Jimmy might jump out at him from some dark corner and scare him into fits. Finally he got so jittery that he went back to the cellar and hid in the coal bin all night.

The following days were just as bad for the ghost. Several times he tried to scare Jimmy's aunt while she was working, but she didn't scare worth a cent, and twice Jimmy managed to sneak up on him and appear suddenly with a loud yell, frightening him dreadfully. He was, I suppose, rather timid even for a ghost. He began to look quite haggard. He had several long arguments with Jimmy's aunt, in which he wept and appealed to her sympathy, but she was firm. If he wanted to live there he would have to pay rent, just like anybody else. There was the abandoned Miller farm two miles up the road. Why didn't he move there?

When the house was all in apple-pie order, Jimmy's aunt went down to the village to see a Mr. and Mrs. Whistler, who were living at the hotel because they couldn't find a house to move into. She told them about the old house, but they said, "No, thank you. We've heard about that house. It's haunted. I'll bet," they said, "*you* wouldn't dare spend a night there."

She told them that she had spent the last week there, but they evidently didn't believe her. So she said, "You know my nephew, Jimmy. He's twelve years old. I am

243

so sure that the house is not haunted that, if you want to rent it, I will let Jimmy stay there with you every night until you are sure everything is all right."

"Ha!" said Mr. Whistler. "The boy won't do it. He's got more sense."

So they sent for Jimmy. "Why, I've spent the last week there," he said. "Sure. I'd just as soon."

But the Whistlers still refused.

So Jimmy's aunt went around and told a lot of the village people about their talk, and everybody made so much fun of the Whistlers for being afraid, when a twelve-year-old boy wasn't, that they were ashamed, and said they would rent it. So they moved in. Jimmy stayed there for a week, but he saw nothing of the ghost. And then one day one of the boys in his grade told him that somebody had seen a ghost up at the Miller farm. So Jimmy knew the ghost had taken his aunt's advice.

A day or two later he walked up to the Miller farm. There was no front door and he walked right in. There was some groaning and thumping upstairs, and then after a minute the ghost came floating down.

"Oh, it's you!" he said. "Goodness sakes, boy, can't you leave me in peace?"

Jimmy said he'd just come up to see how he was getting along.

"Getting along fine," said the ghost. "From my point of view it's a very desirable property. Peaceful. Quiet. Nobody playing silly tricks."

"Well," said Jimmy, "I won't bother you if you don't bother the Whistlers. But if you come back there——"

"Don't worry," said the ghost.

So with the rent money, Jimmy and his aunt had a much easier life. They went to the movies sometimes twice a week, and Jimmy had all new clothes, and on

Thanksgiving, for the first time in his life, Jimmy had a turkey. Once a week he would go up to the Miller farm to see the ghost and they got to be very good friends. The ghost even came down to the Thanksgiving dinner, though of course he couldn't eat much. He seemed to enjoy the warmth of the house and he was in very good humour. He taught Jimmy several more tricks. The best one was how to glare with fiery eyes, which was useful later on when Jimmy became a doctor and had to look down people's throats to see if their tonsils ought to come out. He was really a pretty good fellow as ghosts go, and Jimmy's aunt got quite fond of him herself. When the real winter weather began, she even used to worry about him a lot, because of course there was no heat in the Miller place and the doors and windows didn't amount to much and there was hardly any roof. The ghost tried to explain to her that heat and cold didn't bother ghosts at all.

"Maybe not," she said, "but just the same, it can't be very pleasant." And when he accepted their invitation for Christmas dinner she knitted some red woollen slippers, and he was so pleased that he broke down and cried. And that made Jimmy's aunt so happy, *she* broke down and cried.

Jimmy didn't cry, but he said, "Aunt Mary, don't you think it would be nice if the ghost came down and lived with us this winter?"

"I would feel very much better about him if he did," she said.

So he stayed with them that winter, and then he just stayed on, and it must have been a peaceful place for the last I heard he was still there.

The Crossways

L. P. Hartley

Once upon a time there were two children, called Olga and Peter, and they lived on the edge of a huge forest. Olga was nine and Peter was seven. Their father was a woodman and very poor. Their mother's name was Lucindra. She came from another country; their father had met her in the wars. She was beautiful and had fine golden hair. Though she was sometimes dreamy and absent-minded and would suddenly speak to them in her own language, which they didn't understand, she was very fond of them and they loved her.

But Michael their father was a stern man and they were both a little afraid of him. Even Lucindra was afraid of him, for when he was angry he would scold her and sometimes tell her he wished he had never married her. And when this happened she wished she had never married him, but she did not dare to say so; besides he was strong and handsome and could be kind and loving when his fits of bad temper were over.

One thing he had always told his children, they must never on any account go farther into the forest than where they could still see the sunlight shining through the edges. The trees were so thick and the paths so few and hard to follow that even the foresters themselves sometimes lost their way. And there were dangerous animals as well, wolves and bears and wild boars. Michael still carried a scar from a gash that a bear had given him; it ran all the way from his elbow to his shoulder, making a bluish groove in his skin which you could feel with your finger. When he wanted to impress on them the danger of going too far into the forest he would show them the scar. Olga used to try not to look at it but Peter said he would like to have one like it.

Michael would not let even Lucindra wander about in the forest alone though sometimes he took her with him when he went out with his horse and cart. Then they would eat their dinner together under the trees, and she looked forward to that. But he usually went on foot, for the road soon came to an end and branched off into foot-paths which lost themselves among the trees. So she did not know much more about the forest than the children did. But like them she wanted to know more, for their cottage was miles away from any town, and sometimes weeks passed without her seeing anyone.

One afternoon, however, when Michael was away at work, a stranger called. He was a young man, slight and slim, with hair as fair and eyes as blue as hers, which was not surprising for he came from her own country and had heard of people whom she knew. He was a pedlar who sold bead necklaces and brooches and bracelets and ribbons. These did not interest Peter very much but he also had pocket-knives and scissors and many other things. He brought them all out of his bag and laid them on the table in the kitchen which was their living-room; they shone and glittered and suddenly the whole place seemed much more cheerful, though Lucindra kept shaking her head and saying she was much too poor to buy anything. The young man said he didn't expect her to, but he went on bringing more and more things out of his bag, even after it looked to be empty, and he was so gay that soon they were all laughing, Lucindra most of all; the children had never seen her laugh like that. And finally she went out of the room and came back with some money, and bought a bracelet for Olga and a pocket-knife for Peter and a necklace for herself. Then she told the young man he must be getting on his way, otherwise it would be dark; and he laughed and said he was in no hurry, because he knew the forest quite well. But greatly to the children's disappointment she would not let him stay. So, telling her how unkind she was, he began to gather together his bits and pieces and put them back into the bag. The children could not take their eyes off him as one by one he packed the treasures away; and every now and then, if something was specially pretty, he would raise his eyebrows as though inviting them to buy it; but each time Lucindra shook her head. "You must go, you must go," she kept saying. "All in good time," he answered and looked slyly at the children, who knew that he was delaying his departure on purpose. But at last he got up and swung his sack over his shoulder and they followed him to the door where his horse was nibbling the grass; and he fixed the sack on a sort of pannier on its back and jumped into the saddle and wished them goodbye.

"Which way are you going?" Lucindra asked.

"To the Crossways," he answered, smiling down at them.

"Where's that?"

"Don't you know?" They didn't, and then he told them that in the heart of the forest there was an open space where many roads met; "and one of those roads," he said, "leads to the land of your heart's desire."

"But how would anyone find the place?" Lucindra asked.

"Easily," said the pedlar. "Just follow the full moon until you come to it." He pointed upwards and there was the full moon hanging low over the forest.

"But how do people know which road to take?" Lucindra asked.

"Oh, it's marked with a signpost," said the pedlar. He laughed again and rode off, and they went back into the house, which seemed very dull and empty.

Soon after that their father came in and the children at once began to tell him about the pedlar. They were still very excited and could think of nothing else, for they had never had such an adventure in their lives before. "Did you see him in the forest?" they asked. "I saw no pedlar," he answered frowning. "I believe you dreamed the whole thing."

"Oh, no, we didn't. Look, look, look." And disregarding their mother's warning glance they showed him the bracelet and the penknife, and made Lucindra go and fetch her necklace, for she had already put it away. When he saw the necklace he grew still more angry and upbraided her bitterly for spending so much money. "We're hard up as it is," he said, "and you must needs go buying things from this smooth-tongued scoundrel. Never let me see you wearing them." Peter and Olga began to cry, and their mother let the necklace slip through her fingers on to the floor. "If ever I catch him I shall know what to do with him," Michael said. So they never told him the rest of the story or spoke of the pedlar any more.

It was a hard winter and it set in early, but in spite of that people did not seem to want wood as they used to, and Michael grew more and more morose and sour. Often when he came home he would not speak to them at all, and sat apart brooding, or went out again mysteriously and did not come back till after midnight. There was no pleasing him. If they sat quiet as mice he would complain of their silence; if they talked he would tell them to shut up. This was not so bad for the children as it was for their mother, for they now went to the village school and so had company. It was a long way to walk but they enjoyed it; they felt free the moment they got out of the house, and rather dreaded coming back, to find their mother drooping and listless, and their father, if he was at home, not lifting his head when they came in. Sometimes they lingered and talked to their friends, but they never spoke of the state of things at home, because they had promised their mother not to.

One evening they had stayed away later than usual and were beginning to feel hungry and look forward to the hot, steaming supper their mother always prepared for them; so in spite of everything they found themselves longing for the moment in their homeward walk when they could first see the light shining through the windows. But there was no light and when they got into the house it was empty. They called and called but nobody answered, so they began to feel rather frightened and went out of doors again. It was much lighter out of doors because there was a moon.

"It's a full moon," whispered Peter to Olga, "like that evening the pedlar came."

They went back into the house and found some matches and lit the lamp, and felt a little more cheerful, for it showed them their supper keeping warm on the hearth. They did not go to bed when they had eaten their supper; they sat in chairs like grown-up people. But Peter had gone to sleep before their father came in.

"Where's Cindra?" he said in a thick voice. (He called her Cindra sometimes.) "I asked you, where's Cindra?"

Peter woke up and began to cry. They told him all they knew. "But she can't be gone," said Michael disbelievingly. "She wouldn't leave us." He got up and went into the bedroom and stayed there a long time. When he came back his hand shook and he was so pale that his hair looked quite black. "It's true," he said, "she has gone. I found a letter. She says I'm not to try to follow her. She's gone where her heart calls her. What shall we do? What shall we do?"

When Olga saw that he was frightened she suddenly felt sorry for him and much less frightened herself.

"Don't worry," she said. "We know where she's gone to, don't we, Peter?"

"Where, where?" their father asked, his eyes darting at them.

"To the Crossways."

"Nonsense," he snapped. "There is no such place."

"Yes, there is," said Olga patiently, "in the middle of the forest. You can find it by following the full moon."

"The full moon!" he echoed scornfully. "I know every inch of the forest and I tell you there isn't any Crossways."

"Please, please don't be angry," Olga begged him. "Let Peter and me go, if you don't believe us."

"Let you go," he said, "and lose you too? Haven't I told you that the forest is dangerous? Do you want to send me mad? Sit still and don't stir from here till I come back."

He went out and they heard him calling "Cindra! Cindra!" until his voice died away.

"There's only one thing to do," said Olga. "We must find her and bring her back."

"But what about the bears and the wild boars?" said Peter.

"Oh, I shouldn't worry about them," said Olga. "I'd much rather you went with me, of course, but if you're afraid I'll go alone."

This made Peter feel much braver and they started off. They met with no difficulty in finding the way, for the moon made a pathway through the leafless trees; and at first they were not at all frightened, for when they looked back they could still see the light in the cottage windows. They walked hand in hand and their feet made a pleasant rustling on the fallen leaves.

"Will she be pleased to see us?" Peter asked.

"Of course she will, we're her children," Olga answered.

"But suppose we don't find her at the Crossways?"

"Then we must go on until we do find her. The signpost will say which way she went."

Whiter and whiter grew the moon as it swung into the heavens, and colder grew the air.

"I don't think I can go on much longer, Olga," Peter said.

"You can if you try."

It was then that they saw the bear. It was walking on all fours when they saw it, but when it saw them it stood up.

"Oh, it's going to hug us!" Peter cried.

"Nonsense," said Olga, but her voice trembled. "Perhaps it'll give you a scar like the one Daddy has," she added, hoping to encourage him.

"I don't want a scar now," sobbed Peter.

"All right," said Olga. "I shall just tell it why we've come."

She went up to the bear and explained that they were

looking for their mother, and the bear seemed satisfied, for after swaying a little on its feet and shaking its head, it got on to all fours again and shambled off.

After this escape they both felt very much better, and as if nothing could now go wrong. And suddenly they found that they were not walking on a path any longer, but on a road, a smooth straight road that led right out of the forest. On either side the trees seemed to fall back, and they were standing on the edge of a great circular plain which the moon overhead made almost as bright as day.

"Now we shall soon see her," Olga said. But it wasn't quite so easy as she thought, for the plain was dotted with small, dark bushes any one of which might have been a human being; and Peter kept calling out, "Look, there she is!" until Olga grew impatient.

They saw the Crossways long before they came to it. It was shaped like a star-fish only a star-fish with fifty points instead of five; and the place where they met was like white sand that has been kicked up by the feet of many horses.

But their mother was not there and they walked slowly round the centre, looking at each signpost in turn to see which led to the Land of Heart's Desire. But not one gave any direction; they were all blank, and presently the children found themselves back at the signpost they had started from.

Then in the silence they heard a little sound like a moan, and looking round they saw their mother, lying in a hollow beside the road. They ran to her and she sat up and stretched her arms out and kissed them many times.

"We've come to fetch you back," they said.

She smiled at them sadly. "I can't come back," she said. "You see, I've hurt my foot. Look how swollen it is.

I've had to take my shoe off." They saw how swollen her foot was, and it was bleeding too. "You'd better go home, my darlings," she said, "and leave me here." "But we can't leave you," they both cried. And Peter said, "Look, there are some people coming. They will help us."

He ran towards them crying, "Please help us," but they paid no heed and did not seem to see him. One after another they found the signpost they were looking for, and went the way it pointed, laughing and singing.

"They can't see us," Lucindra said, "because they are going to the Land of their Heart's Desire, and we don't belong to it."

Then both the children felt cold and frightened, much more frightened than when they had met the bear.

"Couldn't you walk if you leaned on both of us?" Peter asked. She shook her head. "And how should we find the way?" she said. "The moon won't help us to go back."

They lay down beside her, clasping her in their arms, and tried to keep awake, for the cold was making them drowsy. Just as they were dropping off they heard a footstep coming down the road; they did not pay much attention for they knew they would be invisible to whoever came. But Olga roused herself. "I'm going to try again," she said, and standing up she saw a long shadow like a steeple, and in front of it a man, walking very fast.

"Oh, Daddy, Daddy!" she cried. But his eyes were wild and staring, and bright with the empty shining of the moon. Terrified lest he too should not recognize them, she seized his hand. He stopped so suddenly that he nearly fell over.

"Where is your mother?" he cried.

"Here! She is here!"

She pulled at his hand, but he shrank back when he saw them, and without looking at their mother he said, "Cindra, I came to say good-bye."

"But it isn't good-bye," cried Olga. "We want you to take us home."

He shook his head. "No, no," he said. "I have been unkind to her. I am not worthy of her. She must go where she wants to go."

"But you must take her, you must!" Olga besought him. "Look at her, she has hurt her foot and can't walk."

For the first time he brought himself to look at her, and went up to her and wonderingly touched her foot.

"Do you really want to come with me?" he asked.

"Yes, yes," she murmured. "But do you know the way?"

"I know the way all right," he said with a touch of his old arrogance, and stooping down he lifted her in his arms.

Suddenly they saw written on the signpost, which had been blank before, "The Land of Heart's Desire".

It pointed straight back the way they came. And the moment their feet were turned towards home they began to laugh and sing, just as the others had.

Master Ghost and I

Barbara Softly

Nathaniel Dodd, the steward who had served our family for as long as I could remember and who had not seen me for close on five years, stared disapprovingly over the roll of parchment in his hand. His eyes, squinting in the sunlight that danced through the window to make a mockery of the sullen atmosphere, became mere pinpricks that tried to pierce my thoughts. His stare moved from my tanned features to the buff coat of my officer's uniform, travelled down the sleeve and paused on the edge of plain linen at my wrist. Involuntarily, and immediately ashamed of the action, I curved my fingers under my gloves so that he would not notice the nails I had split that morning while mending a broken bridle. From my hands the stare glided to my sword, slid from hilt to tip and came to rest on the spurs of my muddied riding-boots.

"I left as soon as I received your message," I began in weak apology for my unkempt looks, and feeling momentarily like the refractory schoolboy he still considered me to be.

The squinting eyes swung from my boots to my face again.

"You may sit down," he said.

Four cold words; not "Good day" or any remark on the change in my appearance which the half decade of soldiering with the Parliamentary Army must have made. I checked the rising comment, for I had no wish to make a greater enemy of the man who was the sole link with my family who had disowned me.

What had I done? Rebelled. The only one of my parents' four children who had dared to disobey their wishes. My two brothers had, not willingly, directed their lives into the ways chosen for them and my sister, at an early age, had been given in marriage to an elderly landowner of wealth in order to provide him with much-wanted heirs. But I, at fifteen as I then was, had seen little glamour or excitement in the life of a priest when I learned that I was destined for the Church. Glamour, life, excitement were to my mind to be found in my youthful pleasures, my sword, my horse, and the prospect of fighting; but not fighting for King Charles, who had just raised his standard at Nottingham, and who was head of that very Church from which I wished to escape.

A few months after I had run away from home I was tracked down by Nathaniel Dodd. That was the first time I was summoned to receive his disapproving stare and the four cold words—"You may sit down". On that occasion I had remained standing, a silent but defiant fifteen-year-old, my hair cropped as short as the most fanatical Roundhead's, determined to retain my freedom. It was not my freedom that Master Dodd wanted. It was to tell me that I could go the way I had chosen and live on the meagre pay of a common soldier because my family had disowned me, and there would never be any forgiveness for me.

"Callous young puppy," Nathaniel Dodd had hissed at my apparent composure.

"What do you expect me to say?" I had asked, goaded into speech by his contempt. "If I show sorrow now for the distress I have caused my parents for not entering the Church, you will be the first to tell me my repentance is too late. The Church is not for me. Why should a boy's life be stunted to suit his parents' whim? If they prefer to exile me and make me homeless, they are to blame for their own unhappiness now, not I."

They were hard words, and they came from a heart that was steeling itself to do without kindred and home for the bitter years of civil war.

Now, five years later, Nathaniel Dodd had sent for me again saying that he had important family matters to divulge. By this time there was a lull in the fighting and I, no longer a common soldier but a captain of a troop of horse in the New Model Army, was able to leave my quarters without a moment's delay. Believing that my father or both my parents were dying, if not dead, I covered the many miles to Master Dodd in two hot summer days, to arrive tired and travel-stained on a well-nigh lamed horse in the mid-afternoon.

"You may sit down." The words were repeated.

"Thank you," I replied, and obeyed, flinging my hat and gloves on the floor beside me.

For an instant the pinprick eyes wavered, then dropped to the parchment and began to read. I was conscious that, at the end of every line, Master Dodd's attention wandered from the black script to my relaxed figure, noting my hair, now long like an ordinary officer's, not shorn like a fanatic's, and the air of maturity and experience.

"Are my parents well?" I asked.

He started as if he had not expected me to have the temerity to address him first.

"In exceptional health, I believe," he said, and there was a hint of acidity in his voice showing that neither I nor what he read on the parchment was to his liking.

"This is your uncle's will," he continued in the same sour tone. "Your father's only brother Edward Knapton, who, until within a few months of his death fought loyally at the King's side." He glared at me over the parchment again and I wondered why he was at pains to tell me this. "He has left his fortune, which was considerable, not to your father, your brothers or your sister—but—to a rebellious, ill-favoured, traitorous"—and here his list of adjectives failed him—"ne'er-do-well—to yourself." He tossed the document in contempt on to the table in front of him.

I hid my amazement at his news and replied with as little sarcasm as possible that my uncle must have known the others were well provided for. If Master Dodd had been a common soldier he would have spat out his disgust.

"The man was mad," he exploded, "mad! He destroyed his previous will and made that—that travesty —only a short while ago." His fingers quivering with fury, he pulled some keys from a drawer and went to a small coffer under the window. "If you need money now I can let you have some, and the rest can be sent when and where you want it later. The house can be sold and then I——"

"What house?" I interrupted.

"Your uncle's," he barked. "Now yours. A new house——" And he named a village deep in a part of the West Country which had been torn by the campaigns during the early years of the war. "He finished building it this spring and planned to live in it at once, but——" He hesitated, lifting the lid of the chest and burying his hand in its contents. "It's no place for anyone and you'll not be needing a house when you are on the march all the time—you chose to give up one Royalist home and

this will only be another. It will fetch a good price
and——"

"I do not wish to sell it," I replied firmly. His ready
acceptance of the fact that I neither needed nor wanted
the house roused my obstinate nature, although I was not
really inclined to be saddled with the property. "You can
give me the keys and I will go down there."

He straightened up, his eyes blinking nervously.

"You'll not like it. Your uncle could not abide it in
the end."

"No doubt that was why he left it to me," I said. "If
he had been fond of it he would have given it to a more
worthy recipient. In any case, I should like to see the
servants. They might not be willing to serve a rebel
master after a Royalist one."

"There are no servants." He spoke slowly in order to
convey some deeper meaning. "The place is empty, no
one will stay there. Your uncle was driven from it—by
some power, some evil—he believed the place was
haunted."

"Haunted?" I laughed. "What—a house not a year old
with a ghost? Who is it? One of the bricklayers fallen
from the scaffolding or did they wall up the master
carpenter in the chimney because of his prying ways?"

Nathaniel Dodd eyed me with awe and a strange
fascination.

"Heaven be praised you never entered the Church,"
he muttered. "The supernatural is to be feared not
mocked."

He passed a bag of money and some keys from the
coffer to my outstretched hand. Then smoothed his
glistening forehead with a damp palm.

"I shall be ready to sell the property when you have
changed your mind," he said.

I slipped the bag and keys into my pouch, swung my hat and gloves from the floor, and bowed my thanks.

"Maybe I won't change my mind," I smiled, and I was conscious of the shaft of sunlight dancing joyously across the sombre room. "For perhaps Master Ghost and I will become well acquainted."

Forty-eight hours later, on a day that had turned from high summer to the cloud and steady wind which had prevailed for most of the season, I sat surveying my inheritance—or what I could see of its chimneys showing above a high, uncut hawthorn hedge and an iron-studded gateway. Dismounting, I glanced all round, back along the grassy track which had led from the road a mile away; to the right where the deep hills were folded in peace, and to the left where, from a distant, tree-lined hollow, the smoke from hidden cottage fires was being swept like pennants across the countryside.

I hitched my horse to a stake in the hedge and, leaving him there to graze, fitted one of Master Dodd's keys to the lock on the gate. The key grated, the lock was stiff and the gate had to be pushed over uneven ground where I had thought there would be a smooth drive. There was no drive and I stood staring in bewilderment. There was nothing, nothing but grass, rough and knee-deep or in hummocky tufts and the whole vast hayfield, in which the house and outbuildings seemed to have been dropped, was scattered with mature trees. Only under the nearest line of windows was there a terrace of freshly laid flag-stones, and even they were edged with weeds, littered with wisps of straw and flutterings of dead leaves.

What is it that is so uncanny about an empty house? As I moved softly on the carpet of turf every window seemed to be watching, every stone to be listening and the air of desolation was so heavy and still that my ears were oppressed with it. Yet there was no stillness; the silence was full of the wind of that dull, clouded summer day, a wind that swept the dry leaves on the flags, that bent the branches of the limes into brooms and brushed them in never-ending motion; a wind full of unseen voices.

The clattering of my spurs striking the terrace steps was enough to unsteady my nerves; my hand flew to my sword while my heart pounded as it had never done in battle.

"Coward," I muttered, remembering Master Dodd's words. "But it seems a day of ghosts; the air could be full of them, crying like lost souls."

"Will you be wanting anything, sir?"

I spun round, back to the wall, sword half drawn, ready to defend myself against the supernatural if need be.

A most unghostlike face, balanced on the haft of a scythe, was glaring at me through the overgrown bushes.

"I be here to cut the grass," it said.

"A pity you did not come sooner," I retorted, angry with myself. "It has not been cut for months."

"I come once a year—the Master only wanted me once a year." The shrubs quivered and a man wriggled on to the stones in front of me. He stood up slowly, stroking the blade of the scythe and eyeing my buff coat with the same look as Master Dodd's—disapproval verging on hatred. "I'm Mallett," he said, "Ned Mallett—and you're a soldier, bain't you." It was a statement not a question. "We don't hold with soldiers in these parts; you'd best be off before anyone else sees you." The scythe tilted in the manner of a battle-axe.

"This is my house," I told him. "The master of whom you speak was my uncle and he has left this property to me."

"That's as maybe," he growled. "Master or no master, you're a soldier, and we've had enough of soldiery in these parts whether they be King's men or Parliament's. You leave peaceful folks be."

"The previous owner, Edward Knapton, was a soldier, too," I replied.

"Maybe he was." The man's attitude became more threatening. "But we don't want no more of you, trampling our crops, eating our food, burning our barns, taking all, and paying nothing. We fought you once with pitchforks and clubs and we'll fight you again whether you be the Master, the King, or the Parliament.

I knew what he meant. Villagers all over that locality, driven to desperation by the plunder of war, had banded together to fight the common enemy, Royalist and Roundhead. Both sides had tried to woo their friendship with promises of better-disciplined troops and gifts of muskets and carbines. The Clubmen, we had called them, because of their primitive weapons.

"You'd best be going," he said again before I could speak. "Master Knapton wouldn't stay here. Worried wellnigh out of his wits, he was, though it wasn't us what drove him away. It might have been," he added menacingly, "if the devil hadn't done it for us. 'I'll not come again,' that's what he told me. 'Ned Mallett,' he said, 'the place is evil and I'll not——' "

"Never mind what he told you," I interrupted, my temper rising. "You and your Clubmen, the devil and all his demons, I am staying here the night at least. So you 'had best be off' down to those cottages and find someone who can come up and cook my supper for me. My horse needs stabling, too, and you can do that on your way back."

He wavered under the decisive tones, but, as his eyes shifted swiftly over my shoulder, something more like cunning crept into his voice.

"My missus'll come up like she did for Master Edward," he muttered. "She'll do the fires and air the linen —though she'll not——"

"I am not asking anyone to sleep here," I forestalled him, and immediately thought that I should feel safer in my bed with my hostile neighbours on the other side of a barred door. "I am not afraid of being alone."

Without another word, he jerked the scythe into his hands and went towards the outbuildings on a path that was evidently the shortest route to the cottages in the hollow. I moved to recross the terrace to the main porch, intending to explore the house, for I was anxious to examine it thoroughly before the man and his wife returned or darkness fell.

With an exclamation of annoyance, I saw another prying villager standing behind me, a boy of about fifteen years of age.

"Who are you?" I snapped.

"Ro-Roger," he stammered.

"And you live here, too, I suppose?"

"S-sort of."

We looked each other up and down.

"You—you're a soldier," he said. "A soldier in the New Model Army, an officer."

"A captain of a troop of horse, and before that I served under Waller in most of his campaigns here in the West; and I have been a soldier for the past five years."

I rolled the words out in fury, waiting for the inevitable disapproval, but it did not come. The boy was staring at me with an odd mixture of incredulity, wonderment, and admiration. His hair was cropped shorter than mine had ever been and he was wearing a shabby doublet and breeches of a faded blue-grey colour. On second thoughts, as I continued to study him, I decided that his clothes were not shabby with the wear of work as Ned Mallett's had been. They were faded with disuse, the lace of his shirt yellowed, dust lines in the creases of folding, and it seemed probable that he was dressed in a discarded suit of my uncle's.

"You knew Master Knapton?" I asked. "Master Edward Knapton who lived here?"

"He only came once, a short while ago. I met him then," was the quick reply.

"And he gave you those clothes."

A momentary glimmer of astonishment showed in the boy's eyes and he glanced down at his doublet.

"They came from the chest at the foot of his bed," he explained, and then more eagerly, "Why are you here—you're a soldier, and there's no fighting now——"

"Because the house is mine." Soon these villagers will be aware of that fact, I thought. "Edward Knapton was my uncle, and I am John Knapton, his nephew, who——"

"John Knapton?" he broke in. "You are John Knapton? But—but you're a soldier—a captain in the Army——" His astonishment was not hidden now. "But no one would ever have dreamed you were a Roundhead soldier as well."

"As well as what?" I asked.

He flushed, hesitated, and shrugged his shoulders.

"As well as—being—being——"

"As well as being the nephew of a loyal subject of the King," I finished for him.

He smiled and the flush deepened.

"That's as good a reason as any."

He laughed, and I could not help liking the boy; his disarming friendliness and his quaint, clipped way of speaking, which was quite different from Mallett's broad dialect or my slight country drawl.

Taking out another of Master Dodd's keys, I went towards the door at the front of the house, and as I reached the porch I heard Roger padding softly after me.

"This is tansy, isn't it?" he asked.

I turned and saw him running his hand up a feathery-leaved yellow flower which was growing in a straggling clump at the edge of the steps. He buried his nose in his palm.

"What a scent!" he exclaimed. "It reminds me of blazing borders and summer gardens."

"It reminds me of fleas," I said, "and doses of bitter physic when I was a child."

His guffaw of laughter warmed me. It was good to hear such a sound in the atmosphere of cheerlessness which had so far been my greeting. When I opened the door, wrinkling my nose at the musty smell, Roger was close at my elbow.

He wriggled past my arm. "Look," he whispered in excitement. "It's new—so new. Look at that panelling and this floor." He darted across the hall to smooth his fingers down the freshly carved woodwork on the walls.

"Of course it's new, boy," I replied. "It was only finished this year. Didn't you see it when my uncle was here?"

He shook his head. "I—I didn't come in," he murmured, and with an effort seemed to check his eagerness.

After that, with firmly compressed lips, he followed me like a dog, through the living-rooms and kitchens, stopping when I stopped, and pausing to look out of a window whenever I opened one. Upstairs, in one of the bedrooms which was more fully furnished than the rest of the house and had obviously been intended for my uncle's use, the sour staleness was overpowering. As I strode to the window, out of the corner of my eye, I saw Roger drop on his knees in front of the linen chest at the foot of the four-poster bed. With a sigh of pleasure, he let his fingers caress the dull wood as they had caressed the panelling and the yellow herb.

"It's the same," I heard him hiss. "It's unbelievable that it's still the same only so much darker."

"If it's the one Master Knapton took your suit from I'm not surprised it's the same," I said, glancing round at him. "But as you did not come indoors when he was here, I don't see how you can recognize it."

He dropped back on his heels as if caught in some guilty thought or action.

"The date is on it here," I said quietly, for he did not reply, and I seemed to have damped his enthusiasm. "On the lid—1620. I've no doubt it was made for my uncle when he was a young man. It's old by his standards now, over twenty-five years."

"Twenty-five years! That's not old," Roger protested. "It won't look like that in over three hundred years, that I know."

"Neither will you," I retorted.

He stared at me. There was silence, a second's silence while the wind of that dull, clouded summer day blew in the narrow window and sent only its voices sweeping through my uncle's room.

" '*Tempus edax rerum*'," I commented.

"What?" asked Roger sharply. "What does that mean? It's Latin, isn't it?"

"Latin, boy!" I exclaimed. "Of course it's Latin, and at your age you should know what it means."

"I don't," he confessed. "I don't take Latin at my school. I take other subjects."

I refrained from another exclamation. For all I knew he might be some ignorant local lad that my uncle had befriended and he was trying to cover his lack of knowledge by blaming it on to his schoolmaster.

" 'Time, the devourer of all things,' is a fair enough translation," I explained.

Roger's eyes met mine, and again I was conscious of the wind, the rustle of the dead lime flowers on the flags. Then he chuckled—and the sound of hoofs clopping on the terrace beneath us told me that Ned Mallett had returned to stable my horse. I hurried to the head of the stairs to see if the man's wife was with him, too. Before I called down I glanced back at Roger. He had not moved but he was watching me, that strange look of wonder, near affection on his face. Although I pretended not to have noticed, it was with growing feelings of uneasiness and foreboding that I made my way to the kitchen.

Who was he, this boy? He seemed familiar with my uncle's possessions, and yet he said he had only met him once. Was his friendliness genuine or was it a cloak for something deeper? Ned Mallett's antagonism had unsettled me. I recollected his hasty glance to where the boy must have been standing behind me and I began to wonder if, ever since Edward Knapton's death, the villagers had set a spy to wait for the new unwanted soldier-owner of the property; a spy who would gain his confidence, as this boy was gaining mine, and then, at the chosen moment—— My fingers sought the hilt of my sword. With that alone, for I now realized my foolishness in leaving my pistols on my saddle, I reckoned I could withstand any treachery.

In the kitchen Mistress Mallett had already lighted the fire and blown it into a blaze. There were clean sheets, which she told me she had brought herself, draped across a bench; but her sullen greeting added to the wave of depression that had come over me at the top of the stairs.

Strong hands smoothed the folds of her petticoats down her broad hips as she regarded me with the eyes of Nathaniel Dodd and Ned Mallett.

"So—you're a soldier," she sniffed. "We've seen more than enough of the likes of you."

"So I understand," was my quick rejoinder and, leaving her at the oven, I went into the living-room.

"There's bread and cheese and ale for your supper," she called out. "I'll make up the beds and then you must shift for yourself. I'll not stay after dusk in this God-forsaken place."

I did not trouble to reply, but dropped my hat and gloves on the settle as I passed and dragged a high-backed chair up to the table in the window. Sitting there, gazing out over the windswept terrace and the unending grass of that vast field, my depression deepened. Master Dodd had been right; I should have to sell "the God-forsaken place". The villagers, even if they intended me no real harm, would never accept me without a struggle, and no doubt, one night spent alone in the house would be enough to drive me away. It would not be difficult to decide which had the most power, the supernatural or the ill-wishes of Master Mallett.

And what of Roger? Was I to be completely alone? It was unlikely after Mistress Mallett's use of the word "beds". As far as I could see the boy had no intentions of leaving me, which seemed further confirmation of my suspicions. He had followed me to the kitchen, through to the living-room and now, without turning my head, I was able to watch his form, grey-blue in the growing shadows, where he was crouching on the settle. My hat and gloves were in his lap and he was engrossed, examining both in minute detail—furtively fingering the felt, the leather, even the lines of stitching.

"It's getting dark in here," I said abruptly.

He started in alarm.

"D-dark?" he stammered. "I'll switch the light on."

He sprang across the room to the door and put his hand to the wall. Then he stood still, his hand slipping to his side.

"What's the matter?" I asked, shaken by his words and attitude.

"Candles—I'll fetch the candles," he murmured.

I stood up to follow him, but hesitated at the strident tones of Mistress Mallett's voice.

"There's candles and tinder in the dresser in the living-room, I'll be bound. Don't you be bothering me, now. The supper's out here and I'll be gone in less than a minute."

Roger returned. He walked past the dresser, straight to the table, and sat down.

"She doesn't want me in the kitchen at the moment," he explained. "There are plenty of candles out there and I'll light them from the fire when she has gone. "

It was a barefaced lie.

"One candle will be sufficient," I remarked coldly, and sat down opposite.

"I don't mind being in the dark," he said.

No, I thought in agreement, I do not suppose you do. So much can be accomplished in the dark with an unwary opponent, but I am as watchful as you, my lad.

Suddenly he leaned across and looked searchingly up into my face.

"You know what you said just now, about time," he began. " 'Time the devourer of all things'—'*tempus*', something or other?"

" '*Tempus edax rerum*'," I repeated, wedging my knee under the table so that it could not be tipped unexpectedly and send me off my balance.

"Do you believe that?"

"That time devours everything?" I asked, and I heard the click of the latch as Mistress Mallett left the kitchen. "It is obvious it does. Look at the grass out there and the hedge. A few months and the place is a wilderness, a few years more of neglect and the whole house will be a tangle of briars, the woodwork rotten and the plaster fallen in. That's time; time devours and——"

"I know," he interrupted impatiently. "That's one sort of time—but I'm trying to talk about something else—a—a time that is only a cover, that we have to live by in hours and days, but which doesn't really exist."

If you are spinning out the time, I thought, you are going about it in a very odd way.

"I'm so hopeless at expressing myself," he went on with a hint of desperation. "Something like it comes in a piece of poetry, though I'm not much good at the stuff and I can never remember it properly—

> '*In every land thy feet may tread*
> *Time like a veil is round thy head.*
> *Only the land thou seek'st with me*
> *Never hath been nor yet shall be——*' "

An uneasy cold crept over my whole body as I listened, held against my will by his glowing eyes and the tense

face so white in the half light. If he had wanted to put me off my guard, he had succeeded.

"Don't you believe that time is only a veil and if you lift it, you can be anywhere at any period of existence?" he whispered.

Uncertainty, vague fear, and a presentiment of some unknown power gripped me.

" 'Time like a veil is round thy head.' " The slow words he repeated dropped into the hollow stillness of the empty house.

My question hovered on the air.

"Who wrote that?" I breathed.

"Henry Newbolt," he said, and even before he spoke I sensed it would be a poet of whom I had never heard.

A sudden flicker of light beyond the hedge in the darkening garden jerked me from my stupor. One hand flew to my sword, the other instinctively closed over Roger's slim wrists on the table.

"Don't move," I hissed as I pressed him to the chair.

"I can't," he growled. "And there's no need to hold me down. I'm not frightened of them."

The injured tone was reassuring. The boy was no accomplice, of that I was sure, though what he was I had not the courage to admit. I was only concerned at that moment with the need for speedy action.

"I'll wager it's Ned Mallett with his scythe and half the village too, come to drive the soldier from his stronghold," I muttered in rising anger. "And this soldier will not be driven. I'll go of my own free will, and neither man nor devil shall frighten me out of my own house."

I released Roger who was writhing under the strength of my arm.

"Get down to that gate opposite the terrace steps. See that it's locked and bolted," I commanded. "They'll not venture over this hawthorn hedge without ladders yet."

"Can't we barricade the house?" he asked eagerly. "We could block all the doors and shutter the windows and pour buckets of blazing tar on their heads. That's what they do in sieges——"

"This isn't a siege," I snapped, ignoring his flippancy although he appeared to be in earnest. "And it is not going to be one. Attack first, defence afterwards is the order in my troop of horse. There must be another gate behind the stables and I'll wait for you there."

He darted away and sent the chair flying in his impetuous dash.

"Don't be foolhardy," I called. "If they are armed they'll fire."

"What?" He paused in the doorway. "With one of those old carbines? Those things wouldn't hit a cow at five yards."

"They've been known to kill a man at twenty," I retorted.

"Oh for a Winchester, and I'd pick 'em off like flies," he cried.

"I want no bloodshed," I ordered. Again his remark was incomprehensible, but time enough to ask him what he meant later, I thought. "If they want to live in peace, far be it from me to start a fight, but they must learn to leave me in peace, too."

If I could retrieve my pistols—if Master Mallett had not had the wits to remove them from the holsters in anticipation of this attack—and could fire over their heads to frighten them into parleying, we might be able to come to amicable terms after all.

As the outer door banged behind Roger, I groped through the dim kitchen to make my way to the stables and barns—but I never reached either. The moment my foot stepped into the sullen darkness of that clouded evening, a bullet shattered the window at my side. I ducked, slid beneath the covering bushes, and flattened myself against the wall waiting for the next shot. None came; no sound, no movement but the trees in the wind and my own shallow breathing. So much for the prospects of peace without bloodshed, I thought, and this was a form of fighting I despised. With my pistols or sword, even my bare hands, I would tackle any numbers if they refused to listen to words of reason, but this game of hide-and-seek, with an enemy who had already spotted me, was not to my liking.

Cautiously I edged sideways, aware that my disadvantage lay in the fact that I was not familiar with the courtyard, and that the stables might be any of the shapes that rose up in the gloom. If my enemy meant to kill, once I was in the open I was an easy target, and so until I could catch a glimpse of him, it was wiser to hug the wall. My fingers, spreading along the bricks, touched first climbing tendrils, a snail—then, something warm and rough—a hand! I froze. My fingers crept upwards to touch a sleeve. With an exclamation of alarm the owner of the sleeve jerked backwards, and before another hand could drop on mine I sprang at the hidden figure. Nose to nose, knee to knee, we struggled under the bushes betraying our whereabouts to the unseen marksman. His second shot speeding through the branches over my head so startled my antagonist that, in his momentary hesitation, I wrenched myself free, swung my fist and gave him a crushing blow on the jaw. As his sagging body toppled another shape leapt for my throat, received the toe of my jackboot in his stomach and fell winded and writhing to the ground.

Two, I thought quickly, and how many more? Off balance and reeling from my shelter I nearly slipped beneath the double onslaught of a burly figure in front and little, leech-like arms which clasped my wrists behind me. With a vicious kick to the rear, I felt my spurs gouge deeply into a stockinged shin—there was a scream of pain and the third assailant dropped from the fight. But the fourth was taking all my strength; he tripped my feet and sent me sprawling to the dust, bruised and entangled by my own sword, and there we rolled, locked in each other's arms until I became conscious of a light wavering towards us from the darkness of the hedge. It was Master Mallett, a flaming torch held high, and at his side was the marksman with his carbine.

"This is your doing," I bellowed in a brief moment

when I was uppermost. "I came in peace and if any of these men are dead, may it lie on your conscience for ever."

I saw the light glinting along the raised barrel and I saw Roger leaping into the circle of yellow flame.

"Get down—he'll fire!" I gasped.

For a moment he stood there poised, a pace from the carbine's mouth—a shot—silence—a feather of smoke—a quiver from the torch as Ned Mallett turned, too late, and struck the gun from the man's hands. The fellow gripping my shoulders loosed them, sat back and eased his bruised muscles; other shapes rose and shambled towards the gate. I lurched to my feet and stumbled forward.

Roger had not moved; upright and as firm as a rock, he watched me coming, a faint smile on his lips. His eyes, as he glanced up into my face, wore an odd, distant look.

"That must be like the silver bullet in the fairy stories that's supposed to kill the devil," he said quietly. "It doesn't really kill him, it just gets rid of him for a while."

"You're hurt," I said.

I slipped my arm round his shoulders and he did not resist. Slowly I led him to the long grass at the edge of the terrace, where I pulled off my coat and spread it on the ground. He sank down and let his head droop on to the improvised pillow. Kneeling by his side I fumbled with the worn cloth of his doublet, feeling through his shirt to his chest. There was not a mark on him nor a speck of blood.

"There's no wound," I whispered.

"There won't be," he murmured. "I'm not going to die yet. I shall be alive long after you are dead—more than three hundred years."

I gazed into that still face which glimmered among the grasses like a white moth at rest.

He raised one hand; his fingers touched my hair, my cheek, my linen shirt, the hilt of my unused sword.

"John Knapton—Captain John Knapton," and I sensed that he was smiling. "I have always wanted to know what you were really like—and now I know you were a Roundhead soldier as well, while everyone else just believes you to be the man who laid out the gardens."

"What gardens?" I asked, a great fear gripping me.

"The gardens here," he replied. "Gardens that everyone comes to see—the sundial on the terrace where you carved your name and put those strange words along its rim, in English, too. I wonder why you did that; most people of your time would have put them in Latin. It's so short, so short a time," he whispered desperately. "There was so much I wanted to see, to know, to ask— and I never guessed how it could end—I—I thought I could be here for ever, if I wanted. The suit was in the chest; I found it there, all folded and old just as he had put it away and then, I hoped I might meet you." He chuckled. "I frightened him, the old man, your uncle, though the villagers thought I was some boy of his. It was too soon and I pestered the life out of him asking what he was doing in your house—everyone knew it was yours—they hadn't a clue it belonged to him first—they even thought you built it."

His fingers slipped from my sword and lay, a feather-weight on my own.

"He was afraid of me," he murmured. "I was something out of this world to him, I suppose."

I heard the wind bending the lime branches, the leaves tapping the flagstones, but there were no voices, only peace in that clouded night.

"The supernatural is to be feared not mocked," Master Dodd had said—and I was not afraid.

I watched him, how long I watched him, I cannot tell. His slight form lay, a shadow in the flattened grass, his face fading, until, as the moonless hours crept by, he drifted like a moth into the darkness.

My coat was warm when I took it up and stumbled into the house. I lit a candle with the tinder that I believed Roger had not known how to use and mounted the stairs to my uncle's room. There I opened the chest and there I found the blue-grey doublet and breeches, the fine lace shirt, fresh-folded in lavender, just as my uncle had laid them away a few months ago; the dust and creases, the yellowing of age and faded colours that Roger had put on would form with the years, three hundred years of time.

I knelt there, my head bowed in my arms while the candle burned low in its socket. I, who had never allowed myself to feel the need for a home, now wanted this, my inheritance, though willed to me in fear; and wanted to create out of its wilderness something living to take the place of the destruction which had been five years of my life.

Was it possible, I asked myself, to raise a memorial to a ghost from the future, to a boy not yet born, a memorial that would endure until he came?

"A wall would last longer than that hawthorn hedge," I thought. "And oaks are slower growing than limes or elms; flagged paths and stone seats would weather the centuries; shrubs of rosemary and lavender—they spring from slips quick enough although the mother plant may not thrive more than a decade and—"I laughed aloud— "he shall have his tansy and as many herbs as he wants, descendants of the ones already here; and his blazing borders, banked by yew—that's almost everlasting."

I stubbed the flaring candle in its pool of grease and, fired with enthusiasm, strode to the open window. The limes were still, only an early thrush was rustling the limp leaves.

"A dial on the terrace," I mused, "where it will catch the sun most of the day; and my name on it with some Latin maxim carved along its rim, *Tempus Fugit* or——"

A chuckle of merriment burst from me. "But the boy doesn't know any Latin!" I exclaimed. "Roger, Roger, what an ignorant lad you are—but for your sake, I'll put the words in English."

I gazed out across that vast field of rampant grass, already seeing in my mind the beauty it was to become. And Roger? I should look for him in vain, for he would not come in my lifetime any more; but come, at last, he would, and love that garden as I was beginning to love it.

" 'Long looked for—come at last.' " I breathed into that first dawn the words which were to be inscribed in stone.

The sun's gold touched the latticed panes.

"I have lived three centuries in half a day," I thought, and then a mischievous smile curved my lips because I knew I should have to write to Nathaniel Dodd.

The house would not be sold for—Master Ghost and I had become well acquainted.

BARBARA IRESON studied at the University of Nottingham and now lives in Yorkshire, England, with her husband and their three children. She has edited *Shadows and Spells, Verse That Is Fun, Come to the Fair,* and other books. While Mrs. Ireson was researching *Haunting Tales,* she and her husband were engrossed in renovations for their present house, which was built in 1620, or thereabouts. At that time there was a series of electricity cutbacks and she often found herself reading in a heavily beamed sitting room by candlelight.